THE MAIDEN IS POWERFUL

Two men the singer knew had died of blood loss. Now she kissed his neck in the very spot where the other men had had punctures and bruises and he felt himself weakening. With a profound shock of horror and revulsion, he realized why. Lane Barber was sucking his blood . . . He opened his mouth to yell for help. Her hand clamped across his mouth.

In desperation, he bit at her hand to make her let go. He sank his teeth in deep, using all his fading strength. Skin gave way. Her blood filled his mouth, burning like fire. Convulsively, he swallowed, and his throat burned, too. . . .

The horror escalated. A sheet over him blocked the vision of his eyes; temperature had become all one to him, unfelt; and the lack of breath prevented him from smelling anything, but he knew he lay in the morgue. . . .

BLOOD HUNT

BLOOD HUNT

LEE KILLOUGH

A TOM DOHERTY ASSOCIATES BOOK

BLOOD HUNT

Copyright © 1987 by Lee Killough

First printing: March 1987

A TOR Book

Published by Tom Doherty Associates, Inc.
49 West 24 Street
New York, N.Y. 10010

Cover art by Tom Galasinski

ISBN: 0-812-50594-8
CAN. ED.: 0-812-50595-6

Printed in the United States of America

0 9 8 7 6 5 4 3 2 1

*For Pat, who has had to hear
more about vampires than he
ever wanted to know, and for
Jane Wallace, who did me the
ultimate compliment of sometimes
forgetting Garreth Mikaelian
isn't a real person.*

The Body
in the Bay

1

Where do they begin, the roads that lead a man to hell?

... *With a ritual* ...

Lien Takananda sits at the kitchen table wearing her bathrobe, her short helmet of gray-touched black hair still rumpled from sleep. She holds three Chinese coins in her hand and concentrates, only subconsciously aware of her husband, Harry, in the bathroom, singing a lascivious parody of a saccharine popular song as he shaves. Almond eyes on the copy of *I Ching* before her, she asks the same question of the sage that she has asked every morning for over fifteen years, since Harry joined the San Francisco police: "Will my husband be safe today?" And she throws the coins.

The hexagram produced by the six throws is number 10, *Treading. Treading upon the tail of the tiger*, the text reads. *It does not bite the man. Success.*

She sighs in relief, then smiles, listening to Harry sing. After a minute, she gathers the coins again, and as she has done for most of the past year, asks on behalf of Harry's partner, "Will Garreth Mikaelian be safe today?"

This time the coins produce hexagram number 36, *Darkening of the Light*, with two moving lines. She bites her lip. The text of both the hexagram and the individual lines is cautionary. However, the moving lines produce a second hexagram, 46, *Pushing Upward*, which reads: *Pushing upward has supreme success. One must see the great man. Fear not.*

She reads the interpretation of the text just to be certain of its meaning. Reassured, Lien Takananda rewraps the coins and book in black silk and returns them to their shelf, then begins preparing Harry's breakfast.

... With nagging grief ...

Garreth Mikaelian still feels the void in his life and in the apartment around him. Through the open bathroom door he can see the most visible evidence: the bed, empty, slightly depressed on one side but otherwise neat. Marti's sprawling, twisting sleep used to turn their nights into a wrestle for blankets that left them in a tangled knot every morning.

He looks away quickly and concentrates on his reflection in the mirror. A square face with sandy hair and smoky gray eyes looks back at him. Burly, he fills the mirror ... a bit more so than he would like, admittedly, but the width does give the illusion of a big man, larger than his actual five foot eight.

And makes you look like a cop even stark naked, my man, he silently tells the reflection.

He leans closer to the mirror, frowning as he works the humming razor across his upper lip. He looks older than he would like, too. Barely twenty-eight and already he can see lines etching down his forehead between his eyes and around the corners of his mouth ... lines not visible six months ago.

Don't I ever stop missing her? He had not cared this way when Judith walked out. There had been more relief than anything, in fact, though he had missed his son. But, then, Marti was different from Judith. He could talk to her. After what she saw as a nurse in the trauma unit at San Francisco General every day, he had not been afraid of shocking or frightening her by talking about what happened to him at work, or of the examples he witnessed of man's unrelenting and fiendishly imaginative inhumanity to man. He could even cry in front of her and still feel like a man. They were two halves of the same soul.

His fingers tighten around the razor, dragging it under his chin. His vision blurs. *Fate is a bitch!* Why else give him such a woman and then put her in an intersection when an impatient driver tried to beat the light . . .

When does the pain stop? When does the emptiness fill?

At least he has the department. He can bridge the void with his work.

. . . With a corpse . . .

The body floats facedown in the bay, held on the surface by air trapped under its shirt and red suit coat. Carried on the tide, supported by its chance water wings, it drifts into the watery span between Fisherman's Wharf and the forbidding silhouette of Alcatraz Island. Bobbing, it awaits discovery.

2

"Lien says you need to be careful today, Mik-san." From where he stood pouring himself a cup of coffee, Harry Takananda's voice carried to Garreth above the homicide squad room's background noise of murmuring voices, ringing telephones, and tapping typewriters.

Squatted on his heels pawing through the bottom drawer of a filing cabinet, Garreth nodded. "Right," he said around the pencil in his mouth.

Harry added two lumps of sugar to the coffee. "But she says there is good fortune in acting according to duty."

"Devoted to duty, that's me, Harry-san." Now, where the hell was that damned file?

Harry stared into the coffee, then added two more lumps of sugar before carrying the cup back to his desk. He sat down at the typewriter. The chair grunted in protest, bearing witness to how many times Harry had added those extra lumps over the years.

Rob Cohen, whose desk sat just around a pillar from Harry's, asked, "Do you really believe in that stuff?"

"My wife does." Harry sipped his coffee, then hunched over the typewriter. "I went through the book once and found that of the sixty-four hexa-grams, only half a dozen are outright downers. The odds are she'll throw a positive hexagram most mornings, so, Inspector-san"—he steepled his fingers and bowed toward Cohen, voice rising into a singsong—"if it give honorable wife peace of mind, this superior man should not object, you aglee?"

Cohen pursed his lips thoughtfully. "Maybe I should introduce *my* wife to *I Ching*, too."

At the filing cabinet, Garreth grinned.

The door of the lieutenant's office opened. Lucas Serruto stepped out waving a memo-pad sheet. His dark, dapper good looks always made Garreth think of an actor cast to play the detective lieutenant in a movie where the cop was the hero. Garreth envied the way Serruto could make anything he wore appear expensive and custom-tailored. "Any volunteers to go look at a floater?"

Around the squad room, heads bent industriously over papers and typewriters.

Serruto surveyed the room for a minute, then shrugged. "Eenie, meenie, minie—Sergeant Takananda, the Cicione killing is in the hands of the D.A., isn't it? That leaves you with just the Mission Street liquor store shooting."

Harry looked up. "Yes, but that's so—"

"Good. You and Mikaelian take the floater." He handed Harry the memo sheet. "The Coast Guard is waiting for you bayside."

With a sigh, Harry gulped his coffee. Garreth shoved the file drawer closed and stood up. They left, pulling on coats.

Driving out of the parking lot, Harry headed toward the Embarcadero. The city flowed past the car, muted by fog, swathed in it. The radio crackled and murmured, dispatching officers across the city. Foghorns hooted.

"Let's try to get out before midnight tonight, shall we?" Harry asked. "Lien wants to feed us supper before it mummifies keeping warm."

"*Us?* You're asking me over again?" Garreth shook his head. "Harry, I can't keep eating your groceries. If nothing else, Lien's cooking is changing my name to Girth Mikaelian." He ruefully ran a thumb inside his snug belt.

"She'll have my hide if I *don't* bring you. Lacking a houseful of kids"—Harry's smile did not hide an old regret in his voice—"she has only you and her art class kids to mother. Don't fight it."

There had been several weeks after Marti's death when Lien's mothering was all that saved him from becoming a basket case. Garreth owed her a great deal. "I'll come."

The car swung onto the Embarcadero. Harry hugged the wheel, as though leaning forward would help him see through the fog better. "Sometimes I wonder what it would be like living somewhere that has a real summer, and maybe even sunshine in August."

"Come along the next time I go to Davis to visit my kid and find out."

They turned in at the pier number on the memo sheet and drove down to a barrier of vehicles. There they climbed out. Fog enveloped them, cold and damp. Garreth shoved his hands in his trench coat pockets and huddled deeper in the collar as he and Harry walked the rest of the way.

Out near the end of the pier the usual post-violent-death circus had set up: uniformed officers, Crime Lab, Photo Lab, an ambulance crew from the medical examiner's office along with an assistant M.E., and this time, Coast Guard, too.

"Hi, Jim," Harry said to one of the Coast Guard officers.

Jim Birkinshaw smiled. "Hell of a way to start a morning, Harry."

Garreth moved as close to the body as possible without interfering with the photographer. The victim had been stretched out on his back, but he still looked less than funeral-parlor neat. His rumpled coat had twisted up around his neck, and a spreading stain of salt water surrounded him.

Strange how you could always tell the dead ones, Garreth reflected. They looked different from living people, even different from someone unconscious. They lay awkwardly, slack, collapsed into postures no vital body would assume.

He pulled out his notebook and began taking down a description of the corpse. White male, brown hair of medium length, 160 to 180 pounds. Five ten? Garreth found estimation difficult in a horizontal position. Red suit coat with black velvet collar and lapels, black trousers, black boots with inseam zippers. Evening wear. Garreth moved around the outside of the group at work to look at the face for an age determination.

Birkinshaw said, "I don't think he'd been in the water long. The pilot of the Alcatraz excursion boat spotted the coat on his first run out this morning."

"A wonderful treat for the tourists," Harry said, sighing.

Garreth jotted down the discovery details, then wrote a dollar sign. Even wet, the clothes retained a quiet elegance. That kind of understatement came with a high price tag. The carefully manicured nails on the outflung gray hands matched the clothing.

The photographer stepped back and was replaced by the assistant M.E., a wiry Oriental woman. In the course of examining the dead man, she pulled loose the twisted coat. Garreth caught his breath, a gasp echoed by others around him. The action rolled the dead man's head into an unnatural position and exposed a gaping wound in the throat, a slash stretching from ear to ear and so deep that spine showed.

Deadpan, Birkinshaw said, "Almost took his head clear off. Looks like his neck's broken, too."

Garreth grimaced. Birkinshaw had known . . . had been waiting gleefully for the moment the rest of them discovered it. Garreth knelt down beside the corpse and studied the face with its half-open eyes. *Age, midthirties*, he wrote. *Eyes, blue*. The face showed care, too . . . closely shaved, sideburns and mustache trimmed.

He stopped writing, staring at the dead man's neck . . . not at the puckered gray edges of the wound, but at a mark below it to one side of the Adam's apple, almost black on the pale skin and about the size of a half dollar. A feeling of déjà vu touched him.

The mark caught the attention of others, too. Birkinshaw nudged Harry. "Maybe he was on his way home from a heavy date when he was attacked. That's the biggest hickey I've ever seen."

Garreth did not think it could be a hickey. He had made a few as an adolescent and they never looked like this. It reminded him more of the marks he had seen on people's arms from hemorrhage into the soft tissues from a poor lab tech's venous stick.

"What can you tell us?" he asked the assistant M.E.

She stood up. "I'd say he died between six and nine hours ago. Cause of death seems obvious. It probably happened without warning. The wound is a single continuous incision with no accompanying nicks to indicate that the killer started to cut and was knocked away. No defense wounds on the hands or arms. From the depth of the wound, someone of considerable strength inflicted it. Do you want us to call you when we're ready to start the autopsy?"

"Please," Harry said. "All right, Mik-san, let's see what he can tell us about himself."

Kneeling beside the body, Harry and Garreth searched it. The hands were bare, but pale skin on the left third finger and right wrist indicated the removal of a ring and watch. Probably married, Garreth thought. Left-handed.

In the coat they found a handkerchief, not monogrammed, and a half-empty pack of sodden cigarettes along with a disposable butane lighter. Nothing helpful, like matchbooks that might tell them where he had been.

The items went into a property envelope.

No billfold in the trousers. Nothing in the left front pocket, either.

"Looks like robbery," Birkinshaw said. "Dressed like he is, he'd be a good target. Junkies, maybe?"

"Why break his neck on top of cutting his throat?" Garreth dug into the last trouser pocket. His fingers touched something. "Cross your fingers and hope we're lucky, Harry."

He turned the pocket inside out to remove the object without touching it, on the off chance that the killer might have touched it, too, and left a fingerprint. A key with a plastic tag attached fell into the clear plastic envelope a Crime Lab man held out.

Harry took the envelope. "Jack Tar Hotel. Overlooked by our killer, do you think?"

"Maybe he was interrupted before he could finish searching the pockets," Garreth said.

Harry murmured noncommittally, then looked up at the Coast Guard officer. "Jim, will you check the bay charts and see if you can give us an idea where our boy here went into the water?"

"Right. We'll call you on it."

The ambulance attendants zipped the dead man into a plastic bag and loaded him on a stretcher. Thinking about the bruise, Garreth watched them lift the stretcher into the ambulance. Where had he seen a mark like that before?

He asked Harry about it on the way back to the car.

Harry frowned. "I don't remember a case of ours like that."

"It wasn't our case, I'm sure." But he had still seen that mark, and heard someone else making a snide remark about a super-hickey. He wished he could remember more.

3

The signboard in the lobby of the hotel read: "Welcome, American Home Builders Association."

Harry showed his badge to the desk clerk and held up the envelope with the key. "Who has this room?"

The clerk looked up the registration card and handed it to Harry. "Mr. Gerald Mossman."

Copying down the information on the card, Garreth saw a Denver address and a company name: Kitco, Inc. "Is Mossman a member of the convention here?"

The desk clerk said, "Yes. That's the convention rate for the room."

"Do you know where we can find Mr. Mossman?"

"The convention people might. Their registration table and function rooms are up the stairs there."

They climbed the stairs and showed their badges again, this time to the people at the registration table. "I'm Sergeant Takananda. This is Inspector Mikaelian. Do you have a Gerald Mossman registered with the convention?"

"He's an exhibitor," came the reply. "The exhibition hall is down where you see the open doors."

At the doorway, however, a young man stepped in front of them, barring their way. "No admittance without a badge."

With a quick, wicked grin at each other, Garreth and Harry produced their badge cases and dangled them before the young man.

He looked down his nose at them. "Those are the wrong—" He broke off, coloring, and stammered, "Excuse me . . . I meant—I'm supposed—may I help you? Do you have business here?"

"Yes," Harry said. "Where is the Kitco display?"

"There's a floor diagram just inside." He hastily stepped aside for them.

The diagram located Kitco at the far end of the hall. There they found a woman and two men, smartly dressed and flawlessly groomed, working before a photographic montage of kitchen cabinets. Leaflets and catalogs lay on tables at the front of the booth.

The woman turned a brilliant, professional smile on them. "Good morning. I'm Susan Pegans. Kitco manufactures cabinets in a wide variety of styles and woods to fit any decor. May I show you our brochure?"

Harry said, "I'm looking for Gerald Mossman. He's with this exhibit, isn't he?"

"Mr. Mossman is our sales manager, but he's not here at the moment."

"Can you tell me where he is?"

"I'm afraid not. Is there anything I can do for you?"

Garreth opened his notebook. "Does he fit this description?" He read off that of the dead man.

Her smile faltered. "Yes. Steve . . ."

The taller of the two men left the people he was talking to and came over. "I'm Steven Verneau. Is there a problem?"

Harry showed his identification. "When did you last see Gerald Mossman?"

The blusher on the woman's face became garish paint over a bloodless face. "What's happened to him?"

Harry eyed her. "Could we talk somewhere away from this crowd, Mr. Verneau?"

"Sure."

"Steve," the woman began.

Verneau patted her arm. "I'm sure it's nothing. This way, Sergeant." He led them to a lounge area off the exhibition hall and moved into a corner away from the few people there. "Now, what's this about?"

There never seemed to be any easy way of saying it. Harry made it quick. "We've found a man in the bay with Mossman's hotel key in his pocket."

Verneau stared, shocked. "In the *bay*? He fell in and drowned?"

Garreth said carefully, "We think he was dead before he went in. He appears to have been robbed."

"Someone *killed* him?" Other people in the lounge looked around. Verneau lowered his voice. "Are you sure it's Gary?"

Garreth gave him the description.

Verneau paled. "Oh, no!"

"We need to have someone come down to the morgue and identify him," Harry said. "Can you do it?"

Verneau went whiter yet, but nodded. "Just let me give Alex and Susan some excuse for being gone."

4

Garreth had never liked the morgue, not so much because death filled it as because it felt inhospitable to life. From the first required visits during training at the Police Academy, he had seen it as a place of harsh light and hard surfaces, where sound echoed coldly and people reflected distortedly in the glazed brick, stainless steel, and tiled floors. It reeked of death, an odor that pervaded everything, hitting him as he came in the door and lingering tenaciously in his nostrils for hours after he left. This year he had come to despise the place, particularly the storage room with its banks of refrigerated steel cabinets. No matter that he intellectually recognized the necessity of the morgue, and that the dead here served the living ... every time he heard the click of the cabinet latch opening, the rolling bearings as the drawer slid out, he relived the nightmare when the face under the sheet was Marti's and half his soul had been torn away.

He stood with face set, ready to catch Verneau if need be, but although the salesman went deathly gray, he remained on his feet. "Oh, my God!"

The attendant lowered the sheet and they left the locker area.

"When was the last time you saw him?" Harry asked.

Verneau swallowed. "Last night. The exhibition hall closes at seven and we walked out together."

"Do you know what his plans for the evening were?"

"Eating out with conventioneers, I suppose. He did Monday night, and that was his usual practice . . . to make personal contacts, you know."

"Did he happen to mention any names, or where he was going?"

"I don't think so."

"A watch and ring were taken from him. Can you describe them?"

Verneau shook his head. "Maybe his wife can. She's in Denver." He ran his hands through his hair. "Oh, God; I can't believe it. This was his first trip to San Francisco."

As though that should be some charm against harm. Garreth said, "He had a large bruise on his neck. Do you remember seeing it last night?"

"Bruise?" Verneau blinked distractedly. "I—no, I don't remember. Who would do something like that? Why?"

Harry caught Garreth's eye. "Why don't I take Mr. Verneau back to the hotel and start talking to people there? You get on the horn to Denver P.D. and have them contact the wife. See if she knows his enemies. And tell them we need a description of his jewelry ASAP to put out to the pawnshops. Come on back to the hotel when you can."

5

Garreth hung up the phone. Denver was sending someone to break the news to Mossman's wife. They promised to get back about the jewelry. A message from the Coast Guard lay on Harry's desk. According to their charts, the body had most likely gone in somewhere along the southern end of the Embarcadero and the China Basin, although probably not as far south as Potrero's Point. Garreth noted the information in his notebook while he munched on pink wintergreen candy from the sack in his desk. They would need to start talking to people in that area, too. Perhaps someone had seen something.

Serruto came out of his office to sit on a corner of Garreth's desk. "What's the story on the floater?"

Garreth told him what they had so far.

Serruto frowned. "Robbery? Odd that the thief wouldn't take the hotel key, too, so he could rifle the room."

"Unless it's only supposed to look like a robbery."

The lieutenant tugged at an ear. "You have other thoughts?"

Garreth ate another piece of candy. "There's a bruise on his neck." He held a circle of his thumb and first finger against his own neck to indicate the size and location. "I remember another case with the same kind of mark, also with a broken neck. It's been within the last couple of years."

23

Serruto pursed his lips for a minute, then shook his head. "I'm afraid I don't remember anything like that. Keep thinking. Maybe you'll remember more." He went back into his office.

Garreth looked around the room. Evelyn Kolb and Art Schneider worked at their desks. He asked them if they remembered the case.

Kolb pumped the top of the thermos she brought to work every day, filling her cup with steaming tea. "Not me. Art?"

He shook his head. "Doesn't ring any bells."

Nor did it for anyone else in the squad room. Garreth sighed. *Damn.* If only he could remember something more. If only he could remember who worked the case.

Loud footsteps brought his attention around to the door. Earl Faye and Dean Centrello stormed in. He raised his brows. "You two didn't wreck another car, did you?"

Faye flung himself into his chair. Centrello snarled, "You know the Isenmeier thing? Turkey tried to cut up his girlfriend? Well, we have everything set to arrest the dude, statements from the neighbors and a warrant in the works. Then the lady says it's off. She refuses to press charges. Seems he asked her to marry him."

"Save the warrant," Schneider said. "You can use it next time."

"Lord, I'd hate to see this fox chopped up," Faye said. He rolled his eyes. "Everything she wears is either transparent or painted on. The first time we went to see her—"

Kolb cocked a brow at Garreth. "Comes a pause in the day's occupation that is known as the fairy-tale hour."

Faye frowned but continued talking. Garreth listened with amusement. Faye was walking proof that the art of storytelling had survived the age of electronic entertainment. If short on anecdotes, he waxed eloquent on women or sports, or described crime scenes in graphic detail.

That thought nudged something in Garreth's head. He suspended all other thought, hunting for the source of the nudge. But the telephone shattered his concentration. The feeling of being close to something faded.

With a sigh, Garreth reached for the receiver. "Homicide, Mikaelian."

"This is the coroner's office, Inspector. We're starting the autopsy on your floater."

Garreth gathered a handful of wintergreen candy to eat on the way over to the wing where the coroner's office was located. He knew he would not feel like eating later.

6

Not every room in the morgue echoed, Garreth reflected. The autopsy room with its row of troughlike steel tables did not. It always sounded horribly quiet . . . no footsteps or casual chatter, only the droning voices of the pathologists dictating their findings into the microphones dangling from the ceiling and the whisper of running water washing down the tables, carrying away the blood.

The Oriental doctor had already opened the abdominal cavity and removed the viscera when Garreth came in and stood at the head of the table, hands buried in his suit coat pockets. She nodded a greeting at him, never breaking her monologue.

The water ran clear this time, Garreth noticed. Even that in the sink at the foot of the table, usually rosy from the organs floating in it awaiting sectioning, sat colorless. The doctor examined the organs one at a time, slicing them like loaves of bread with quick, sure strokes of her knife and peering at each section . . . and tossing some slices into specimen containers. She opened the trachea its full length and snipped apart the heart to check each of its chambers and valves. As Garreth watched, a crease appeared between her eyes. She moved back to the empty gray shell that had been a man and went over the skin surface carefully, even rolling the body on its side to peer at the back. She explored the edges of the neck wound.

The neck had another mark, too, Garreth noticed, one that had been hidden before by the dead man's shirt. A thin red line ran around, biting deep on the sides. A mark from a chain ripped off?

"Trouble?" he asked.

She looked up. "Exsanguination—blood loss—is indeed the cause of death. However . . ."

Garreth waited expectantly.

"It did not result from the throat wound. That was inflicted *after* death. So was the broken neck. The cord is completely severed but there's no hemorrhage into it."

Déjà vu struck again. Death by bleeding, wounds and a broken neck inflicted after death. Now he *knew* he had knowledge of a previous crime with similar circumstances. Garreth bit his lip, straining to remember *what* previous case.

"He didn't bleed to death internally and I can't find any exterior wound to account for—"

There had been something else strange about that bruise on the other man. Now, what had it been? "What about the bruise?" he interrupted.

". . . for a blood loss of that magnitude," the doctor went on with a frown at Garreth, "unless we assume that the punctures in the jugular vein were made by needles and the blood drained that way."

That was the other thing about the bruise! "Two punctures, right? An inch or so apart, in the middle of the bruise?"

She regarded him gravely. "I could have used your crystal ball before I began, Inspector. It would have saved me a great deal of work."

Garreth smiled. Inside, however, he swore. He remembered that much, those facts, but still nothing that could help him locate the case in the files, not a victim or detective's name.

The remainder of the autopsy proceeded uneventfully. Lack of water in the lungs established that the victim had been dead before entering the water. The skull and brain showed no signs of bruises or hemorrhage to indicate that he might have been struck and knocked unconscious. The stomach contained no food, only liquid.

"Looks like he died some time after his last meal. We'll analyze the liquid," the doctor said.

Garreth bet it would prove alcoholic.

When the body was on its way back to its locker, Garreth prepared to leave. He had missed lunch but had no appetite. Perhaps he should just go on to the hotel. At least the fog had burned off, leaving a bright, clear day.

Before leaving the morgue, he called up to the office. Kolb answered. "Is there a message from the Denver P.D. with descriptions of some men's jewelry?" he asked her.

She went to look and came back on the line in

a minute. "No, but there's a message to call—
damn, I wish Faye would learn to write legibly. I
think the name is Ellen or Elvis Hague or Hugie.
I can't read the number at all."

"Never mind. I think I know." Mrs. Elvira
Hogue was one of the witnesses to the Mission
Street liquor store shooting. He looked up the
number in his notebook and dialed it. "Mrs.
Hogue? This is Inspector Mikaelian. You wanted
to talk to me?"

"Yes." Her thin, old-woman's voice came back
over the wire. "I saw the boy who did it, and I
learned his name."

Garreth whooped silently. Once in a while the
breaks came their way! "What is it?"

"You remember I told you I've seen him in the
neighborhood before? Well, he was here this
morning again, bold as brass, talking to that
Hambright girl up the street. I walked very close
to them and I heard her call him Wink."

"Mrs. Hogue, you're a wonderful lady. Thank
you very much."

"You just catch that shtunk. Mr. Chmelka was
a nice gentleman."

Garreth headed for R and I—records and
identification—to check the name Wink through
the monicker file. They came up with a make, one
Leroy Martin Luther O'Hare, called Wink, as in
"quick as a," for the way he snatched purses in
his juvenile delinquency days by sweeping past
victims on a skateboard. Purse snatching had
been only one of his offenses. Wink added burglary and auto theft to his yellow sheet as he
approached legal adulthood, though he had not
been convicted of either charge.

With Wink's photograph tucked among half a
dozen others of young black males, he drove to
Mrs. Hogue's house.

She quickly picked out Wink. "That's him; that's the one I saw this morning and the one I saw coming out of the liquor store after I heard the shooting."

Garreth called Serruto.

"We'll get a warrant for him," the lieutenant said.

Garreth visited Wink's mother and the Hambright girl, first name Rosella. He also talked to the neighbors of both. No one, of course, offered any help. Garreth gained the impression that even Wink's mother hardly knew the person Garreth asked about. The neighbors denied any knowledge of comings and goings from Mrs. O'Hare's or Miss Hambright's apartment.

"Hey, man, I gots enough to do chasin' rats over here without wachin' someone else over there," they said, or else: "You wrong about Wink. He no good, but he no holdup man. He never owned no gun."

Garreth dropped word of wanting Wink into a few receptive ears whose owners knew he could promise some reward for turning the fugitive, then he headed for the Jack Tar. He would see Serruto about staking out the mother's and girlfriend's apartments. For now, he had better check in with Harry before his partner put out an APB on him.

7

"So we both came up empty today," Harry said, hanging up his coat in the squad room.

"Except for identifying our liquor store gunman and the odd results of the autopsy."

"I'd just as soon do without the autopsy." Harry grimaced. "Who needs a bled-out corpse who died before his throat was cut?"

Garreth had arrived at the hotel just in time to follow Harry back to Bryant Street.

"The meetings are breaking up for the day," Harry had said. "Everyone will be going out to play. We'll start in on them again tomorrow, and this time you can join the fun."

In the squad room Garreth rolled a report form into his typewriter. "Did I miss anything interesting at the hotel?"

"Just Susan Pegans fainting dead away when we told her about Mossman. No one I talked to, conventioneers or other exhibitors around Kitco's booth, saw him last night or knew where he was going."

Garreth began his report. "Did you go through Mossman's room?"

"Right away. There was about what you'd expect ... a couple of changes of clothes and a briefcase full of company propaganda. A return plane ticket to Denver. He traveled light in the city; there's a false bottom in his shaving kit where I found his credit cards, extra cash and traveler's checks, and personal keys. No billfold, so he must have had that on him when he was killed. He made two calls, one Monday and one last night, both a little after seven in the evening and both to his home phone in Denver."

"Tomorrow why don't I check with the cab companies to see if one of them took a fare of Mossman's description anywhere last night?"

"Do that."

Garreth remembered then that he needed to talk to the lieutenant. He knocked on Serruto's door. "May I see you?"

"If it's about the warrant on O'Hare, we have it. There's an APB out on him, too."

"I'd like to stake out his mother's and girlfriend's apartments. He's bound to get in touch with one or the other."

Serruto leaned back in his chair. "Why don't we see if the APB and your street contacts can turn him first? Two stakeouts use a lot of men." He did not say it, but Garreth heard, nonetheless: *We can't spend that much manpower on one small-time crook.*

Garreth nodded, sighing inwardly. All are not equal in the eyes of the law. "Yes, sir." And he went back to his typewriter.

An hour later he and Harry checked out for the night.

8

Garreth always liked going home with Harry. The house had the same atmosphere Marti had given their apartment, a sense of sanctuary. The job ended at the door. Inside, he and Harry became ordinary men. Where Marti had urged him to talk, however, Lien bled away tensions with diversion and serenity. A judicious scattering of Oriental objects among the house's contemporary furnishings reflected the culture of her Taiwanese childhood and Harry's Japanese grandparents. The paintings on the walls, mostly Lien's and including examples of her commercial artwork, reflected Oriental tradition and moods.

Lien stared at them in disbelief. "Home before dark? How did you do it?"

Harry lowered his voice to a conspiratorial tone. "We went over the wall. If someone calls, you haven't seen us." He kissed her with a great show of passion. "What's for supper? I'm starved."

"Not lately." She patted his stomach fondly. "Both of you sit down; I'll bring tea."

Strong and well laced with rum . . . an example of what Garreth considered a happy blend of West and East. Between sips of tea, he pulled off his shoes and tie. One by one his nerves loosened. These days, he reflected, Harry's house felt more like home than his own apartment did.

During dinner Lien monopolized the conversation, heading off any threat of shop talk with anecdotes from her own day. She brushed by the frustrations of finishing drawings for a fashion spread in the Sunday paper to talk about the art appreciation classes she taught at various grade schools in the afternoons. Garreth listened bemused. Her kids came from a different world from the one he saw every day. They never took drugs or shoplifted. They were well fed and well dressed, bright-eyed with promise. Sometimes he wondered if she deliberately told only cheerful stories, but he never objected; he liked hearing about a pleasant world populated by happy, friendly people.

Not that he regretted becoming a cop, but sometimes he wondered what he would be doing now, what kind of world he would live in, if he had finished college . . . if he had been good enough to win a football scholarship like his older brother Shane, if he and Judith had not married so young, if she had not gotten pregnant his sophomore year and had to stop working, leaving them with no money to continue school.

Or would things have been any different? He had always worshiped his father and wanted to be just like him. He loved going down to the station and watching the parade of people and officers. While Shane had been starring in backyard scrimmages and Little League football, Garreth played cops and robbers. Police work had seemed a natural choice when he had to go to work.

After dinner, helping Lien with the dishes, he asked, "Do you believe people really have free choice, or are they pushed in inevitable directions by social conditioning?"

She smiled at him. "Of course they have choices. Background may limit or influence, but the choices are still there."

He considered that. "Consulting *I Ching* isn't a contradiction of that?"

"Certainly not. If anything, the sage supports the idea that people have control over their futures. He merely advises of the possibilities." She looked up in concern. "What's the matter? Are the dreadful broody *what-if*'s chewing at you?"

He smiled at her understanding. "Sort of."

Or maybe what really chewed was the thought that tonight one man no longer had any choices at all. Someone else had taken them away from him.

The body in the bay with its peculiar bruise haunted him, lurking in the back of his mind the rest of the evening, even through the excitement of watching the Giants win a 1–0 squeaker. He stared at the TV screen with Harry and asked himself who would stick two needles into someone's jugular and drain out all his blood. Why? It seemed too bizarre to be real. And why did his memory refuse to give up the information he wanted on that other case like it?

Garreth had no particular desire to go home to his empty apartment, so after leaving Harry and Lien, he headed his car—a bright Prussian red Datsun ZX he and Marti had given each other their last anniversary—back to Bryant Street. He sat in the near-empty squad room doodling on a blank sheet of paper and letting his mind wander. Bruise . . . punctures . . . blood loss. He recalled a photograph of a man in a bathtub, arm trailing down over the side to the floor. A voice said, "Homicide isn't like Burglary, Mikaelian. This is the kind of thing you'll be dealing with now."

He sat bolt upright. Earl Fay's voice! It had been Faye and Centrello's case. Faye had told Garreth—new to the section, unpartnered as yet, and stuck with paperwork—all about it in elaborate, gory detail.

Garreth scrambled for the file drawers. Everything came back to him now. The date was late October last year, just about Halloween, one of the factors which fascinated Faye, he remembered.

"Maybe it was a cult of some kind. They needed the blood for their rituals."

Methodically, Garreth searched. The file should still be here. The case remained open, unsolved. And there it was . . . in a bottom drawer, of course, clear at the back.

Seated cross-legged on the floor, Garreth opened the file. Cleveland Morris Adair, an Atlanta businessman, had been found dead, wrists slashed, in the bathtub of his suite at the Mark Hopkins on October 29, 1982. The death seemed like suicide until the autopsy revealed two puncture wounds in the middle of a bruise on the neck, and although Adair had bled to death, his wrists had been slashed postmortem by someone applying a great deal of pressure. That someone had also broken Adair's neck. Stomach contents showed a high concentration of alcohol. The red coloring of the bathwater proved to be nothing more than grenadine from the bar in his suite.

Statements from cabdrivers and hotel personnel established that Adair had left the hotel alone on the evening of October 28 and gone to North Beach. He had returned at 2:15 A.M., again alone. A maid coming in to clean Sunday morning found his body.

Hotel staff in the lobby remembered most of the people entering the hotel around the time Adair had. By the time registered and known persons were sorted out, only three possible suspects remained, and two of them were eventually traced and ruled out. That left the third, who came through the lobby just five minutes after Adair. A bellboy described her in detail: about twenty, five ten, good figure, dark red hair, green eyes, wearing a green dress plunging to the waistline in front and slit to the hip on the side, carrying a large shoulder bag. The bellboy had seen her on occasion before, but never alone. She usually came in with a man . . . not hooking, the bellboy thought, just a very easy lady. He did not know her name.

What interested Faye and Centrello about her was that no one saw her leave. Their efforts to locate her failed, however.

Nor did they find any wild-eyed crazies who might have made Adair their sacrifice in some kinky ritual.

The Crime Lab turned up no useful physical evidence, and robbery was apparently no motive; Adair's valuables had not been touched.

Garreth reread the autopsy report several times. Wounds inflicted by someone applying a great deal of pressure. Someone stronger than usual? The deaths had striking similarities and differences, but a crawling down his spine told him that his gut reaction believed more in the similarities than in the differences. Two out-of-towners staying at nice hotels whose blood had been drained through needles in their jugulars, then the bodies doctored to make it seem that they had bled other ways. It had a ritual sound about it. No wonder Faye and Centrello had hunted cultists.

After a jaw-cracking yawn, Garreth glanced down at his watch and was shocked to find it almost three o'clock. At least he would not notice the emptiness of the apartment now. He would be lucky to reach the bedroom before he collapsed.

9

Every eye in the squad room turned on Garreth as he tried to sneak in. From the middle of the meeting, Serruto said, "Nice of you to join us this morning, Inspector."

Garreth tossed his trench coat onto his chair. "Sorry I'm late. A potential witness wouldn't stop talking. Have I missed much?"

"The overnight action. Takananda can fill you in later. Now we're up to daily reports. Let's start with your cases. You've identified the Mission Street holdup man. Any word on him yet?"

"On my way in this morning I rattled some cages close to him," Garreth said. "We'll see what that produces."

"So we're just waiting to collar him, right? How about the floater?"

Garreth let Harry answer while he tried not to yawn. Despite the hour he had fallen into bed, sunrise woke him as usual.

"I've been awake since six," he complained to Harry after the meeting broke up. "So I went to work. After I rattled cages, I went by China Basin and talked to people there. So far no one seems to have seen a body being dumped in the bay." He poured himself a cup of coffee. *Do your stuff, caffeine.* "Where are the lab and autopsy reports you said we have back?"

Harry picked them up from his desk and tossed them at Garreth. In return, Garreth handed Harry the Adair file. "I finally remembered where I saw a bruise like Mossman's before. Take a look at this."

The lab and autopsy reports told Garreth nothing new. No bloodstains on the clothes, confirming that Mossman could not have had his throat cut on the street. However, there had been soiling which analyzed as a mixture of dirt, residue of asphalt and vulcanized rubber, and motor oil. It would seem Mossman had gone to the bay in the trunk of a car. No surprise there.

The autopsy report merely made official what Garreth had seen yesterday. Analysis of the stomach contents found a high percentage of alcohol, as he had thought there would be.

He glanced at Harry, who sat staring at the Adair reports. "What do you think?"

Harry looked up. "I think we'd better get with Faye and Centrello on this."

They made it a five-man meeting in Serruto's office.

With both files in front of him, Serruto said, "I can see definite similarities." He looked over at Harry and Garreth. "Do you want to pool resources with Faye and Centrello on this?"

Harry said, "What I want to do is give Earl and Dean a chance to take over this case if they want it. After all, the Adair thing was theirs."

Centrello grimaced. "I don't want it. You two play with the cult crazies for a while. I'll be glad to give you anything I know that isn't in the reports, but if you solve it, the glory is all yours."

Faye looked less certain, but he did not contradict his partner.

Serruto frowned at the Adair file. "Are you thinking cults on the Mossman thing, too, Harry?"

"I'm certainly going to check out the possibility."

"Don't get too tied into it; it didn't solve the Adair killing."

"Words of wisdom," Harry said as they left for the hotel.

"You know, both men had alcohol in their stomachs, so they were drinking not long before they died." Garreth pursed his lips. "I wonder if they drank in the same place?"

Harry punched for the elevator. "Adair went to North Beach. When you visit the cab companies, check for North Beach destinations on those trip logs."

Garreth sighed. "You know every jack man of those conventioneers went to either North Beach or Chinatown that night."

Harry grinned and slapped Garreth's shoulder. "You'll sort them out. That's detective work, Mik-san. Think about me, trying to find someone who knows where Mossman went. I can't believe he didn't mention something to *someone*."

A thought struck Garreth. He frowned at Harry. "You talked to quite a few people?"

"It seemed like hundreds."

"And no one knew a thing. Maybe he didn't want people to know. He's a married man and if he had something hot going . . ."

Harry pursed his lips. "Verneau said this was Mossman's first trip to San Francisco and he didn't make any local calls from his room. If he had a lady, she would have to be either a member of the convention or someone he met Monday. Susan Pegans fainted when we told her Mossman was dead, and that wasn't even telling her *how*. Skip the cab companies for a bit and help me at the hotel. We'll start with our saleswoman."

10

Susan Pegans stared at the detectives with eyes flashing in outrage. "No! Absolutely not! I didn't go anywhere with Gary. He's a very happily married man. He calls his wife every evening when he's away from home."

But Garreth heard the note of regret in her voice as she said it. He was willing to bet she would have gone with Mossman in a moment, given an invitation.

"Alex Long and I had dinner in Chinatown with a couple of Iowa contractors and their wives. Ask Alex."

They would, but for the moment, Garreth continued to press her. "Have you seen him spending an unusual amount of time with any single person here?"

"He spent time with everyone. What does it take to make you understand that Gary doesn't—" She broke off, eyes filling with tears. She wiped at them with the handkerchief Garreth handed her. "Gary didn't play at conventions, not ever. He worked. Why do you think he was sales manager?"

"But you knew where he was going Monday night. Verneau said he told all three of you," Harry said.

"Yes, so we would know who had been contacted and not duplicate efforts."

"Yet you didn't think it strange when he said nothing to you about Tuesday night?"

She shrugged, sighing. "I wondered, yes, but
... I thought he'd tell us Wednesday. I—" She
broke off again, shaking her head.

"Pity unrequited love," Harry murmured as
they left her. "Well, do we take her at her word
or start questioning some of the other ladies?
You'll have noticed how many really beautiful
ones there are here."

"Maybe we ought to think about guys, too,"
Garreth said. "That would be a better reason for
keeping it quiet."

"You talk to beautiful young men, then; I'll
stick to the ladies. Just find *someone* who went
out with him."

Garreth found no one. He worked his way
straight down the section of the membership list
Harry gave him and heard negative answers in
every interview. As far as Garreth could determine, Mossman had said to hell with the convention on Tuesday. Checking with Harry later, he
found his partner having no better luck.

"Maybe you ought to start on the cab companies," Harry said. "I'll keep working here."

"Let me bounce one more idea off you. You
mentioned that he may have met someone Monday evening. So let's talk to the people he was
with Monday. Do you have their names?"

"Verneau gave them to me." Harry checked off
two names on the membership list. "You take
this half of the group."

Garreth made it easy on himself. He rounded
up both and talked to them at the same time,
hoping one might stimulate memory in the other.
"Where did you go?" he asked them.

Misters Upton and Suarez grinned at each
other. "North Beach. That's some entertainment
up there."

"It offers a little of something for everyone. Do you remember the names of the clubs you visited?"

"Why do you want to know about Monday?" Suarez asked. "Wasn't Gary Mossman robbed and killed on Tuesday night? That's what's going around."

"We need to know about people he met Monday. Please, try to think. I need the club names."

They looked at each other. "Big Al's," Suarez said.

Between them, Suarez and Upton named half a dozen of the better known clubs. Garreth jotted the names down. "Any others?"

"Oh, yeah. We must have hit a dozen or more. We'd just walk down the street and drop in, see a girl or two dance, and go on."

"Did you talk to anyone?"

Their eyes narrowed. "What do you mean?"

Garreth gave them a man-to-man smirk. "You were five guys out on the town alone. Didn't you buy drinks for any girls?"

The contractors grinned. "Well, sure. We kind of collected four and took them along with us."

Four. Garreth raised a brow. Who had not had one? "Did Mossman pay special attention to any of them? Did he ask any of them back to the hotel?"

"No."

"Are you thinking he met someone Monday he might have seen again Tuesday and gotten killed by?" Suarez asked.

"We're checking all the possibilities. Can you give me the names of the girls? I also need to know if he met anyone outside your group."

"The girls only told us their first names, and Mossman didn't talk to anyone except us and the girls," Upton said.

"Give me the girls' names then and their descriptions." Inwardly, Garreth groaned. Track down four girls in North Beach by first name and description. Shit.

"Except the singer," Suarez said.

Garreth blinked, feeling he had missed a connection somewhere. "Except what singer, Mr. Suarez?"

The contractor shrugged. "We were in this club—I don't remember the name—and Mossman couldn't do anything except stare at the singer. She kept looking at him, too, giving him the eye. I remember he hung back a bit as we left, and when I looked around, he was talking to her. It was just for a minute, though."

"What did this singer look like?"

Suarez grinned. "Spectacular. Tall, and I mean *really* tall, man. Her legs went on forever. She was built, too."

Something like electric shock trailed up Garreth's spine, raising every hair on his body. He stared at Suarez, hardly breathing. "Do you think she was five ten?"

"Or taller. She had on these boots, see, and—"

"What color was her hair?"

"Red. Not that bright color but darker, like mahogany."

Red-haired
Woman

1

Harry was dubious. "He had a few words with a red-haired singer Monday night. What makes you think he went back to do more on Tuesday?"

"A hunch."

Certainly he could think of no other reason. No real evidence connected Mossman to this woman any more than evidence connected Adair to that other redhead. Only the similarity in height and coloring suggested that the two women might be the same. Still ... two mysterious deaths and two memorable redheads. He had a feeling about it.

"My Grandma Doyle gets what she calls Feelings ... that's with a capital F. She's Auld Sod stock, full of blarney and superstition, but—well, that Green Bay–L.A. game that wiped out my brother's knee, we were all watching the TV and at halftime she went to her room. She said she didn't want to watch Shane get zapped. And sure enough, in the middle of the third quarter . . . scratch one knee and one Rams end."

"Coincidence?" Harry suggested.

"Except that's just one instance. My grandmother's Feelings are famous in our family. On the other hand, maybe my hunch is nonsense, but crazies come in all shapes and sizes so we'd better check the redhead out."

Harry nodded. "That reason I'll go along with. But let's eat first; I'm starved."

So was Garreth. Lunchtime had long passed. "How about Huong's?"

Huong's, though a hole-in-the-wall greasy chopsticks eatery up a side street off Grant Avenue, served some of the best fried rice and egg rolls in San Francisco. For love of them, Garreth had learned to ignore the greasy smoke that seeped out of the kitchen and covered the walls and Chinese signs on them with a uniform coat of dingy gray, and to beg silverware from waitresses who understood little English and barely more of Harry's and his fractured Chinese.

Harry considered. "It'd be too much trouble to drive over there when we have to come back here again. How about settling for less this time?"

With stomach longing for fried rice, Garreth settled for a club sandwich in the hotel coffee shop.

"One thing," Harry said while they ate. "Whether the redhead is in it or not, we need to know where Mossman went."

"I'll get on the cab companies."

He called them from the assistant manager's office. To be on the safe side, he expanded the time limit and asked for single fares picked up at the hotel between 7:00 and 8:30 P.M. Garreth expected to develop writer's cramp, but while it appeared that fleets of cabs had picked up passengers Tuesday evening, most trips carried groups. Less than a dozen cabs made single-fare trips in that time period.

He wrote down the cab number, destination,

and cabdriver's name for each trip. Then it became a matter of having drivers on duty stop by the hotel to look at a picture of Mossman that the Kitco booth supplied him or calling on them at home. "Was this man a passenger in your cab Tuesday night?" He particularly pressed the five whose destinations had been in North Beach. However, none could identify Mossman.

"That doesn't mean I couldn't have taken him," one female cabbie said. "I just don't remember him, you know?"

Garreth met Harry back at the hotel. "Zero. Zip."

Harry looked at his watch. "Well, let's call it quits here, then."

Garreth seconded the motion and they headed back to Bryant Street.

While they typed up reports at the office, Harry said, "What do you say to taking Lien out for a change? I'll call her, and you make reservations for three somewhere."

Garreth shook his head. "Tonight you have her to yourself. I'm going to eat at Huong's and fall into bed early."

"You sure?" Harry whipped his report out of the typewriter and signed it after a fast proof-reading.

"Go home to your wife."

Harry waved on his way out.

Garreth kept typing. Some time later Evelyn Kolb came through. She said, "There's a telex for you from Denver. I think Art put it under something on your desk."

"Under?" He dug through the pile of papers on the desk, frowning. Under, for God's sake. It could have gone unseen for days.

The telex, when he found it, had the descriptions of the jewelry. He read quickly. A man's gold Seiko digital watch with expansion band and enough functions to do everything but answer the telephone; a plain gold man's wedding band, size 8, inscribed: *B.A. to G.M. 8-31-73.*

"Oh, God," he sighed, feeling his chest tighten. "Today was their wedding anniversary. What a hell of a present."

Kolb grimaced in sympathy.

Garreth made himself go on. A sterling silver pendant two inches long, shaped in the outline of a fish with the Greek word for fish inside the outline. "Is that enough silver to bother stealing?" he asked.

Kolb pumped tea out of her thermos. "If some kind of cult killed your man, they might not like Christian symbols."

Garreth toyed with the telex. "It's almost too bizarre." He wondered if it was possible that instead of a cult, they were dealing with someone who wanted Mossman dead, but made it as weird as possible to confuse everyone. The telex also said the wife knew of no serious enemies her husband had, but of course that would have to be checked out. For now, he typed up the jewelry descriptions for a flier to distribute to the pawn-shops, then finished his reports.

2

"No more. *Bu yao*," Garreth said to the waitress who extended the coffeepot toward his half-empty cup.

He could not be sure he had the Chinese pronunciation right, but it came close enough to convey his meaning. With a nod and a smile, the girl turned away.

He drained the cup and stood, reaching for the check with one hand and into his pocket for the tip with the other. He left the girl a generous one; she had struggled hard to overcome the language barrier between them. At the cash register he paid the withered little old woman almost hidden from sight by the machine. "Delicious, as always, Mrs. Huong."

She smiled in return, bobbing her head. "Come back again, Inspector."

"Count on it."

Outside, he walked down the steep half block to Grant Avenue and stood on the sidewalk there, surrounded by passing evening throngs of tourists and the bright kaleidoscope of shop windows and neon signs with their Chinese pictographs, contemplating alternatives to going home. Perhaps he should turn over a few rocks in Wink O'Hare's neighborhood. This was about the time of day the little vermin was most likely to stick his head out of his hole. On the other hand, just a few blocks up the hill, Grant Avenue intersected with Colum-

51

bus Avenue and Broadway in the beginning of North Beach's bright-lights section, and somewhere among the bars and clubs sang a tall red-haired woman who might or might not be involved in murder.

He stared up the hill, weighing the choices. Finding Wink should have priority—he still had the gun he had presumably used to shoot the liquor store clerk—but evening in North Beach frankly appealed to Garreth far more than the despairing poverty of Wink's turf. He had his sources keeping eyes and ears open, and as long as he was on his own time anyway . . .

He turned uphill.

Chinatown gave way to blocks of glittering, garish signs proclaiming the presence of countless clubs. Barkers paced the sidewalks, calling to passersby in a raucous chorus . . . beckoning, wheedling, leering, each promising the ultimate in exotic entertainment inside his club. Garreth absorbed it all, color and noise, as he threaded his way through the crowd, but also kept alert for unnecessary bumps against him and fingers in his pockets. He spotted some familiar faces . . . about the time they recognized him, too, and swiftly faded into the crowd.

He hailed a barker he had met on previous occasions. "How's business, Sammy?"

"All over legal age, Inspector," Sammy replied quickly. "Come on in and see the show, folks! All live action with the most gorgeous girls in San Francisco!"

"Any redheads, Sammy?"

Sammy eyed him. "Sure. Anything you want."

"Maybe a very tall redhead, say five ten, with green eyes?"

The barker's eyes narrowed. "This redhead got a name? Hey, mister!" he called to a passing couple. "Your timing is perfect. The show is about to start. Bring the little lady in and warm up together. What do you want her for, Mikaelian?"

"A date, Sammy. What else? Who do you know with that description? She sings in the area."

Sammy laughed. "Are you kidding? We've got more showgirl redheads than the stores have Barbie dolls. Come on in and see the show, folks! Real adult entertainment, live on our stage! Our girls have curves in places most girls don't have places, and they'll show you every one!"

"I need names, Sammy," Garreth said patiently.

Sammy sighed, not patiently. "Names. Who knows names? Try the Cul-de-Sac across the street. There's a red-haired singer I seen there. And maybe in the Pussywillow, too. Now, will you move on, man? You're spoiling my rhythm."

Grinning, Garreth moved across the street into the Cul-de-Sac. Yes, a barmaid said when he ordered a rum and Coke, they had a red-haired singer. She came on after the dancer.

He sat down at the bar, which ran around the edge of the stage. A blonde dragged an enormous cushion out onto the stage and proceeded to writhe nearly naked on it in simulated ecstasy. In the midst of her throes, she rolled over, saw Garreth watching her with amusement, and said in a bored monotone, "Hi, honey. And what's your day been like?"

"About like yours, unfortunately, hours wasted grinding away at thin air," he replied.

A fleeting grin crossed the blonde's face.

The singer appeared presently. Garreth left. The redhead's hair color was bottle-bred brass and she looked old enough to have sung on the Barbary Coast itself.

He talked to barkers on down the street, collecting a notebook full of possibles, but in check-

ing them out, he found women with the wrong
color of red, wrong height, and wrong age. In two
hours he checked over a dozen clubs with no
success and stood on the sidewalk outside of the
last with an ache working its way up from his
feet. He looked around, seeking inspiration.

"Hi, baby. All alone?" a husky voice asked
behind him.

Garreth turned. A woman in her thirties with
elaborately curled dark hair arched a plucked,
painted eyebrow at him. "Hi, Velvet," he said.
Her real name, he knew from busting her when
he worked Vice, was Catherine Bukato, but on the
street and with the johns, she always went by
Velvet. "How's your daughter?"

Velvet smiled. "Almost twelve and more beautiful every day. My mother sends me pictures of
her regularly. I may even go home to see her this
winter. You up here working or playing tonight?"

"I'm looking for a woman."

Velvet hitched the shoulder strap of her hand-
bag higher. "You're playing my song, baby."

"The woman I want is red-haired, young, and
very tall. Taller than I am. She sings somewhere
around here. Would you happen to know anyone
like that?"

Velvet's eyes narrowed shrewdly. "I tell you
what. My feet are killing me. Why don't you play
like a john who has to work up his courage? Buy
me a drink where I can sit down for a while and
I'll think on it."

Garreth smiled. "Pick somewhere."

She chose the nearest bar and they found seats
in a rear booth. She ordered, then kicked off her
shoes and stretched her legs out, propping her
feet up on the seat on the far side of the booth.
She closed her eyes. "That's what I needed. You
know, for a cop, you're almost human, Mikaelian."

"Every Thursday night." In the right quarters, inexpensive kindness could reap valuable benefits. Velvet's sharp eyes and ears missed little on the street.

A fact she knew he knew. Opening her eyes, she said, "So let me pay for the drink. Who's this woman you're looking for?"

Garreth gave her a detailed description.

Velvet's drink came. She sipped it slowly. "Tall? A singer? Yeah, I've seen someone like that. I can't remember where, though. What did she rip off?"

"I'm in Homicide now, not Burglary. I just want to talk to her."

Velvet's drawn brows rose again, skeptical. "Oh, sure."

"If you have a chance, will you ask around? It's important that I find her."

Velvet eyed him a moment, but then nodded. "How can I refuse someone who always asks about my kid? You have a kid, Mikaelian?"

"An eight-year-old boy named Brian."

For the remainder of the time it took her to finish her drink, they talked children and exchanged the pictures they carried. As Garreth handed back Velvet's snapshot of her daughter, the prostitute started to laugh.

"What's funny?" Garreth asked.

Her teeth gleamed in the dimness of the bar. "What a pair we are, a cop and a hooker, sitting in a bar talking about our kids." She drained her glass, sighed, and fished around under the table for her shoes. "Well, time to go back to work. Thanks for the coffee break."

They headed for the door.

"I hope this won't make trouble for you with Richie, getting nothing for the time," Garreth said.

She looked up at him. "Look, if it isn't too much trouble, maybe you could give me a little something, a kind of advance on information I'm going to give you? It'll help with Richie."

He dug into his pocket for his billfold and came up with two tens. "One for Richie Soliere and one for you to buy something for your daughter, all right?"

She folded away the bills with a smile. "Thanks a lot." Then she tossed her head and dropped back into her husky "professional" voice. "Good night, baby."

He watched her walk off into the crowd, then counted what remained in his billfold. The impulsive generosity had nearly cleaned him out. It would make the rest of the swing through North Beach a dry trip. He hoped Velvet gave him a good return on his investment.

3

Rob Cohen raised a brow at Garreth. "That's the third time you've yawned in the last five minutes. You single guys sure lead a fast life."

Harry regarded Garreth sharply, however. "You worked all night after all?"

Garreth shrugged. "I couldn't sleep." He gave Harry a recap of the North Beach canvas. "It was a waste of good shoe leather, though; I didn't find her."

"Maybe you're lucky. Your hexagram this morning was number forty-four, *Coming to Meet*. 'The maiden is powerful. One should not marry such a maiden.' "

A sudden chill raised the hair down Garreth's spine. He wondered at it. *I Ching*'s prophecies usually neither disturbed nor encouraged him. He thought of Grandma Doyle's Feelings. However, he made himself slap Harry's shoulder. "Don't worry, Taka-san. I have no intention of marrying *any* maiden in the near future."

Too late he realized that the flip response had been wrong. Harry's almond eyes went grave. "You know the text isn't to be taken literally. What's the matter?"

The chill bit deep into Garreth's gut. "Nothing." A lie? He could not be sure. His chest felt so tight he had trouble breathing. "Guess I'm just superstitious enough not to like having that caution turn up when I'm hunting a woman." He hurriedly changed the subject. "Here's the flier on Mossman's watch, ring, and pendant that's going out to the pawnshops."

Harry read it over. "Good."

The tightness and chill eased in Garreth. "What do you want to do this morning?"

"I think one of us ought to get started checking out cults and the other take China Basin. Shall we flip for it? Loser takes the cults."

Garreth chose tails. The quarter came up heads. Harry grinned as he left for China Basin.

Garreth sat down with the Adair file and read through the reports to see which groups Faye and Centrello had investigated. On the half dozen he found reports on, only one had a formal name, Holy Church of Asmodeus. The others were listed by leaders' names. The groups varied in size, organization, and object of worship. Some seemed to be satanists or devil worshipers. Others appeared to be variations of witchcraft and voodoo.

One group claimed to be neo-druids. All, however, had been rumored to use blood in their
ceremonies. A few admitted it, but insisted it was
either animal blood or small amounts from members, voluntarily given. Analysis of blood samples
on altars and instruments confirmed that most
was animal blood. One of the few human samples
proved to be A positive like Adair's, but investigation of the group failed to establish opportunity
for any of the members and, further, more detailed analysis of the blood sample found enough
differences in minor factors to rule out the possibility of the blood being Adair's.

Nevertheless, Garreth turned all the names in
to R and I for a check of current activities, then
called Sergeant Dennis Kovar in Fraud.

"Denny, what complaints have you had in the
past year about oddball church and cult groups?"

Kovar laughed. "How much time do you have
to listen? I don't need to lift weights after picking
up the current file a few times a day. Parents and
neighbors are all out for the blood of these
groups."

"What about the groups? Do you have any
word that any of *them* are using blood?"

Silence came over the line for a moment before
Kovar answered. "What are you looking for?" He
listened silently to Garreth's reply, then said, "I
don't have many complaints about those groups.
They aren't asking for monetary donations. They
keep a low profile so they won't be noticed. But
you might talk to Angelo Chiarelli. He's undercover full-time and officially attached to Narco,
but he's fed information to me on some of these
fraudulent church groups and contacted a few
kids in the cults for Missing Persons. Maybe he
can help you."

A call to Narcotics produced a promise to pass

on Garreth's request. "You understand we can't just go calling on him every day, and he's pretty busy doing his own job to run errands for other sections."

Garreth sighed. "He doesn't have to work on my case. I just want any possible information on blood-using cults that he may know about."

"We'll get back to you."

He even called the Humane Society about complaints of people killing and mutilating animals and went out to buy underground papers. When Harry came back to the office around two, they exchanged notes over coffee and doughnuts.

Harry's interviews in China Basin produced nothing for them. The underground classifieds had some cult ads, but no direct route of contacting the groups.

"We'll have to get some scrawny kid straight out of the Academy, who can get past their security," Garreth said. "The ASPCA has some complaints of animal mutilation we might follow up on, too."

"What about Chiarelli?"

"Still no word back from Narco yet. Here's everything R and I has currently on the cults Faye and Centrello investigated."

And what, Garreth wondered, leaning back in his chair with a sigh, did it mean until they knew where Mossman had been? Until they knew, they had no way of establishing opportunity for the cults. Checking movements was treadmill work.

Still, it needed to be done, and over the next four days they visited the cult groups Faye and Centrello listed, then those with ads that their rookie contacted for them. They visited people who had reported animal mutilations to the Humane Society. Garreth did not like most of the cultists he met—some he detested on sight—but he found them very educational: women who simultaneously attracted and chilled him, people who he would have taken for dull businessmen on the street, and some, too, who looked like escapees from Hollywood horror movies. No group, though, had a very tall red-haired female member.

None of Mossman's jewelry appeared in the pawnshops.

At the same time, they hunted up the four girls who had joined Mossman's group on that Monday night—and cleared all four of any Tuesday night involvement with Mossman—and kept prodding their contacts for Wink O'Hare's hiding place. Garreth spent his evenings in North Beach on a systematic search for the singer. On Tuesday, September 6, one week after Gerald Mossman died, Garreth found her.

4

Calling the singer tall seemed an understatement. In boots with four-inch heels, to go with the satin jeans, shirt, and Stetson of her urban cowgirl outfit, the redhead towered over the patrons of the Barbary Now as she walked between the tables singing a sentimental Kenny Rogers song. The red hair, black in shadow, burning with dark fire where the light struck it, hung down her back to her waist and framed a striking, square-jawed face. Watching the long legs carry her between the tables, Garreth remembered the description the bellboy had given of the woman in the Mark

Hopkins lobby. She had to be the same woman. Surely there could not be two like this in San Francisco. He would slip something extra to Velvet, above the usual, to thank her for finding this woman.

The hooker had called the office that afternoon. He and Harry had been out, but she left a message: *If you're still looking for that redhead, try the Barbary Now after 8:00 tonight.*

So here he and Harry were, and here was a redhead.

"Nice," Harry said.

Garreth agreed. *Very* nice. He beckoned to a barmaid. "Rum and Coke for me, a vodka collins for my friend, and what's the name of the singer?"

"Lane Barber."

Garreth watched the singer. He did not blame Mossman for having stared at her. Most of the present male eyes in the room remained riveted on her throughout the song. Garreth managed to take his own off just long enough to see that.

The barmaid brought their drinks. Garreth tore a page out of his notebook and wrote on it. "When the set finishes, will you give this to Miss Barber? I'd like to buy her a drink."

"I'll give it to her, but I'd better warn you, she has a long line waiting for the same honor."

"In that case"—Harry took out one of his cards— "give her this instead."

The girl held the card down where the light of the candle on the table fell on it. "Cops! If you're on duty, what are you doing drinking?"

"We're blending with the scenery. Give her the card, please."

Three songs later, the set ended. Lane Barber disappeared through the curtains behind the piano. She reappeared five minutes later in a strapless, slit-skirted dress that wrapped around her and stayed on by the grace of God and two buttons. She made her way through the tables, smiling but shaking her head at various men, until she reached Garreth and Harry.

She held out the card. "Is this official or an attention-getting device?"

"Official, I'm afraid," Harry said.

"In that case, I'll sit down." Garreth felt her legs rub against his under the small table as she pulled up a chair. She smiled at Harry. "*Konnichi wa*, Sergeant Takananda. I've always enjoyed my visits to Japan. It's a beautiful country."

"So I hear. I've never been there."

"That's a pity." She turned toward Garreth. "And you are—?"

"Inspector Garreth Mikaelian."

She laughed. "A genuine Irish policeman. How delightful."

She was not really beautiful, Garreth realized with surprise, studying her as well as he could in the flickering candlelight, but she moved and talked and dressed to seem that way, and something radiated from her, something almost irresistible in its magnetism. She looked no more than twenty or twenty-one.

"Now, what is this unfortunately official visit about?" she asked. "It can't be a traffic ticket; I haven't driven anywhere in weeks."

"Were you working last week?" Harry asked.

She nodded. Oddly, the flame of the candle reflected red in her eyes. Garreth had never seen that in humans before. He watched her, fascinated.

"Do you remember speaking to a man on Monday who was in his thirties, your height when you're barefoot, and wearing a red coat with black velvet lapels and collar? He was with four other men, all older than him."

She shook her head ruefully. "I must have

talked to over a dozen different men that night, Sergeant. I do every night. I like men. I'm afraid I can't recall any particular one."

"Maybe this will help." Garreth showed her the picture of Mossman.

She tilted it to the flickering light of the candle and studied it gravely. "Now I remember him. We didn't really talk, though. I flirted with him while I sang because he was nice-looking, and as he left, he came over to say how much he liked my singing." She paused. "You're from Homicide. Is he a suspect or a victim?"

The lady was cool and fast on the uptake, Garreth reflected. "A victim," he said. "Someone cut his throat Tuesday night. Did he come back here at any time on Tuesday?"

"Yes. He asked me out, but I didn't go. I don't date married men."

Harry said, "We need to know exactly what he said and did Tuesday. What time did he come in?"

"I don't really know. He was here when I did my first set at eight. He stayed all evening and we talked off and on, but not too much. I didn't want to encourage him. Finally I told him I wasn't interested in going out with him. The bartender, Chris, can confirm that we sat there at the end of the bar. About twelve-thirty he left."

Garreth made notes by the light of the candle. "Was that the last you saw of him?"

"Yes. Lots of men don't know how to take no for an answer, but he did."

"I suppose you have a fair number of guys try to hustle you. Do you ever take anyone up on the offer?"

She smiled. "Of course, if the man interests me. I don't pretend to be a nun. What business is it of yours?"

"Where do you usually go, your place or his?"

Her eyes flared red in the candlelight, but she replied evenly, "Yes."

Garreth dropped the subject, recognizing evaporating cooperation. There would be time enough later to question her about Adair, if need be. "I'm sorry; that was irrelevant. I'll need your name and address, though, in case we want to talk to you again."

"Of course." She gave him the address, an apartment near Telegraph Hill.

"Are you a permanent resident of the city?" Harry asked.

"I travel a good deal, but this is home base, yes."

"Are you a native like Harry there, or an immigrant like me?"

"Yes," she replied, and when their brows rose, she smiled. "Women are more fascinating with a bit of mystique, don't you think? Leave me mine until you absolutely must have the information, can't you?" She glanced at her watch. "It's almost time for the next set. Please excuse me."

She rose and left, walking gracefully toward the piano. Garreth looked after her, sighing. He could not see her as a bloodthirsty cultist.

Harry grinned at him. "Do you still want to involve her in two murders?"

She began a song in sultry tones that jostled Garreth's hormones pleasantly. "I'd rather date than arrest her," he admitted.

"She seems cooperative enough and she didn't hesitate to admit she'd seen Mossman Tuesday. Still ..."

"Still," Harry agreed. "You never know, so we'd better check her out."

5

In the darkness of his bedroom, lying awake, Garreth heard the foghorns start. The years living here had taught him to recognize the patterns of a few, like the double hoot of the one on Mile Rocks and the single every-twenty-seconds blast of the one on Point Diablo. *Fog moving in*, he thought.

He stopped consciously listening when the horns and diaphone on the Golden Gate Bridge joined the chorus. The dial of his watch glowed on the bedside table, but he resisted the urge to look at it. Why see how long he had lain awake?

He sat up, hugging his blanketed knees. What was wrong? Why should he be bothered that their interviews with the manager of the Barbary Now and the singer's neighbors last night and today turned up nothing to connect her with the murders?

"I wish everyone I hired were as dependable," the manager had said. "She's always on time, always polite to even the biggest asshole customers, never drunk or strung out. Lane never causes trouble."

Her neighbors echoed the sentiment. One said, "You'd hardly know she's there. She sleeps all day and comes home from work after we've gone to bed. If she brings anyone home, I don't know it because she never makes a sound. She's away on

tour sometimes and it may be a week before I
realize she's gone."

"Do you ever see any of her friends?" Garreth
had asked.

"Once in a while. They're men, mostly, leaving
in the morning, but all very well dressed . . . none
of the dirty, hairy, blue-jean types."

Altogether, their questions produced a picture
of an ideal neighbor and employee. So what did
he find so disturbing about that? Maybe just *that*.
He had an innate suspicion of people who kept a
profile low to the point of invisibility. Even
granting differences between professional images
and private lives, he could not quite reconcile
such a life-style with the sexy, coolly sophisti-
cated young woman from the Barbary Now. *The
maiden is powerful*, I Ching said. *One should not
marry such a maiden*. Beware of that which seems
weak and innocent.

And yet, he could not picture her threading a
needle into Mossman's jugular, either . . . not
with his present knowledge of her.

"I need to know more," he said aloud into the
darkness.

The midchannel Golden Gate diaphone sounded
out of the fog in its bellow-and-grunt voice, as
though replying to his remark.

He would talk to her landlord, he decided,
lying back in bed, and then to more of the
Barbary Now personnel. He would see if all their
opinions matched the ones he had already heard.

That decided, he lay relaxed, listening to the
hooting and bellowing of the foghorns reverberate
through the night. The rhythmic chorus carried
him into sleep.

6

The woman inside the protective grille across the doorway wore a bathrobe and slippers. She blinked through the grille at Garreth's identification. "Police? This early?"

"I'm sorry about the hour, Mrs. Armour, but I need to ask a few questions about a tenant of yours." He himself had been up for hours, finding out who owned the house where Lane Barber lived.

Mrs. Armour opened the grille with a frown and led the way up a steep flight of stairs to a sunny kitchen looking out over the fog that shrouded the lower marina and bay. "Which one, and what have they done?"

"I don't know that Lane Barber has done anything. She merely knows someone involved in a case I'm investigating."

The frown faded. She sat down at the table, returning to the toast and coffee that Garreth's ring had obviously interrupted. "Coffee, Inspector?" When he accepted with a nod, she poured a cup for him. "I'm glad Miss Barber isn't in trouble. Actually, I would have been surprised if you'd said she was."

Mrs. Armour, too? Garreth added cream and sugar. "You know her well?"

"Not personally, but she's one of my best tenants. I have a number of properties in that area and most of them are rented by restless

67

young people who are here this year and gone the next. I wish you could see the state they leave their apartments in. It's appalling. But Miss Barber pays her rent on time every month and when I go in with the painters to repaint her apartment, as I feel ought to be done every few years, her place is always spotless. She takes beautiful care of it."

Garreth stopped stirring his coffee. "Every few years? How long has she been a tenant?"

Mrs. Armour pursed her lips. "Let's see. I think I've had her apartment done three times. She must have been with me about ten years. No . . . I've painted four times. She's been there twelve years. She's my oldest tenant."

Twelve years? Garreth blinked. "How old was she when she moved in?"

"Very young, but at least twenty-one. I remember she told me she was singing in a club."

Garreth stared at her. The singer was twenty-one *twelve years* ago? He clearly remembered the face above the candle; it had not belonged to a woman in her thirties, although her level of sophistication certainly seemed more commensurate with that age than with twenty-one. Had she had a face-lift, perhaps?

"What has her friend done?" Mrs. Armour asked.

For a moment, Garreth struggled to think what the woman was talking about. "Oh . . . he died. In the time Miss Barber has been your tenant, have you ever had any trouble with her? Has the apartment . . . smelled strange, or have neighbors complained of strange people coming and going?" Cult types. It occurred to him that if she lived in the middle of a shifting population, former neighbors may have seen things present ones could not know about.

"Smelled strange? Like marijuana?" Mrs. Armour sat bolt upright in indignation. "Certainly not! I've never had a single word of complaint about her."

Garreth could not believe in this paragon. It was obvious, however, that Mrs. Armour was not going to add any clay to the lady's feet, so he thanked her for her help and headed for Bryant Street.

As he came into the squad room, Harry said, "You're supposed to call Narco."

Garreth peeled out of his trench coat. "I hope it's about Chiarelli."

He called after the squad meeting. It was about Chiarelli. A Sergeant Woodhue said, "It's arranged for you to meet him. Join us in the garage at twelve-thirty."

Garreth hung up. "Let's hope Chiarelli can help us."

"Maybe. But my hexagram this morning said, 'In adversity, it furthers one to be persevering,' and yours read, 'Success in small matters. At the beginning good fortune; at the end, disorder.' "

Garreth grimaced. "Thanks. I really needed to hear that."

He thought about his conversation with the landlady on the Barber girl's age. A strange lady, this redhead. He ran her name through R and I. It came back negative for local and state, even negative NCIC—the FBI had nothing on her. She did not even have a traffic ticket. In fact, he discovered that she had no driver's license. That brought a frown. She had said something about driving when they talked to her. Had she been only joking?

"Do you think she can be thirty-three years old?" he asked Harry. "She looks much younger."

"In the lighting of that bar, Methuselah would

look like an adolescent; it's designed that way. How else could some of those hookers snag a john?" Harry raised his brows at Garreth. "Why so concerned about her age? Isn't that part of the mystique?"

"Maybe there's such a thing as too much mystique." The first chance he had, Garreth decided, he would ask the lady a few pointed questions and dispel some of it.

7

A voice over Sergeant Woodhue's walkie-talkie said softly, "It's going down now."

Suddenly the old warehouse filled with narcotics officers. Garreth hung on Woodhue's heels, the sergeant's words at the briefing echoing in his head: *This is the drill. We're busting a buy. Chiarelli, who's going by the name Demesta, will be there. You're a hot-dog cop along for the fun. When Chiarelli bolts, you go after him.*

The men involved in the buy scattered like cockroaches before a light. Garreth searched among them hurriedly, looking for someone who matched the description Woodhue had given him—a lean runt in an oversize old army jacket—but he could not see Chiarelli. In the melee and half dark, he had trouble distinguishing any particular individual.

Then Woodhue pointed and barked, "Get Demesta!"

Garreth saw the army jacket then, faded to pale

green, with dark patches where the insignia had been removed. It dwarfed the man inside it, a man who bowled over an officer and was vanishing into the junk littering the building. Garreth took after it.

Chiarelli went out of a broken window in a shower of flying glass from remaining shards in the frame. Trying to avoid cutting his hands as he followed, Garreth swore. *See the stupid cop jump out the window*, he thought sardonically. *See him break his leg.*

But somehow he landed outside without crippling himself and looked up in time to see his quarry scramble across a set of railroad tracks and disappear into a passage between two more warehouses. Garreth pounded after him. At the beginning, good fortune? The hell. It looked more like disorder all day.

A hand reached out of a narrow doorway to grab Garreth's coat and jerk him inside the building. "Let's make this fast, man," Chiarelli said. "You're interested in cults?"

Garreth nodded, panting slightly. "I have two men who've been bled to death through needles stuck in their necks. We think maybe a cult did it."

"Like the Zebra murders? Christ!" Chiarelli shuddered and crossed himself. "So you want the names of people or groups who might use blood in their rituals."

"Right. Can you help me?"

Chiarelli sighed. "I'm not really next to that scene, you know, not unless some group also uses drugs, but ... I guess I've heard a few things. Give me paper and a pen."

Garreth handed him his pen and notebook.

Chiarelli printed with the speed of a teletype and talked almost as fast as he wrote, passing on

more information than he had time to write.
"Some is just addresses, not names. There have
been weird stories about this house on Geary.
Screaming and smells like burning meat." He
had similar comments on every person or address
he wrote down. When finished, he handed the
notebook back. "Will that help?"

Garreth glanced over the pages, amazingly legi-
ble for the speed at which they had been written.
"I hope so. Thanks." He started to turn away.

"Wait a minute," Chiarelli said. "We have to
make it look good for me or I'm blown."

"I'll just say you outran me."

He shook his head. "Not good enough. You
don't look like you've been chasing me all this
time."

"How do you want to handle it, then?" He saw
Chiarelli's fist double and stepped back, shaking
his head. "Hey, not that—"

But the fist was already in motion. It sank into
Garreth's stomach. He went down onto hands and
knees in a wheeling galaxy of pain and light. His
gut rebelled at the treatment by rejecting what
remained of his lunch and he huddled retching on
the dusty floor.

A wiry arm slipped under his and helped him
to his feet as the paroxyms subsided. Chiarelli's
face floated beyond a blue haze. "Take it easy.
You'll be all right in a couple of minutes," he
said cheerfully.

Garreth would have gone for Chiarelli's throat,
but he could only lean against the wall and
concentrate on breathing. He could not even
swear at Chiarelli, just gasp and groan.

"Sorry, man, but it has to look real."

Chiarelli did not have to worry about that,
Garreth reflected bitterly.

"See you around, man." Chiarelli slipped out the door.

Garreth continued to lean against the wall for several more minutes, then made his way slowly back to the site of the bust.

Seeing him coming, Harry exclaimed, "Garreth!" and rushed to catch his arm. "What happened? Are you all right?"

Garreth leaned against a handy car, holding his stomach. "Bastard ambushed me. I thought I was never going to make it up off that damned floor."

"So you let him get away, hot dog?" Woodhue said.

Several prisoners snickered. Garreth glared at them. "Next time I won't bother chasing him. I'll hobble the son of a bitch with a piece of lead . . . permanently."

Harry helped him to a car. "Nice acting," he whispered.

Garreth climbed into the car, remembering Chiarelli's smirk. "Who the hell is acting?"

He sat silent all the way back downtown. Not until they had left the Narco officers and returned to Homicide did he give the notebook to Harry. "We'd better run these names through R and I, then find out who owns or lives in these houses."

Harry regarded him with concern. "Are you sure you're all right? Maybe you ought to go home and take it easy the rest of the day."

"I'm fine. We have work to do." He started to take off his coat and winced as the motion stretched bruised muscles.

Harry hustled him toward the door. "Go home. I'll tell Serruto what happened."

"I don't want to go home. I'll be fine," Garreth protested.

"No one who refuses time off can possibly be

fine. I'm a sergeant, but you're just an inspector, so I'm pulling rank and ordering you out, hear? Or do I have to have someone take you in handcuffs?''

Garreth sighed. "I'll go quietly, papa-san."

He left Chiarelli's pages of his notebook with Harry and headed for his car. He slipped the key into the ignition but did not start the engine immediately. As much as he hurt, he hated the thought of going home. He ought to give up the apartment with all of its sweet and painful memories and find another. Perhaps one of those places around Telegraph Hill that Mrs. Armour had mentioned.

The thought of them told him what he really wanted to do. He wanted to see Lane Barber again, to talk to her by daylight and find answers for the increasing number of questions she raised about herself. Then he started the engine.

8

She did not come to the door until Garreth had rung the bell five times. He realized that she must be sleeping and would find his visit inconsiderate and inconvenient, but he remained where he stood, leaning on the bell. She finally opened the door, wrapped in a robe, squinting against the light, and he discovered that even by daylight, she looked nothing like a woman in her thirties. If anything, she seemed younger than ever, a sleepy child with the print of a sheet wrinkle across one pale, scrubbed cheek.

She scowled down at him. "You're that mick detective. What—" Then, as though her mind woke belatedly, her face smoothed. He watched her annoyance disappear behind a facade of politeness. "How may I help you, Inspector?"

Why did she bother to swallow justifiable irritation? Did police make her that nervous? Perhaps it was to observe this very reaction, to see what she might tolerate to avoid hassles, that he had persisted on the bell.

"I'm sorry to wake you," he lied. "I have a couple of important questions to ask."

She squinted at him from under the sunshade of her hand, then stepped back. "Come in."

Moving with the heavy slowness of someone fighting a body reluctant to wake up, she led the way to the living room. Heavy drapes shut out the afternoon light, leaving the room in artificial night. She switched on one lamp and waved him into its pool of light. She herself, however, sat in shadow in a suspended basket chair across from the chair by the lamp. A deliberate maneuver on her part?

"This couldn't wait until I got to the club?" Weariness leaked through the careful modulation of her voice.

"I'll be off duty by that time. I try not to work nights if I can help it; the police budget can't stand too much overtime."

"I see. Well, then, ask away, Inspector."

With her face only a pale blur beyond the reach of the light, Garreth found himself listening closely to her voice, to read her through it, and discovered with surprise that she did not sound like he felt she should. Inexplicably, the voice discorded with the rest of her.

"Can you remember what you and Mossman talked about Tuesday night?"

She paused before answering. "Not really. We flirted and made small talk. I'm afraid I paid little attention to most of it even while we were talking. Surely it isn't important."

"We're hoping that something he said can give us a clue to where he went after leaving the Barbary Now. Did he happen to mention any friends in the city?"

"He was far too busy arguing why *we* should become friends."

Suddenly Garreth realized why her voice seemed at odds with the rest of her. She did not talk like someone in her twenties. Where was the slang everyone else used? Just listening to her, she sounded more like his mother. What was that she had called him at the door? A mick. Who called Irishmen *micks* these days?

Garreth looked around, trying to learn more about her from the apartment, but could see little beyond the circle of lamplight. The illumination reached only to a Danish-style couch which matched his chair and a small desk with a letter lying on it.

He said, "He told you he was married, didn't he?"

"He wore a wedding ring. I could see that even in the Barbary Now's light."

"Of course." Garreth stood up and moved toward the door. "Well, it was a slim chance he'd say anything useful, I suppose. I'm sorry to have bothered you." On the way, he detoured by the desk to read the address on the letter. Knowing someone she wrote to might be useful.

"It's a price I pay for my unusual working hours." She stood and crossed to the lamp. "I'm sorry I couldn't help."

BLOOD HUNT   77

Garreth had just time enough to read the
ornately written address before the light went
out, leaving the room in darkness.

On the steps outside, after her door closed
behind him, he reread the address in memory.
The letter had to be incoming; it had this address. However, it had been addressed not to
Lane Barber, but to Madelaine Bieber. The similarity of the two names struck him. Lane Barber
could well be a stage name, "prettied up" from
Madelaine Bieber.

He eyed the garage under the house as he came
down the steps to the sidewalk. Did she drive or
did she not?

He tried the door. Locked. However, by shining
a flashlight from his car through the windows, he
made out the shape of a car inside and illumi-
nated the license plate. He wrote down the
number.

Motion above him brought his attention up in
time to see the drape fall back into place in the
window over the garage. Lane, of course, watching
him, but . . . out of curiosity or fear? Maybe the
license number would help provide an answer to
that.

Back at Bryant Street, he ran Madelaine Bieber
through R and I, and asked for a registration
check on the license number.

"The car is registered to a Miss Alexandra
Pfeifer," the clerk told him. The address was
Lane's.

"Give me a license check on that name."

The picture from DMV in Sacramento looked
exactly like Lane Barber. Miss Pfeifer was described as five ten, 135 pounds, red hair, green
eyes, born July 10, 1956. Which would now make
her twenty-seven.

Then R and I came back with a make on

Madelaine Bieber. "One prior, an arrest for assault and battery. No conviction. The charges were dropped. Nothing since. She's probably mellowed with age."

Garreth raised a brow. "Mellowed with age?"

"Yeah," the records clerk said. "The arrest was in 1941."

Garreth had the case file pulled for him.

Madelaine Bieber, he read, had been singing in a club in North Beach called the Red Onion. A fight started with a female patron over a man, and when the woman nearly had her ear bitten off, she preferred charges against the singer. Miss Bieber, aka Mala Babra, was described as five ten, 140 pounds, red hair, green eyes. Birth date July 10, 1916. The picture in the file looked exactly like Lane Barber in a forties hairstyle.

Garreth stared at the file. If Lane were born in 1916, she was now sixty-seven years old. No amount of face-lifting would ever make her look twenty-one. This Bieber must be a relative, perhaps Lane's mother, which would explain the likeness and similar choice in professions. But why was Lane receiving her mother's mail? Perhaps the mother was a patient in a nursing home and the mail went to her daughter. It was something to check out. But another question remained: Why have a false driver's license and a car registered to that false license name?

Mystique? Lane generated nothing but, it seemed. The lady definitely deserved further attention.

9

At eight o'clock, when Lane came out through the curtains for her first song, Garreth sat at a table talking to a barmaid while he ordered a drink. "How long has she been singing here?"

The barmaid, whose name tag read *Nikki*, shrugged. "She was here already when I came last year."

"What do you think of her?"

Nikki sighed. "I wish I had her way with men. They fall all over themselves for her."

Lane worked her way through the club as she sang. On one turn, she saw Garreth. For a moment, her step faltered and a musical note wavered, then she smiled at him and moved on.

After the last song of the set, she came over to his table. "We meet again. I thought you weren't going to work overtime tonight."

He smiled. "I'm not. I'm here for pleasure. I'd also like to apologize again for disturbing you this afternoon."

She smiled back. "That isn't necessary; I realize you were only doing your job."

"Then may I buy you a drink?"

"Later, perhaps. Right now I've already promised to join some other gentlemen."

Nikki, passing the table, said, "Don't waste your time; you're not her type."

Garreth watched Lane sit down with three men in flashy evening jackets. "What *is* her type?"

"Older guys in their thirties and forties. Guys with bread to throw around. And her man of the evening is always a tourist, an out-of-towner. She only likes one-night stands."

Garreth recorded it all in his head. He asked casually, "Man of the evening? She lets herself be picked up often?"

"Almost every night, only *she* does the picking up. The suckers just think they picked her up."

"Really?" *Be an audience. Keep her going, Garreth, my man.*

"Really. She chooses one, see, and tells him to leave but that she'll meet him later. She never goes out the door with one of them."

"Then how do you know that's what happens?" He kept his voice teasing.

"Because," Nikki said, lowering her voice, "I've overheard her giving them instructions. She tells the guy that the boss is her boyfriend, see, and that he's very jealous, but then she tells the sucker he's turned her on so much, she's just *got* to see him. He leaves thinking he's really a superstud. Every night she tells a different guy the same thing."

"Always a different guy? No one ever repeats?"

Nikki shook her head. "Sometimes they try. She's polite, but she never goes with them again." Nikki sighed. "She must do something they really dig. I wonder if I should try the tigress bit, too."

"Tigress bit?" *You're doing great, honey; don't stop.*

"Yeah. If they come back for another try, the guys she's gone with always have this huge hickey on their necks. I've never—"

The whole world screamed to a halt for Garreth. He felt electricity lift the hair all over his body. "Hickey?" he asked breathlessly. "About this size and located here?" He demonstrated with a circle of thumb and finger.

The barmaid nodded.

She's dirty! But for a moment Garreth could not be sure whether he felt satisfaction or disappointment at proof of her involvement. Perhaps both. Wanted or unwanted, this gave him a legitimate excuse to ask all the questions of her he liked.

He gave Nikki a five-dollar bill. "For you, honey. Thanks."

He made his way to the table where Lane sat. Nodding to the three men with her, he said, "Sorry to interrupt, gentlemen, but I need to speak with the lady for a minute."

Lane smiled. "I said, later, perhaps."

"It can't wait."

One of the men frowned. "The lady said later. Bug off."

Ignoring him, Garreth leaned down to Lane's ear. "I can use my badge and make it official."

She glanced up sharply at him. Her eyes flared red in the candlelight again. Why did her eyes reflect when most people's did not? Garreth wondered. Lane stood, smiling at the men, cool and gracious. "He's right; it can't wait. I won't be a minute." As they walked away from the table, though, the tone of her voice became chiding. "So you're on duty after all. You lied, Inspector."

"So did you. You said you didn't see Mossman after he left the club on Tuesday, but we found him with a bruise on his neck just like the ones the girls here tell me you put on all your men."

She glanced around. "May we talk outside?"

They left the club. Outside, the street stretched away from them in both directions, glittering with the lights of signs and car headlights, smelling of exhaust fumes and the warmth of massed humanity. Like accents and grace notes, whiffs of perfume and male cologne reached them, too. Voices and cars blended into a vibrant roar. *My city*, Garreth thought.

Lane breathed deeply. "I do so love the vitality of this place."

Garreth nodded agreement. "Now, about Mossman . . ."

"Yes, I saw him. What else could I do? He would have waked all the neighbors, pounding on my door that way. He got the address from the phone book."

"So you invited him in?"

She nodded. She strolled down the street and Garreth followed. "I invited him in," Lane said, "and then . . . well, he was a charming man and . . . we ended up in bed. He left about three, alive, I swear. But he insisted on walking, even though I warned him not to and offered to call a cab."

Garreth counted two possible flaws in the story. Three o'clock lay on the edge of the limits given by the M.E. for Mossman's time of death. He would have had to die very soon after leaving Lane's apartment. And would a man careful enough to leave his keys and extra money and credit cards hidden in his hotel room ignore the offer of a cab and walk down a street alone in the middle of the night?

They turned the corner. Once around it, the traffic thinned and the noise level dropped dramatically. Garreth asked, "Why didn't you tell me this before?"

She sighed sheepishly. "The usual reason: I didn't want to be involved."

"The autopsy found puncture wounds in the middle of the bruise on Mossman's neck. How did they get there?"

"Punctures?" She stared down at him. "I don't

have the slightest idea. They weren't there when he left me."

Garreth said nothing in response to that. Instead, he waited, curious to see what more she might say to fill the conversation gap.

But unlike most people, who felt uncomfortable with silence and would say anything, often incriminating things, to avoid silence, she did not rise to the bait. She walked wordless beside him as they turned another corner.

Now almost no traffic passed. Garreth found himself preternaturally conscious of the near-empty street. Here on the back side of the block, they seemed a hundred miles from the crowds and lights.

He asked, "Did you ever meet a man named Cleveland Adair?"

Her stride never faltered. "Who?"

"Cleveland Adair, an Atlanta businessman. We found him dead last year with a bruise and punctures just like Mossman's. A woman matching your description was seen in the lobby of his hotel shortly before his estimated time of death."

He expected denial, either vehement or indignant. He was even prepared for her to try running away. Instead, she stopped and turned to look him directly in the eyes. "How many deaths are you investigating?"

Her eyes looked bottomless and glowed like a cat's. Garreth stared into them, fascinated. "Two. After all, it looks like the same person killed them both."

"I suppose it does. Inspector," she said quietly, "please back up into this alley."

Like hell I will, he thought, but found he could not say it aloud. Nor could he act on the thought. Her eyes held his and his will seemed paralyzed.

Step by step, as commanded, he moved backward, until he came up short against a wall.

"You're here alone." Her hands came up to his neck, loosening his tie and unbuttoning the collar of his shirt. Her hands felt cool against his skin. "Have you told anyone where you are or about my little love bites?"

Yes, he thought, but he spoke the truth. "No." Should he have admitted that? He could not find concern in him; all he cared about at the moment was staring into the glowing depths of her eyes and listening to her voice. "I haven't told anyone."

"Good boy," she crooned, and kissed him gently on the mouth. She had to bend down her head to do it. "That's a very good boy." Her voice dropped to a whisper. "I don't think you should ever tell."

He barely heard her. Her voice reached him from a great distance, like all sensation at the moment: the rough brick of the wall at his back, the chill of the evening, the increasing rate of her breathing. Somewhere deep inside, uneasiness stirred, but listening to it seemed too much trouble. He found it easier to just stand passive and let her tip his head back against the wall.

Her lips felt cool on his mouth and cheek, and her fingers on his neck as she probed to one side of his windpipe. His pulse throbbed against the pressure.

"That's a nice vein," she whispered in approval. Her breath tickled as she spoke between kisses. "You're going to like this. You'll feel no pain. You won't mind a bit that you're dying." She kissed him harder and he felt the nip of her teeth. Her mouth moved down over his jaw to his neck. "You're a bit short for me so this will be awkward unless you stand very still. Whatever happens, don't move."

"No." It emerged in a sigh.

"I love you, Inspector. I love all men of power."
Her teeth nipped harder, moving toward the spot
where his pulse beat against her fingers. "You
don't have money or position like the others,
but you have knowledge, knowledge I can't afford
to have spread around, so that gives you more
power than most of my lovers. Still, I have more. I
have the power of death, and the power to take
your power from you. I love doing that."

She bit harder. A distant sensation told him her
teeth had broken his skin, but he felt no pain,
only a slight pressure as she sucked.

"What—" he began.

Her finger brushed across his lips, commanding
him to silence. He obeyed. All desire to talk had
left anyway. A wave of mixed warmth and cold
moved outward through his body from where
her mouth touched him. He shivered in pleasure
and moved just a little, straining toward her mouth.
Yes. Nice. Go on. Don't stop.

Presently, though, he wondered if maybe she
should. He felt very weak. He needed to sit down
before he collapsed.

His knees buckled, but her hands caught him
under the arms and held him against the wall.
She must be very strong, a languid thought came
through the tingling of his nerves . . . certainly
stronger than she looked, to be holding up someone of his weight so easily. Dreamily he thought,
The maiden is powerful, just like the sage said.

But with the thought of *I Ching*, lassitude disappeared. Fear rose up through him like a jet of ice
water. Two men the singer knew had died of
blood loss. Now she kissed his neck in the very
spot where the other men had had punctures and
bruises and he felt himself weakening, too! With
a profound shock of horror and revulsion, he
realized why. Lane Barber was sucking his blood!

He shuddered and tried to pull loose, pushing at her shoulders with his hands. His body obeyed only sluggishly, however, and when she noticed his effort, her body pressed harder against his, pinning him to the wall.

Use your gun, you dumb flatfoot.

But her hand easily kept him from reaching it.

Abandoning pride in favor of self-preservation, he opened his mouth to yell for help. Her hand clamped across his mouth, silencing him.

Garreth's breath caught in fear. He did not have the strength to fight her. Only her weight against him held him upright. She was killing him, as she had killed Adair and Mossman—were human teeth really sharp enough to bite through skin into veins? Where had she learned such depravity? —and he could do nothing to stop her. He was dying, helpless to save himself.

In desperation, he bit at her hand to make her let go of his mouth. He sank his teeth in deep, using all his fading strength. Skin gave way. Her blood filled his mouth, burning like fire. Convulsively, he swallowed, and his throat burned, too . . . but with the fire came a surge of new strength. Lane jerked the hand to free it, but he hung on, making the most of the opportunity to hurt her. More blood scorched down his throat. He managed to bring both hands up to her shoulders and push her back.

But it was too little effort coming too late. She tore loose from him, her hand from his mouth and her mouth from his throat. He felt her teeth rip through his flesh. As she backed away from him, he fell, collapsing to the ground.

The pain of striking the ground barely reached him. He only saw, not felt, the blood streaming from his torn throat to make a crimson pool around his head. A suffocating fog muffled all sensation ... touch, sound, and smells.

"Good-bye, lover," a distant, mocking voice said. "Rest in peace."

Her footsteps receded into the darkness. Garreth tried to move, to drag himself to the mouth of the alley where he might find help, but a leaden heaviness weighted him down, leaving him helpless. He could not move, only stare into the growing, cooling pool of blood. He cursed his stupidity ... for coming after her alone, for not letting someone know what he had found out, but most of all, as his breathing and heartbeat stumbled, faltered, and faded, he cursed himself for underestimating her ... just what *I Ching* warned against. How could he explain this to Marti when he saw her?

See the idiot cop, he thought bitterly. *See him bleeding to death ... dying alone in a cold and dirty alley.*

Passage

1

Rest in peace. Like hell. Death is not peace. It leads not to Marti, nor to any kind of heaven . . . not even to oblivion. Death is not that kind. Death is hell.

It is dreams . . . nightmares of suffocation and pain, of restless discomfort, of aches when one cannot move to ease them, of itches impossible to scratch. It is hallucination invading the void, playing blurrily before half-open eyes that are unable to focus or follow . . . imaginary hands on him, patting him, then lights, footsteps, sirens, voices. *Oh, God! Call the watch commander . . . I didn't kill him, Officer! I'd never kill no cop, and anyway how could I do that to him? I just took the gun and stuff out of his pockets. Would I show you where the body was if I'd done it? . . . Garreth? . . . Easy, Takananda. Garreth! Oh, God, no! . . . He hasn't been dead long; he's still warm . . . Are there loose dogs in this area?*

Death is hell, and hell is dreams, but mostly, hell is fear . . . panic-stricken, frantic. Are all the dead aware? Do they remain that way? Is this to be eternity . . . lying in twilight and nightmares, throat aching with thirst, body crying for a change of position, mind churning endlessly? Does Marti lie like this in her grave, insane with loneliness, begging for peace, for an *end*? *No, not for her . . . please, no.*

He hates giving up life, but accepts that in the jungle, death is the price of carelessness, of error, and he has errored badly. Surrendering life to rejoin Marti would be welcome. He could even accept oblivion. This, though . . . this limbo? The thought of having to endure it for eternity terrifies him.

He screams . . . for himself, for Marti, for all the dead trapped sleepless and peaceless and tormented in their graves. He screams, and because it is without sound, unvoiced, it echoes and reechoes endlessly down the long, dark, lonely corridors of his mind.

2

The horror escalated. A sheet over him blocked the vision of his eyes; temperature had become all one to him, unfelt; and the lack of breath prevented him from smelling anything, but he knew he lay in the morgue. He had heard its cold echoes on arriving, had felt himself slid into a drawer and heard the door close. Now he heard, had lain listening for countless time, the hum of refrigeration units about him while he dreamed nightmares and wished Lane had thrown him in the bay, too. Maybe he would have gone out to sea. Better to be fish food than lie in this hated purgatory of cold and steel. He prayed his parents did not have to see him here.

That was when he thought of the autopsy. One would have to be done. His heart contracted in fear. What would it be like? How would it feel to lie naked in running water on cold steel, sliced open from neck to hips, shelled out like a pea pod . . .

Heart!

He could not cease moving or hold his breath, but his mind paused, waiting. Yes, there it was! Like the distant boom of a drum, his heart sounded in his chest. It squeezed. A slow ripple moved outward from it along his arteries. He felt almost every inch of them. A long pause later, the drum beat again, then again.

He listened in wonder. If his heart beat, he could not be dead. His body lay leaden, held unmoving to the surface beneath him, but a silent cry of joy banished the darkness inside him. Alive Alive!

He drew a breath . . . slow, painfully slow, but a breath nonetheless.

He could have sworn he was not breathing before, nor his heart beating. He had felt—how he had felt!—the silence of his body. What miracle caused the heart and lungs to resume function? He could not imagine, and at the moment, over-joyed with the sound and feel of them, he did not give a damn about the reason.

But he remained in a morgue locker, naked in a refrigerated cabinet. Unless he found a way out, the cold would kill him again. Could he attract attention by pounding on the locker door?

He tried, but the weakness that had held him motionless the past—how many?—hours persisted. He still could not move.

Could he survive until they came to take him

out for the autopsy? He did not feel the cold of the locker right now. Perhaps if he kept alert, he could fight off hypothermia.

He wished, though, that he could change position. His body consisted of one continuous, unrelenting ache, stiff from neck to toes.

By concentrating and straining, he finally managed to move. Like the first heartbeat and the first breath, it came with agonizing slowness. Still, by persisting, he managed to shift his weight off his buttocks and turn on his side. Not that that helped a great deal; he still felt uncomfortable, but at least the position of the aches changed.

He tried again to knock on the locker door, but he moved in slow motion, and the sound he produced was barely audible even to him. He would just have to wait for them to open the door.

He fought his way onto his stomach to change the pressure points once more.

He did not sleep. Certainly he did not rest, but in spite of himself, he must have dozed because the motion of the drawer sliding out startled him. He had not heard the door open. Light flooded him blindingly as the sheet came off.

"What clown put this stiff in on his belly?" a voice demanded irritably.

If he raised upright, would they faint? Garreth wondered. He wished he could find out, but gravity dragged at him, weighting him. He went without resistance as they rolled him onto the stretcher and rearranged the sheet over him.

"Hurry," another voice said. "This one's a cop and Thurlow wants to get him posted as soon as possible."

Garreth worked his hands to the edges of the stretcher and clamped his fingers around the rubber bumper. Even if he could not move fast enough to attract their attention and they missed the faint motion of his chest, they could hardly overlook this.

The stretcher stopped. An attendant pulled off the sheet. Hands took him by the shoulders and legs and pulled . . . but Garreth's grip held him on the stretcher.

"What the hell is going on?" snapped the voice of the medical examiner.

"I don't know, Dr. Thurlow. His hands weren't like that when we put him on the gurney."

Now that he had their attention, Garreth forced open his eyes. Half a dozen gasps sounded around him. He focused on Dr. Edmund Thurlow. "Please." The whisper rasped up out of his throat with a plea from his soul. "Get me out of here."

3

Were the doctors at the far end of the intensive-care unit speaking in unusually loud voices? Garreth wondered. He heard every word clearly.

"I tell you he was dead," Thurlow insisted. "I detected no vital signs, no heartbeat or respiration, and his pupils were fixed and dilated."

"I think it's obvious he couldn't have been dead," another doctor said. "However, that's beside the point now. The question is, can we keep him alive? His blood pressure is nonexistent and we have bradycardia as well as a reduced temperature and respiration rate."

"Well, he's getting blood just as fast as we can pour it into him. We'll just keep running bloodwork on him and see how he does."

Garreth looked up at the suspended plastic bag with its contents the same dark red as Lane Barber's hair. His eyes followed the tubing down to his arm. The blood made him feel better, but still not good. Exhaustion dragged at him. He desperately wanted to sleep, but he could not find a comfortable position, no matter how he shifted and turned.

"What about the throat injury?" a doctor asked.

"I think the skin sutures we put in will be sufficient," came the reply. "The trauma doesn't appear nearly as severe as what you described, Dr. Thurlow."

"We have photographs of what I saw." Thurlow's voice sounded defensive. "Both the left jugular and common carotid suffered multiple lacerations, almost to the point of complete severing. There were also multiple lacerations of the trachea and left sternocleidomastoid muscles."

"And yet just over twelve hours later the vessels and trachea appear intact. The muscle is healing, too. I can't believe that this is a recent injury."

"I don't pretend to understand it; I only know what I found when I examined him in the alley."

They went on talking, but Garreth tried to ignore them. Careful not to move the arm with the needle in it, he shifted position again. The cardiac monitor above his bed registered the effort with an extra bleep. Moving proved point-less, however. Nothing made him comfortable. His bed stood near the window, and the glare of sunlight added to his discomfort.

Footsteps approached. If it was the nurse, he decided, he would beg for something to drug him to sleep. Then he smiled weakly as Harry and Lieutenant Serruto appeared around the curtain. "Hi," he whispered.

"Mik-san," Harry replied in a husky voice. His hand closed hard over Garreth's.

Serruto said, "They're letting us ask you a few questions."

"Yes. What the hell were you doing up there?" Harry demanded. "I'm your partner. Why don't you tell me what you're doing?"

"Easy, Harry," Serruto said.

Garreth did not mind. He heard the frantic worry beneath the anger and knew how he would have felt in Harry's place. "Sorry."

"What happened?" Serruto asked.

Talking hurt. Garreth tried to find a short answer. Reaching up to the heavy collar of bandages around his throat, he managed to whisper, "Lane Barber bit me."

They stared. "*She* bit you! Did she overpower you or what?"

How could he explain the loss of will that allowed her to stand him passively against a wall and tear his throat out? Damn, that light hurt. He shut his eyes.

"Please. Close the curtains. Sun's too bright."

"There's no sun," Harry said in a tone of surprise. "We've been socked in with heavy fog since midnight."

Garreth opened his eyes again in astonishment. Noises that sounded overly loud and light that hurt his eyes ... bleeding to death produced one hell of a hangover. But to his relief, Harry closed the curtains. It helped a little.

"Lane bit Mossman and Adair," he said with an effort. "Drank their blood."

"Christ!" Harry shuddered. "The barmaid

thought Barber might be kinky, but she's *really* bent."

Barmaid? Garreth did not ask the question, but he raised his brows in query.

Serruto explained. "We went around to the Barbary Now. Harry thought that you might have been there. The barmaid told us what you two talked about."

If that was so, Harry must have made the same connections *he* had. He looked questioningly at Harry. Harry sighed, shaking his head, indicating to Garreth that they had not arrested Lane.

"She's skipped," Serruto said. "Caught a plane to be at her mother's bedside, she told the manager."

Harry said, "Something spooked her. When she came to work, she told the manager that she might have to leave suddenly. She'd even arranged for another singer to come in. After her walk with you, she sang a second set, then made a phone call—to her family, she told the manager—and said she had to leave."

Garreth's visit had spooked her. She saw him taking down the license number of the car. "Search her apartment?"

They nodded. "Nothing," Serruto said. "No personal papers in the desk or trash. Some had been burned in the fireplace. The lab is seeing what they can recover from them. Refrigerator and cupboards bare. A closet full of clothes, so she didn't take much with her. The manager has no idea where her mother might live."

A nurse pulled back the bed curtains. "Lieutenant, that's enough for now." When Serruto frowned, she slid between him and the bed and herded both the lieutenant and Harry away.

Harry called back, "Lien sends her love. She'll visit as soon as it's allowed."

When they were gone, the nurse moved around the bed, tucking in sheets. "For someone so weak, you're a restless sleeper."

For the first time in his life. "I'm not comfortable. May I have a sleeping pill?"

"Absolutely not. We can't allow anything that depresses body functions." She leaned across him, pulling up the covers. As she did so, the smell of her filled his nostrils ... a pleasant mixture of soap and fabric softener and something with an odd but strangely attractive metallic/salty scent. "A bit later I'll send an aide to give you a back rub. That may help."

The aide, when she came, gave a good back rub, but not even that helped. The sheets felt hot and sticky every place they touched him. He twisted in vain looking for a cool spot.

But though he could not make himself comfortable, he felt better with each unit of blood put into him. The dragging weight of his body lightened and he moved with less effort. A thirst that had persisted all day turned into strident hunger and he looked forward eagerly to supper.

An eagerness which suffered sharp disappointment when he saw the broth, gelatin, and tea they allowed him. "I don't get real food?" He thought longingly of fried rice and Lien's sweet-and-sour pork.

"We don't want to strain your circulation by making it work at digestion."

Maybe *we* did not, but *he* would not have minded. Then again, perhaps he would. After eating, his stomach churned uneasily, as though debating whether to keep the offering or not. Garreth lay quiet, willing the nausea away. Could this be part of last night, or was it an aftermath of Chiarelli's punch?

At length, the nausea subsided ... and Garreth

discovered he felt much better. Full of new blood and a symbolic meal, he felt surprisingly normal. Though he still needed sleep, he found some of the aches had subsided. He wished he had a TV to watch.

A doctor appeared later in the evening, introducing himself as Dr. Charles. Garreth recognized one of the voices from the group that morning.

"You're looking much better, Inspector. I'm very pleased with your blood picture. Now, let's check a few things."

He used a stethoscope and rubber hammer and tongue depressor, listening, peering, tapping, probing. While he worked, he hummed. Occasionally the hum changed key, but Garreth could not tell if that had any significance or not. What he did notice was the same metallic/salty odor about the doctor that he had noticed on the nurse, and the aides, too, come to think of it. Did they all wear the same antiperspirant or something?

"Oh, you're doing much better. What you need now is a good night's sleep, and if you're doing this well in the morning, we'll move you out of Intensive Care," the doctor said.

Garreth, however, did not feel the least like sleeping now. He wanted a TV or visitors. Lacking both, he could only lie in bed listening to the heart monitors bleeping in ragged syncopation around the room. He closed his eyes, but opened them again when his mind began replaying the nightmare in the alley. Where *had* she learned that perversion?

Why did they keep Intensive Care lighted so brightly at night? he also wondered. There was enough light to read by. How could anyone sleep in a glare like this?

He still lay awake when dawn came, and then, astonishingly, for what must be the first time in his life, the first rays of the sun were followed by an intense desire *to* sleep. Only he could not. Just as suddenly, he rediscovered all of yesterday's aches. The sheets heated up and Garreth found himself once more in a ceaseless hunt for a comfortable position. Worse, when breakfast came, his stomach voted against it. It came back up almost as soon as it went down.

On his morning rounds, Dr. Charles frowned gravely about that. Garreth told him about Chiarelli.

"We'll schedule for a barium series tomorrow and see about your stomach."

In the meantime, they fed him intravenously. He lay with clear liquid running into one arm and blood—after the morning bloodwork, they decided he needed still more blood—into the other. He would look like a junkie by the time they dismissed him, he reflected.

The air filled with that metallic/salty scent, stronger than ever. Only this time, none of the staff were around him. Sniffing out the source, Garreth discovered that it came from the tube feeding blood into his arm.

The hair on his neck stirred. *That* was what he was smelling, *blood*? He smelled the blood in people? Why now, when he never had before? He shivered uneasily. Weird. What was happening to him?

Before he had a chance to answer the questions about himself, Serruto arrived with a stenographer to ask official ones. Those seemed to go on forever, though objectively he knew the lieutenant made it a relatively short statement. After Serruto left, Garreth was moved to a private room and then left to sleep. He wished he could. He felt exhausted, and ready to cry in frustration at being unable to sleep.

Garreth did not even attempt to eat lunch. The mere scent of it set his stomach lurching.

Lien came for a short visit in the afternoon. "You look terrible," she said, "but at least you're alive. I had a frantic call from your mother yesterday morning."

Garreth's stomach tightened. "They'd heard about me on the news?"

"No, it hadn't been broadcast yet. She said your grandmother dreamed you'd been killed, that Satan tore out your throat." Lien paused. "It's uncanny, isn't it?"

But typical of Grandma Doyle.

"Unfortunately, at that time we thought you *were* dead. The happiest phone call I've ever made was the one later to let her know you were alive after all. She said to tell you they'll be up in a couple of days to visit."

He would like that. Maybe Judith would let them bring Brian, too.

Lien chattered about her job and art classes, relieving him of the necessity of saying anything. While she talked, she distracted him from his discomfort, but once she had left, he went back to fighting aches and hot sheets. To make matters worse, his upper gums started to hurt for no reason.

He eyed the cushioned chair by the window. That might be a helpful change; it would be a change anyway. So he threw back the covers and eased over the side of the bed.

In two steps he had fallen flat on his face, giving himself a bloody nose and—he discovered with horror—loosening his upper canines. They wiggled when he touched them with his tongue. He was trying to crawl back into bed when an aide found him.

Dr. Charles wasted no time being polite or

solicitous. "That was a stupid thing to do. In the first place, you're not ready to get out of bed, and when I decide you are—when *I* decide, Inspector—you will be helped in and out. Under *no* circumstances are you to do it alone. I presume that as a police officer you know how to take orders. Well, I'm giving you one. *Stay in bed.* Do *nothing* without asking permission first. Is that clear?"

Garreth shrank back meekly into the bed. "Yes, sir."

"Good. We have the barium study scheduled for you tomorrow. A dentist will check your teeth as well." He stalked out.

Toward evening Garreth managed to doze some, but he never really slept, never truly rested. With nightfall, though, he felt better, just like the night before. The desire to sleep vanished, though he remained tired. He turned on the TV.

A nurse, coming in to check his vital signs, turned it off. "Dr. Charles wants you to sleep."

As soon as she left, however, he switched the set back on, keeping the volume as low as he possibly could and still hear. That proved to be very low indeed. It seemed that his sharpened hearing was persisting. He also used that hearing to listen for nurses in the corridor, so that he could shut off the set before they caught him with it on.

After midnight, Channel 9 started its *Friday Fright Night* feature, three horror movies in a row. Garreth settled back to watch, as he often had since Marti died. However melodramatic, the movies diverted him. Tonight's offerings began with *Dracula*. He sighed. How appropriate. His entire life these days seemed to revolve around blood, or the lack of it.

Into the movie, with everyone worrying about Miss Lucy's mysterious wasting disease, Garreth reflected that his one complaint with these shows was the way the characters waded up to their necks in clues and yet never realized they had a werewolf, demon, or vampire loose among them. On the other hand, perhaps that was reasonable. In a real-life reaction to such a situation, no one would guess, either. They would hunt for a rational explanation and refuse to accept anything less. Like with Miss Lucy. They thought the broach on the shawl caused the punctures on her neck. No real-life person would consider a vampire bite as—

The thought ended in a paralysis as though he lay in the morgue again, without heartbeat or breath. He could not move, only stare unseeing at the TV screen with mind churning. No, that was impossible. It was a *crazy* thought! *I'm losing my mind*, he thought. Lane Barber might be psychotic and a killer, but a human one, certainly. Nothing more or less. How could she be anything else?

So she slept all day. She worked nights. If she kept no food in her apartment, perhaps she hated to cook and always ate out. She bit men she made love to and some of them died, but two men with punctures in their bruises did not mean punctures in every bruise.

On the TV, Miss Lucy slathered in bloodlust, turned vampire by Dracula's bite.

Thirst started to burn in Garreth's throat and he reached involuntarily for the bandage around his neck. *No.* He jerked his hands away. *That really is impossible!* If every vampire bite made a vampire, the world would be hip-deep in the breed. Look at all the men Lane had bitten.

He turned off the TV with a decisive stab of his finger. The blood loss must be affecting his mind. Vampires did *not* exist. He had no insatiable urge to bite the nurses, did he, despite his thirst and their attractive blood scent? He had not developed a desire to don a black opera cape and take the form of a bat. He just happened to feel better at night.

But cold continued to run up and down his spine, and knots worked uneasily along his gut.

Anger flared in him. This was nonsense! He would end it once and for all. Easing out of bed, he groped his way to the bathroom and peered into the mirror. The face he saw every morning while he shaved stared back at him.

There. Satisfied? Everyone knew vampires did not make reflections. Moreover, barring the drawn appearance and pale color, his square face looked exactly as always. His canines, though sore and loose from his fall this afternoon, looked no longer than usual.

Then he realized he had not turned on the light.

He quickly flipped up the switch . . . and wished he had not. The eyes in the mirror, perceived before as normal gray, now reflected the light as Lane's had, flaring red . . . fire red, blood red, hell red.

Garreth slammed down the switch in a spasm of panic and clutched the edge of the washbowl for support, trembling. No! This was insane. Impossible!

And yet . . .

He sat down on the closed lid of the toilet. And yet, how was it that he, who always woke with the sun, now felt better at night? Why could he see in the dark? Why did he smell the blood in people and throw up solid food? On the other hand, if he had become—

He could not finish the thought. It stumbled and died before a new flood of panic. *Run!* a voice screamed inside him. *Run!*

It brought him off the toilet and to the bathroom door, where he clung to the jamb, breathing hard. He had to get out of here. There was a logical explanation for everything but he needed somewhere to think. Somewhere quiet. He could not do it in this place with its reek of blood and voices shouting up and down the halls and interns and nurses coming in all the time to poke and prod him.

How to get out, though? While they could not keep him against his will, demanding to be released in the middle of the night might make them consider him irrational. And he could not just walk out without clothes.

But he had to get away somehow!

Shaking, he made his way back to the bed and pulled the call-light cord.

"May I help you?" a female voice asked from the speaker above the call light.

"I need to go to the bathroom. Will you send an orderly to help me, please?"

But a female aide appeared a few minutes later, not an orderly. She opened the cabinet beside his bed.

"Please, not the urinal," Garreth said. "I can't use that thing. I feel much better. Can't you let me use the bathroom if someone takes me there?"

"I'll see," the aide replied, and left.

While Garreth waited, crossing mental fingers, he ripped the draw sheet on his bed into several long strips and wrapped them around his waist under his hospital gown. When the door opened again, he smiled in relief at the brawny orderly.

"You're sure you want to try this?" the orderly asked.

Garreth nodded. He had no trouble making the gesture sincere.

"Okay." Putting an arm around Garreth, the

orderly supported him getting out of bed and walking across the room.

The orderly's cheerfulness stabbed Garreth with guilt. He consoled himself with the thought that if all went right, no one would be hurt.

The orderly left him in the bathroom. Garreth waited a few minutes, running the water, then sat down on the floor and called for help.

The orderly hurried in. "Did you fall? Are you hurt?"

"Help me up, please."

As the orderly leaned over to do so, Garreth threw an arm around the muscular neck and tightened down. The orderly collapsed flat on the floor in Garreth's neck lock.

"I don't want to hurt you," Garreth said, "but if you don't shuck your shirt and pants in one minute, you're going to have the biggest pain of your life in your neck."

"Mr. Mikaelian, you—" the orderly began in protest.

"Take off the shirt and pants," Garreth said.

It was not easy with both of them lying on the floor, but the orderly managed. Garreth tied his hands with the strips from the draw sheet, gagged him with another strip and a washcloth, and tied him to the pipes of the washbowl, out of reach of the call-light cord beside the toilet. Then Garreth changed into the orderly's clothes, rolling up a cuff to shorten the trousers to his length. He helped himself to the orderly's shoes and socks.

"I'm sorry about this, but I want a quicker discharge than I think the doctor is willing to give me. At least I'm leaving you your skivvies. I'll see the other clothes are sent back."

The orderly sighed in combined disgust, anger, and bewilderment.

Garreth walked out, shutting off the light and closing the bathroom door.

No one looked twice at him in the corridor. He took the elevator down and walked out of the building without once being challenged. On the street he hailed a cab. The resolution that let him walk without staggering ran out. He slumped back in the seat.

"Hey, buddy, you okay?" the cabbie asked.

Oh, God. The cabbie smelled of blood, too, though with the reek of sweat and a cigar nearly overwhelming it. The combination sent waves of nausea through him. "I'm fine."

The fifteen-minute ride home seemed interminable. Keeping the cab waiting, he unlocked the door with his hidden spare key and went in to change clothes. A sweater with a turtleneck reaching almost to his ears hid the bandage on his throat. He clipped his off-duty Charter Arms Undercover .38 on his belt, then dropped the extra set of car keys and his bank card into the pocket of a sport jacket. He had to endure another ride in the cab to his bank's automatic teller and one last one to the lot where he had parked the ZX.

It was with relief that he paid off the cabbie, adding some extra money along with the orderly's clothes. "See that these reach an orderly named Pechanec at General, will you?"

Then he was free, on his own. He started the car. But he hesitated before backing out of the parking slot. Where did he go now? "On his own," it occurred to him, this time meant alone . . . very, very alone.

4

Garreth drove blindly, not caring where he went. Some place would feel right, and there he would stop, and think. Rational answers he had overlooked before would become apparent. Then perhaps he could make the terrified child within him realize that there was nothing to run from, nothing to be frightened of.

Eventually he found himself in a deserted parking lot, but it was with shock that he looked up and recognized Mount Davidson. The white cross atop the hill loomed above him, his strange new night vision seeing it luminous with icy fire against the night sky.

Relief and triumph followed surprise. This proved his imaginings false. How could he possibly have come to a place like this if he had ... changed.

Climbing out of the car, he made his way up the slope toward the cross. Still no terrible agony engulfed him. If anything, each step made him feel better. Sitting on the ground at the base brought sheer relief, with all the aches of the past several days draining away.

Garreth stretched out full length and buried his face in the grass. The earth felt delicious, so cool, so clean and sweet-smelling. Funny. He had never liked sleeping on the ground as a kid on scouting camp-outs, but now it felt better than any bed, certainly better than that torture rack at the hospital. What a joy it would be to just continue lying here, to pull the earth over him and sleep forever.

Pull the earth— He sat bolt upright, shaking, horror and gut-wrenching fear flooding back. *What the hell are you thinking, man!* He really was going wacko. He had better take himself back to the hospital before his delusions had him jumping some unsuspecting jogger.

But Garreth could not make himself move, even though he suddenly felt as though his presence defiled the hill. The earth drew him. It even soothed the thirst growing more ravenous by the hour. The sun, he decided. He would wait for the sun. If nothing happened when it rose, there was nothing wrong with him except that he had gone bananas and needed a room at the funny farm. And if—well, it would be a clean end with no one having to know what a foul thing he had become.

Garreth crossed his legs, folded his hands in his lap, and waited.

Eventually the sky lightened.

His heart pounded. Feeling it, he scolded himself. *Don't be a fool. Nothing's going to happen.* But his heart continued to slam against the wall of his chest while the sky grew brighter. Pulses throbbed in his aching, burning throat, in his arms and legs and temples.

The upper rim of the sun appeared over the horizon. Garreth braced himself. A beam of light lanced westward to the great white cross above him. He fought an urge to bury his face in his hands and made himself lift his chin to meet the sun.

There was no agony, no searing dissolution. The light burned through his eyes, however, turning the throb in his temples to a pounding headache. A great weight pressed down on him, draining his strength, dragging at his limbs. The earth beckoned to him, called him to the sweet coolness that would shut out this miserable, blinding, exhausting sun—

"No!" He lurched to his feet. "Damn you!" he shouted at the sun. "Kill me! You're supposed to kill me. Please! I won't be—*that*!" He screamed into the terrible blood-red sky of dawn. "I won't be! No! *No! NO!*" Screamed in fury and despair, over and over and over.

Garreth could not recall running down Mount Davidson or fishing trooper glasses from the glove compartment of the car and gunning the ZX out of the parking lot, but he found himself driving again, with mirror lenses hiding the eyes of his image in the rearview mirror. Driving where, though? He slowed down, groping for orientation. And slowed still more as a patrol car passed him going the other direction. He carried no driver's license; that sat in the Property Room along with the rest of his billfold contents, state's exhibits.

A street sign finally told him where he was. From that he guessed where his reflexes were taking him: Lien . . . who had kept him sane the last time his life came crashing down around him.

Garreth parked the car around the corner at the end of the block Harry did not pass on the way to work and followed the narrow footpath between the backyards to the Takananda gate. Slipping over, he sat down behind the big oak tree shading the flagstoned patio and settled against the trunk to wait.

From inside the house came the sounds of morning: a shrill electronic beeping of the alarm clock, running water, the murmur of voices. The telephone rang. Harry's voice rose. Moments later the front door slammed and the motor of the car roared to life. Tires squealed around the corner at the far end of the block.

Garreth pushed to his feet and came around the tree onto the patio.

Lien saw him from the kitchen. Her almond eyes went wide. "Garreth!" She ran out of the house to him. "What on earth are you doing?"

He managed a wry smile. "Visiting."

Her eyes flashed. "Don't lie to me, Garreth Doyle Mikaelian! Harry just had a call about you. Come in this minute and sit down! You look ready to fall on your face."

He followed her gladly and dropped into the closest chair.

She sat on the hassock in front of him, frowning in exasperation and concern. Her nearness brought a warm wash of bath-talcum scent overlying that of blood. "Why did you run away from the hospital?"

He could give a half-truthful answer. "I couldn't eat their food or sleep in their bed. I wanted out."

She stared. "Have you lost—" She broke off to resume in a patient voice, "Garreth, you almost *died*. You're in no condition to be going anywhere. You need medical care. Come on; I'll drive you back."

She started to rise.

Garreth reached out to catch her wrist. "No! I can't go back. I—I'm—" But the words caught in his throat. He could not tell her about the hateful thing he had become. Hell . . . he could not even say the words to himself. Thank God for the glasses so she could not see the animal glow of his eyes. "Lien, I have to sleep and I haven't been able to since I went into that place. Let me stay here today, and promise you won't tell anyone where I am, not even Harry. Please!"

She stared from his face to her wrist and said softly, "Garreth, you're hurting me."

He let go as though stung. *Shit*. "Damn! I'm sorry."

Lien rubbed the marks left on her wrist by his fingers. "I never knew you were so strong. Garreth ..."

How could he be so thoughtless? He had seen some of his strength when wrestling the orderly. "I didn't realize—I never meant—I'm sorry," he said miserably.

"Garreth!"

He looked at her.

She patted his arm. "You can stay on one condition. That you do nothing but rest. Do you promise?"

He nodded.

She smiled. "Fortunately it's Saturday and I don't have to work, so you won't be alone. Harry went off without breakfast so would you like his waffles?"

His throat burned with hunger but the thought of waffles brought a spasm of nausea. He grimaced. "I'm not hungry."

Lien frowned at him. "Garreth, you—" Then she sighed. "All right. Now get yourself into bed in the guest room."

A bed. He would never be able to sleep on a bed. "I'd rather sleep out on the patio."

"Patio!" she said in horror. "It's chilly out there."

"Please. I can't breathe in here."

His desperation must have shown in his voice. Her forehead furrowed but she made no further protests even when he passed the lounge chair to lie down on the grass well in the shade of the tree. His last conscious sensation was of Lien covering him with something.

5

He slept, but not in oblivion. Garreth dreamed
... frantic, terrifying dreams ... of the alley and
Lane tearing out his throat, of being Gerald
Mossman, split open and shelled out on an autopsy table, of chasing joggers through Golden
Gate Park and tearing out *their* throats to gulp
down the salty fire of their blood. He fled from
the murders, running back through the park to
the Conservatory. Inside, though, it had become a
library. Titles of the books glared from the spines
in pulsating red lettering: *Dracula, The Rise and
Fall of the Roman Vampire, Foundation and Vampire, The Vampire Strikes Back.*

Spinning away from the stacks in revulsion, he
found himself among a group of children sketch-
ing bats and wolves under Lien's direction. He
started to back away but Lien caught his arm
and, pushing him down in a chair, cradled his
head against her chest.

"Hush, Garreth, hush." She rocked slightly,
stroking his hair as he remembered her doing
once after Marti died. "The superior man doesn't
panic. Let's try studying this thing calmly. Look."
She released him and began two lists on her
sketch pad. "It's obvious that everything legends
say about vampires isn't true. Yes, you rest best
on earth, you smell and crave blood, and something is happening to your teeth. On the other
hand, while daylight is uncomfortable and debili-

114

tating, it doesn't kill you. There's no nonsense with mirrors, either. That would violate physical laws. The subject needs more research, but perhaps *most* of the legend is false. Maybe you don't have to stop being the person you are, the person Harry and I love. Once your basic needs of rest and food are met, why shouldn't you be able to go on living your life as you always have? Do you understand, Garreth?" Her voice rose, became more insistent. "Garreth?"

That was a real voice, not a dream. He opened his eyes, waking as he had all his life, from sleep to awareness in a breath. That, at least, had not changed. The sky showed crimson through the tree above him and Lien knelt at his side with an expression of relief.

"You're the soundest sleeper I've ever seen," she said. "I don't think you moved all day. I couldn't even see you breathe. I kept coming out to make sure you were still alive." She paused. "Did you know it's almost impossible to feel your pulse? Your skin is cold, too. Garreth, please, *please*, let me take you back to the hospital."

He sat up stiffly, groping for the dream. An exploring tongue found his teeth looser. Had the dream Lien been right? Could he go on being the same person? "Isn't Harry home yet?"

"He called to say he'd be late. They're turning the city upside down looking for you."

Garreth flushed at the reproach in her voice. "Thanks for not giving me away."

"You needed the rest." She stood. "Come inside. It's freezing out here."

It did not seem so to him.

"What do you think you can stomach for supper?"

His throat burned. A cramp contracted his

stomach. He let it pass before answering. "Just tea, please."

She turned around sharply. "This is ridiculous. You have to eat! Are you trying to kill yourself?"

Maybe that would be best. Dreams were often just dreams. He did not want to think about eating. "Please, Lien."

She fixed the tea and stood with arms folded, watching him sip it. "If you won't go back to the hospital, at least show up at Bryant Street long enough to let them know you're alive so they can go back to hunting people who deserve it."

He hated lying to her. He did it anyway. "All right. I'll turn myself in to Harry."

She hissed in exasperation. "Don't be childish. It isn't like that and you know it."

"I'm sorry." The tea curbed none of his hunger, none of the thirst, but at least its warmth soothed the cramps. He stood, clipped on his gun, and put on his coat.

Lien followed him to the door. "Please take care of yourself."

He hugged her. "I will. Thanks for everything. You're a super lady."

Picking up the car from around the corner, he drove to the public library in the Civic Center. The subject needed research, his dream Lien had said. From the books containing information on the vampire legend, he chose some half a dozen and after skimming them, copied a number of pages to study over multiple cups of tea in an all-night café. It went fine as long as he considered the information just research, as long as he did not think of it as applying to him personally. Once he let awareness seep in, though, all the horror, the dread, returned in an icy flood. His hands shook so much he could not hold either cup or papers.

It all seemed so preposterous, a nightmare. If only he would wake up. Or consider it just a delusion born of the trauma of Lane's attack.

He humored the delusion and resumed reading, still shaking. There appeared to be two kinds of vampires, those like Dracula who walked around talking and reasoning, and the zombies like Miss Lucy, mindless, dripping dirt and graveclothes, driven only by their lust for blood. Lucy had been bitten by Dracula, but he, like Mina Harker, had swallowed some of his attacker's blood in turn. Did that make the difference?

A question none of the reading answered, however, was why Lane let him live. She had broken Adair's and Mossman's necks to destroy their nervous system and prevent them from rising again. Why had she not done the same for him?

"Inspector Mikaelian?"

He started. A uniformed officer smiled down at him. "I saw your car out front. We've been looking for you."

It had been only a matter of time. Moving unhurriedly, Garreth folded the copied pages and slipped them into the inside pocket of his sport coat. "What are you supposed to do when you find me?"

"We've already called Lieutenant Serruto in Homicide."

Garreth stood. "Am I under arrest?"

The officer looked young. His eyes widened in shock. "Oh, no, Inspector. It's just an Attempt to Locate. You need medical treatment, the bulletin said."

"I don't, but doctors have to play God. Let's go."

They waited in the parking lot for Serruto. He arrived with Harry driving. The lieutenant did not bother getting out of the car, just rolled down the window. "Give one of the uniforms your car keys, Mikaelian. Drive the car to the lot at Bryant Street," he told the uniformed officers, "and leave the keys on my desk in Homicide. Get in, Mikaelian."

Garreth debated trying to run. Even fasting, he bet he could still outrun the rest of them. He weighed that against the suspicion bolting might raise.

"Get in," Serruto repeated in a voice with steel beneath it.

Garreth climbed in the back seat, eyes on the nonfunctional handle of the door closing behind him. Trapped!

"Thanks," Serruto told the officer, and then, as the car left the parking lot, "You monopolized a lot of manpower hours, Mikaelian."

Garreth slunk down in the seat, flushing guiltily.

"Mind telling me the meaning of this stunt?"

Wishing he sounded less defensive, Garreth said, "I don't like hospitals. I felt better but didn't think they would believe me."

"Really?" Harry said. "Lien called. She told me you were almost comatose all day."

"I won't go back to the hospital."

Serruto turned around on the seat to face Garreth. "We can raise a charge of assault to confine you if need be."

Garreth dug his nails into the palms of his hands. *Be cool, man. Vampires can hypnotize with a look. Do it.* He looked Serruto straight in the eyes, trying to remember what Lane had done to him. "I don't look sick to you, do I?"

Serruto stared back, eyes widening, then said in a flat voice, "No. What you do you want to do, then? You can't come back on duty without an okay from a doctor."

"I know. I just want to rest at home for a few

days. Then I'll go back for a checkup and let them run their blood tests or whatever." He continued to hold Serruto's eyes.

"All right. You have sick leave at home."

"Ah . . . could you arrange a new ID card and badge for me, and a temporary driver's license until I can replace the one in the evidence locker?"

"See me Tuesday about it."

Garreth bit his lip to keep from grinning. It worked!

"Why don't you stay at our place?" Harry asked. "We have a guest room."

That would not do at all. "I'd rather be home."

But Serruto had turned around again and was out of Garreth's influence. "You go to Takananda's tonight or we charge you with assault and take you to the hospital."

Garreth made himself smile. "Yes, sir."

6

Garreth did not really sleep. He felt anything but sleepy and he wanted to be sure he was awake before Harry and Lien, so that he could sneak back inside. Sleeping outdoors during the day was one thing; discovering that he had slept out in a chilly night, even when he did not feel the cold, would disturb them. He rested, though— reminded of the times he had gone camping as a Boy Scout, except that this time he felt comfortable instead of wanting an air mattress between him and the ground—and while he rested, he considered solutions for the sleeping situation. A coffin was ridiculous, but he did need some kind of container for a layer of earth.

He sat up, thinking again of the Boy Scouts. An air mattress might work. As soon as possible, he would leave here and try it out.

In the morning he played with the eggs and toast Lien fixed for him, managing to look like he was eating without actually doing so. He drank only sugared tea and took the vitamins she forced on him.

"Since Harry is on duty today," she said, "will you come to church with me?"

The knot in his stomach came not from hunger this time—he no longer felt hunger, only light-headed euphoria, a common feeling brought on by fasting, he remembered Marti telling him once—but from fear. Church! Well, he might as well find out how it affected him.

"Of course I'll go."

Lien drove. Garreth sat with his hands clenched in the pockets of his coat, his eyes hidden from her and the sun by the mirror-lensed trooper glasses. He could not remember the last time he had actually felt religious, though he still went to church with his mother and grandmother when he visited home. He had gone regularly as a child, sandwiched with Shane between his mother and Grandma Doyle, where he could be thumped on the head with a grandmotherly knuckle if he wiggled too much.

Lien's church was Roman Catholic, but it reminded him of the Episcopal one at home. Garreth could not shake the conviction that he should not be here, but sitting beside Lien, he felt no pain other than that of guilt. Lien touched him with holy water coming in and it did not burn. Would it if he had grown up Catholic? If anything, the light coming through the stained-glass windows and the rhythm of the Mass gave him a kind of peace. He had a feeling that if the tall priest had looked more like Father Michaels—a small, round, laughing man who smelled pleasantly of pipe tobacco and was continually relighting that pipe at the coffee period following Morning Prayer from a seemingly inexhaustible supply of kitchen matches in the pocket of his black coat—Garreth would have been tempted to confess his vampirism and ask for absolution. Or was that cure for his condition pure myth, too?

Leaving, Lien said, "Shall we eat lunch at Fisherman's Wharf?"

His teeth rubbed against the inside of his upper lip, so loose they felt ready to fall out. He had no doubt they would, and that new, sharp ones were even now pushing through his sore gums. A need to be alone overwhelmed him.

"Another time, please? I think I'd like to go home and sleep." If she argued, he was ready to take off his glasses and use his power on her.

But though her forehead creased in concern, she did not fight him. "Call me if you need anything."

He walked her back to her car, then caught a bus for a shopping center, where he bought an air mattress and several bags of earth from the garden section. At home he slit the end of each section of the air mattress and poured in earth a handful at a time until he had a layer of earth an inch or so thick. Mending tape sealed the mattress again.

Garreth lay down experimentally on the resulting pallet. Tension ran out of him like knots untying. The slightly lumpy surface felt as com-

fortable as the softest of beds. He sighed in
satisfaction. It worked.

Before he let himself fall asleep, though, Garreth
worried the loose teeth free. Pushing his tongue
into the spaces left, he felt sharp points coming
through the gums and shivered. Somehow the
teeth signaled a watershed, a point of no return
at which he could no longer doubt the thing he
had become. The chill of that thought followed
him into sleep.

7

Hunger woke him, violent, racking cramps that
doubled him in bed, ravenous thirst which would
no longer be denied. Garreth felt his teeth with
his tongue and found them fully grown, sharp as
needles, though to his surprise, they were no
longer than the teeth they had replaced. His gut
knotted with more than cramps. The metamor-
phosis was complete and he could no longer
avoid the one problem he had refused to think
about: food. Tonight he had to find a solution.

Garreth staggered out of bed to the bathroom
and doubled over the washbowl gulping down
water. But neither hot nor cold water slaked the
burning thirst; it only eased the cramps enough
that he could stand upright.

In the mirror his face loomed gaunt, pale, and
unshaven. He was losing weight, he noticed, and
grimaced bitterly. *After all the times I've dieted
without success, this is a hell of a way to—*

He forgot all about weight and stared at his reflected teeth. With the drawing back of his lips in the grimace, the canines, narrower than his previous ones, had grown, extending nearly half an inch. And as he relaxed, they retracted again. Glancing toward the bed in the other room, he thought of Marti and for the first time, rejoiced in her death. At least she had been saved the agony of seeing him like this!

The length of his beard astonished him, until he thought to switch on the TV and check the programming against the guide—he had better buy another watch to replace the one being kept as evidence. This was *Monday* evening. He had slept nearly thirty hours.

He unwound the bandage from his neck. Without surprise he found the flesh scarred but healed. Count the recuperative powers of the vampire as fact, then. Using a pair of nail scissors, he cut and pulled the sutures. Another turtleneck hid the luminous ivory scars.

Is this proper attire for the hunting vampire? came a bitterly sardonic thought.

He snatched up a coat and headed for the door.

Garreth found he still could not think about what he intended to do, how to do it, or where. He let his body take him, guided by its new instincts. He found himself on a bus for North Beach. Of course . . . Lane's turf, rich with game.

He sat staring out the bus window, heartsick, hating himself. How could he bring himself to do this to other human beings? What if he refused? What happened to the starving vampire since he had never heard of them dying for lack of food?

Leaving the bus at the corner of Columbus and Broadway, he considered the possibility of suicide. It offered a clean solution . . . maybe. If vampires could commit suicide. Driving a wooden stake through his heart or breaking his neck sounded difficult to accomplish by himself.

Humanity streamed around him. He smelled not just their perfume and sweat now but the warm metallic/salty scent of the blood pulsing through their veins. It ignited a frenzy of hunger. His stomach churned. *Dear God, don't let me cramp again and attract attention!* Occasionally someone passed whose blood ran hot and strong and he turned toward her like a compass to north . . . only to pull back, afraid. How long had it been since he last picked up a girl? Before he met Marti. He had been turned down a fair number of times in those days, he recalled. A refusal now meant more than a blow to the ego; it meant no supper. Worse, what if she came with him? What if he killed her?

He could not do it. He just . . . could . . . not . . . do . . . it!

In panic, he turned up a side street and ran, away from Broadway, away from the blood smells fanning his hunger, and did not stop until the next corner. There he leaned against the wall of a building, swearing at himself. Some vampire he made. What *was* he going to do?

Gradually, he became aware of voices around the corner, sharp, full of anger and fear. A man's: "And Richie says you're holding out on him. He don't like that."

"I'm *not*," a woman replied. "I just don't get the action. The johns want *young* girls. I do the best I can. I swear."

Garreth recognized Velvet's voice. Edging up to the corner, he peered around it. The hooker had been backed up against the building by a man waving a switchblade under her nose.

"Well, if you can't convince them you're sweet sixteen and a virgin, you better find something else they want, baby, because Richie says you're running in the red. You ain't cost-effective. So unless you get your act together, you *will* be running in the red. I'll fix your face so you can't get a job ushering at a dogfight."

Good old Richie, Garreth thought.

He came around the corner. In two long strides he was on top of the muscleman, clamping a hand on the wrist of the knife hand just as the man registered Garreth's presence and started to turn. Garreth bent the wrist back. The forearm gave with a sickening *crack*. He let go of the wrist and smoothly took the knife as the muscleman collapsed screaming to the sidewalk.

Garreth stepped over him and put a hand under Velvet's elbow. "Come on; let's get out of here." He hurried her back toward Broadway.

Her eyes looked the size of dinner plates. "Why'd you do that? He wasn't going to cut me this time. Now Richie will get mad."

"Tell Richie the muscle was getting carried away and about to use the knife for fun when a friendly flatfoot came along. Better yet, drop a dime on him and we'll nail him to the wall before he *does* have you carved up."

She bit her lip. "Sometime, maybe. For now, thanks." She glanced sideways at him. "Say, what's the story on you? First I hear they found you stiff in an alley with your throat torn out, then the word is you sat up on the autopsy table and knocked the knife out of the doctor's hand; now here you are walking around breaking arms with one hand. You look younger somehow, too."

He restrained a grimace. *Drink blood, the Elixir of Youth.* "I owe it all to clean living and a pure heart," he said aloud.

The blood ran hot in her. He smelled it:

fear-driven, richly salty, and with it, the near-audible hammering of her heart, just now beginning to slow after the terror. He drew a deep breath and, folding the switchblade, dropped it in his pocket. His hand shook with the driving urgency of his hunger.

He felt her looking at him and glanced over to see her smiling knowingly. She had seen his increase in breathing and misinterpreted it, he realized.

"Hey, baby. Maybe you'd like to party?"

He shook his head. "Don't make me run you in for soliciting a cop, Velvet."

"Did I mention money? This is on the house. Call it saying thanks. Come on." She reached up to ruffle his hair. "Let me show you that blondes really do have more fun."

He started to say no, but something else in him, something controlled by the ravenous thirst, made it to his tongue first. "Okay. Why not?"

She tucked her arm through his. "It isn't far. You'll like this."

He hated it. Not the sex; that felt fine. But afterward, with the blood smell of her filling his head, making him dizzy with need, she looked up and said dreamily, "Did you know your eyes glow red, Mikaelian? They're like rubies."

Hunger overwhelmed him. He kissed her neck, exploring, feeling his canines extend. She sighed in pleasure when his mouth found the throb under her silky skin. The sound goaded him. He bit, and . . . nothing! Only a drop of blood rose to tantalize him where each fang pierced. He had missed the vein!

A scream of frustration echoed through his head, and then it screamed *at* him, demanding that he tear at her throat until he found the blood he needed. Garreth recoiled, and scrambled off her in horror. *No!* The guilt he had felt coming up here paled beside the self-loathing flooding him now. He did not have to stop being the person he was? Like hell. Look at him, turning into a ravening damn animal!

He struggled into his clothes, desperate to leave before his hunger destroyed what humanity remained in him.

Velvet stirred drowsily on the bed. "Don't rush off, baby."

How could he explain? It was impossible. "I'm sorry; I have to go to work." He buckled his belt.

She sat up, frowning irritably. "Well, wham-bam-thank-you-ma'am."

He clipped on his gun, not daring to look at her, breathing through his mouth so that he would not smell the blood in her. "I'm sorry," he repeated. It sounded lame in his ears.

"Cops." She snorted. "Always in a hurry to come and a hurry to go."

He fled the room without even bothering to put on his coat. He finished dressing on the street while he walked away as fast as he could and gulped the night air to clear her scent from his head. He kept walking, paying no particular attention to the direction, as long as it was away from the crowds and bright lights.

Missed! He could not believe it. Who ever heard of such a thing? *See the vampire miss the vein. See him miss supper. Poor hungry vampire. Maybe he should hire a dowser to find veins for him.*

How many necks did a neo-vampire have to mutilate before learning the quick, clean bite? He could not do that. How did he eat, then?

A car's horn blared. Garreth scrambled out of its path. It was then that he noticed where he was going . . . east, down to the Embarcadero. He stopped and stood looking across at the pier buildings, forgetting his problem for a moment to think about the ships moored over there, where they had been and where they might be going, exotic places. He had never even been out of the state.

A man passed him, jogging, with a sleek Doberman running easily at his side. They left the scents of sweat and blood behind them.

Garreth's spine tingled. He turned to watch the dog. They had blood, too. Could he live on animal blood? Lane drank human blood and all the books talked about vampires drinking human blood, but blood was blood, surely.

The idea of preying on dogs did not appeal to him; they were pets, usually loved by someone. Cats, too. Besides, he had no idea how much blood they could lose without dying. However— his eyes moved toward the pier across the street— the city did have one species that existed in profusion, that would not be missed, and that he would not mind killing. Over there lay a bounteous hunting ground.

The idea of touching a rat, let alone biting one, disgusted him, but a growing weakness in him and the return of his stomach cramps provided incentive for overcoming his squeamishness. People learned to eat many things out of necessity, even other people. Better rats than people.

He crossed the street . . . only to find the gate across the entrance locked. He clutched at the grating in frustration. What now? The only open gates led onto piers with activity. He needed to find a way onto an empty pier . . . somehow. He stared into the darkened building longingly.

Something moved in him, a gut-jarring wrench that sent pangs through him from head to hands and feet. He started to lean against the grating for support, to wait for the pain to pass. He almost fell onto his face. The grating had disappeared from in front of him. Looking around, he found, to his astonishment, that it lay *behind* him.

Another truth! Vampires could move through solid objects. He had not noticed that he became mist. How had he done it, then?

Garreth quickly ceased to care about *how*. His stomach said: *hunt*. He started down the length of the building, through a dark that appeared no more than twilight to his eyes, his ears tuned for every possible sound.

The building creaked around him. Outside, traffic mumbled and water slapped the pier and foundations. Then, amid other sounds, he caught the scrabble of tiny clawed feet and the high squeak of a rodent voice. One turn of his head pinpointed the sound. He moved that direction, climbing over a customs barrier in his path. The rat's form appeared among the shadows under the customs counter.

It must have heard him because it grew suddenly still. Only its head moved, turning to look up at him. Garreth froze in place, too. The tiny eyes met his.

"Don't move," he said. Then he had a better idea. "Come here. Come to me." He would see just how far this control went.

The rat continued to stare.

Garreth concentrated on it. "Come here."

One slow step at a time, the rat obeyed. As it came within arm's reach, Garreth squatted on his heels. The smell of the rat reached him, a sharp rodent odor, strong but not quite strong enough to mask the tantalizing scent of blood. He steeled himself to touch the creature. *Blood is blood*. He drew a breath, smelling that blood ... and reached for his prey.

The rat's fur felt rough and spiky in his hand. He waited for it to struggle, but the creature submitted to being picked up, hanging quiescent in his grasp. One wrench would break its neck, or a bend of his elbow bring it to his mouth, but he hesitated. Rats carry disease. How did plague and rabies affect vampires? Were they immune, or would the disease organism be destroyed by passing through his digestive system? This rat looked healthy enough, bright-eyed and fat.

The blood smell of it was overwhelming. Hunger maddened him. He had to risk drinking from it. He remembered the switchblade in his pocket. That would keep him from having to actually bite the rat. But what then?

The rat remained quiet. Garreth stood, carrying it, and looked around for inspiration. Draining the blood into the palm of his hand and licking it up from there sounded not only slow but primitive. He had never liked camping out with all the loss of physical comfort that meant: digging latrines, boiling water, bathing in a bucket. He wanted something more civilized now, too.

His gaze fell on a trash barrel. He carried the rat to it and looked in. Almost on top of the litter inside sat a foam cup of the type used for coffee carry-outs. Lipstick, looking brown in the twilight of his vision, printed one edge of the rim.

After this, he decided, he would bring a cup of his own, maybe one of those collapsing things for camping, something that fit easily and inconspicuously in a pocket. But for now, he set the cup on the customs counter, then, using both hands, broke the rat's neck and brought out the switchblade.

The blade opened with a snap. A pass of it opened the rat's throat, and Garreth held the rat by its hind legs, letting the blood drain into the

cup. Its smell set his stomach churning in anticipation, though his brain still recoiled. *Blood is
blood*, he reminded himself. *Blood is life.*

And when the rat stopped dripping, he reso-
lutely picked up the cup, lipstick away from him,
and gulped down the contents before he had time
to think further.

Any worry that he might throw up vanished
immediately. The first swallow ignited a wild
appetite for more. At the same time, though, it
tasted flat, lacking, as though he drank simple
tomato juice when he expected the peppery fire of
a Bloody Mary. His skin crawled. What he really
wanted, of course, was human blood. *But this will
do and it's all you're getting, beast.* He drained the
cup to the last drop and went hunting another
rat.

8

"Mik-san!" Harry came up out of his desk chair
grinning from ear to ear.

From around the room, other detectives con-
verged on Garreth, pounding him on the back.
Serruto came out of his office. "Is that our
Lazarus behind those Foster Grants? You're looking pretty good, Mikaelian. Did you see the
doctor today?"

"Yes, sir."

"What does he say about when you can come
back?"

"I'm back now. Really," he added, handing

over the evaluation form from the doctor. He took off his glasses and hung them on the breast pocket of his suit coat. "I checked out okay. I'm cleared for full duty." Or at least, he had been after "persuasion" helped the doctor perceive the readings for temperature, pulse, and respiration as normal.

Foreheads furrowed in surprise around him. Harry looked concerned. "Only a week after the attack? You still look pale, and you seem thin."

"I'm on a diet. The doctor approves."

Serruto read the form. "He thinks your neck is healed?"

Garreth tilted back his head to show the scars above his collar, still livid but obviously in no danger of tearing open with exertion. "I agree it's incredible, but my mother's people were always fast healers, and I've been doing nothing since Saturday but sleeping and eating, and drinking an herbal tea my Grandma Doyle swears by."

He saw by their expressions that they put little credence in the herbal tea, but otherwise swallowed the lies. Garreth fought down a pang of guilt. He could not very well tell the truth, could he? That he had slept days but spent nights decimating the rat population on the Embarcadero, feeding the little corpses to the fishes in the bay. He hated admitting it to himself—it seemed like a savage, desperate way to be living, and he had come close to being caught last night by a watchman. He had had to crouch behind a pile of crates with breath held until the man walked out of sight. Garreth's chances of being seen increased with every night. He needed to find some way to hunt less often.

Serruto read the form again. "I don't know," he said doubtfully.

Garreth met his eyes as the lieutenant looked

up and stared steadily into them. "I'm fit, the doctor says. You believe him, don't you?" It was a cheat and Garreth's conscience bothered him because of it, but he used it anyway. He wanted to be working.

Serruto stared back, then returned the form. "If the doctor says you're fit, who am I to disagree? Okay, everyone, the reception party is over. Back to work." He beckoned Garreth toward his office. "Come in. You, too, Harry."

It was about what Garreth expected, a short lecture which could be summarized as: "The doctors may think you're fit for full duty, but I think you should take it easy for a while. Make sure he does, Harry. Here's your new badge, ID card, and gun. Be sure to qualify with it on the firing range. Here's your temporary driver's license. Now, I suppose you want to know how we're doing on your redhead?"

"Yes, sir."

"We haven't found her," Harry said. "The APB is out with the names Barber and Alexandra Pfeifer. Odd alias, isn't it? But I suppose it sounds more authentic than the standard Anglo-Saxon ones.

"It's all crazy. Did you know we dusted her apartment, but the only prints we found belonged to your name on the letter, Madelaine Bieber, but *she* turns out not to be Barber, but a sixty-seven-year-old woman who was arrested for assault in 1941? And we can't find her, either."

Garreth bit his lip to keep from telling them that Lane and Madelaine Bieber were the same woman. Once he accepted Lane as a vampire, it followed that her apparent age bore no relation to her actual one. If he told them, and they believed him, then they would inevitably realize what he had become. He had no desire to learn how they might react to that.

Little wonder, though, that Lane hunted so efficiently; she had had decades of practice.

He asked, "Did you ever learn anything from the burned papers in the fireplace?"

Serruto shook his head. "The lab only managed to bring up a partial postmark with two of the ZIP numbers, a six and a seven."

"Doesn't that help?"

Harry sighed. "It might if we knew for sure whether they're the first or second two numbers. If the ZIP is sixty-seven something, the letter came from the middle of Kansas. If it's something sixty-seven something, it could have been mailed in any one of nine states. I had the fun of going through a ZIP directory to check the possibilities." He laughed. "Isn't being a detective exciting?"

"Show him the picture, Harry," Serruto said.

Harry brought it in from his desk. Studying the photograph, Garreth saw that most of the envelope had burned away. In what remained, he saw a postmark circle with the two numbers at the bottom. At the top of the circle, partials of three letters also remained, and below the postmark, an ornate *M*. He recognized the letter as part of the address on the envelope he had seen. Too bad they were unable to see the return address. Addressed to her real name, it must have come from someone who knew her well and from a long time back.

"Did you learn anything useful from her driver's license or car registration?"

"Just that the information given for the license was false," Harry said.

Serruto frowned. "We ran her through NCIC, even asking for Wants on anyone fitting her description. I know she's dirty. She stinks of 'fugitive.' She must be wanted somewhere for something."

Garreth found satisfaction in knowing that he was no longer the only one who felt that way.

"Anyway, that's where we stand now," Serruto said. "More is up to you two." He eyed Garreth intently. "Are you sure you feel like working?"

Garreth returned his gaze steadily. "I feel just fine."

Serruto waved them toward the door. "Then crack the whip over him, Harry."

Harry nodded, grinning. On the way back to their desks, he said, "I tried calling you a couple of times, to see how you were doing, but you never answered."

Garreth doubted a mere phone could wake him in the daytime. "I turned off the telephone bell so I wouldn't be disturbed." Even the small lie bothered him.

"Lien was so worried I almost drove over to check on you personally."

Garreth breathed a sigh of relief that he had not.

"She's down at City of Paris today. Why don't I give her a call to tell her what the doctor said about you, and ask her to make enough sweet-and-sour pork for three tonight?"

Garreth hoped the stricken plunge of his heart did not show on his face. He could never eat sweet-and-sour pork again, nor eat with Harry and Lien again, for that matter. He did not have to fake the disappointment in his voice. "I wish I could, but . . . I have a date."

Harry's brows went up.

"A nurse I met while the doctor was checking me over."

Harry slapped his shoulder. "That's great. You

get along well with nurses. Glad to see you back in the game."

"Does this mean you'll be playing Cock of the Walk with the rest of the boys now?" Evelyn Kolb eyed him over the cup of tea she was pumping from her thermos.

Garreth paused in the act of putting his glasses back on. "What a sharp tongue you have."

She smiled. He eyed her thermos. That might be how to reduce the number of times he had to hunt. After all, the ability to store food was supposed to be an advantage of civilization.

He walked over to her desk and picked up the thermos. "Does this work very well?"

"Very well. Tea I put in in the morning is still hot enough to burn my tongue twelve hours later."

He toyed with the pump spigot on the top. "How much does it hold?"

"A quart. Why?"

"I'm thinking of bringing tea to work the way you do. They come in larger sizes, too, don't they?"

"Sure, but how much do you expect to drink in a day?"

He shrugged, noting with dismay how easily he lied these days and to how many people. Why? Right now he could have replied truthfully that he was thinking of buying a thermos. *The wicked flee where no man pursueth*, he thought ruefully.

Garreth returned the thermos to her desk and watched her put it away in the kneehole. A thermos full of blood would keep him several days. The flaw in that struck him on the way back to his desk. Outside its owner's body, blood clotted. The thought of ordinary blood still sounded unappealing to his brain, but that of clotted blood turned even his stomach. If he wanted to store blood, he would have to use anticoagulants. Where to come by those, though?

Harry sat at his desk frowning at the lab photo of the postmark. "What do you think these letters are?"

Garreth peered over his shoulder. "The one in the middle has to be either an O or U. Isn't that a slanted foot to the left? That would be an A, K, R, or X."

"And on the right?"

It looked like the bottom end of a straight line. "Man, that could be anything." He checked the keys of the typewriter. "F, H, I, K, N, M, or P." A thought occurred which might solve several problems. "Why don't we ask the lab if they can work on making the letters a little more visible?"

Harry shrugged. "We can ask."

Garreth maneuvered Harry into doing the talking when they reached the Crime Lab. He put in a word or two, then slid away and wandered along the worktables to where a technician was checking bloodstains on a shirt.

The tech looked up with a smile. "Glad to see you back. I'm glad I won't be giving evidence on your bloodstained clothes at a murder trial. I see you got in a few licks yourself."

"Two kinds of blood on the clothes?"

The tech nodded. "Mostly A positive, but some B positive, too."

Casually, Garreth asked, "If you wanted to keep blood fresh, how could you do it?"

The tech shook his head. "I'd rather have it dried. It's easier to analyze. Blood cells decay so fast in liquid or clotted blood."

"What if you wanted to keep it from clotting? Would you use heparin?"

The tech rocked his row of slides back and forth, studying the blood on them. "Heparin?

Probably not. That's about the most expensive product on the market. It's cheaper to use things like oxalates and citrates." He looked up. "I'd probably choose sodium citrate. That's inexpensive and available at almost any chemical supply house. It isn't a drug, so it isn't controlled like heparin."

"How much would you have to use?" Garreth crossed his fingers, hoping the tech would not ask why he was so interested in anticoagulants.

The blood on some of the slides looked clumped. The tech wrote letters on a report form, then stood and reached for a book on a shelf above the cabinet behind him. "Well, let's see. Anticoagulants ... Here we are. You need ten milligrams for a hundred milliliters of blood. I've bought it in a two and a half percent solution. That gives you twenty-five milligrams per cc. So a cc will keep two hundred and fifty milliliters. That help?"

"Yes. Thanks." Garreth hoped so.

9

Jubilation carried him into work on Friday. The citrate worked. Four quarts of blood sat cold and liquid in his refrigerator. A lot of drained rat bodies fed the fishes today but the slaughter was worth it. He would not have to hunt for several days. Rat blood still did not satisfy him; hunger continued to gnaw no matter how much he drank, but at least it took the edge off. He could live with what remained, like the time Marti took him off bread and he survived very well even though he never stopped craving the bread. His thermos of tea would help keep his appetite under control during the day. He was also learning to live with the pressure of daylight. The dream had been right; he could go on living a normal life and no one would ever have to suspect the changes in him.

Not even a useless interview with Lane's agent—*current* agent, Garreth qualified silently; she almost certainly changed them along with her identity—failed to dampen his spirits.

"She phoned and told me not to book her any gigs for an indefinite period of time," the woman said. "She said her mother is critically ill and she intends to stay with her until the crisis is over."

"Where's that?" Harry asked.

"I don't know. She never said."

Harry frowned. "You mean you don't have any background information on your clients?"

The agent frowned back. "Lane has a dozen backgrounds, all probably false. Look, Sergeant, I find her gigs and she pays me ten percent. That was our agreement. She gives me no trouble with performing drunk or strung out, or not showing up at all, and she brings me a small but steady income, so I don't pry into her life." The agent paused. "Once or twice I asked her personal questions and she changed the subject. She looks like a hot, foxy kid, but she's ice and steel underneath."

A very perceptive lady, Garreth reflected.

As they left, Harry asked, "Where do you want to eat lunch?"

The optimism in Garreth faltered only a little. "I'm on a diet, remember? We can eat anywhere you want, as long as I can buy a cup of tea there."

Harry grinned. "You're serious about the diet this time."

"Of course." As though he had a choice.

"North Beach being our Italian Quarter, how about Italian food?"

"Fine." Garreth would hate it, whatever the restaurant. He hated all meals. Tea filled his stomach, but did nothing to neutralize the longings that food smells stirred in him. He envied Harry, happily putting away everything Garreth had loved but could no longer eat.

But the moment they walked in the door of the restaurant, Garreth lost all future appetite for Italian food. At the first breath of inside air, his lungs froze. Instant panic set in as he tried to breathe and could not. He clawed frantically at his tie and shirt collar, yanking them open.

"Garreth! What's wrong?" Harry shook him by the shoulders.

Garreth opened his mouth wide, straining, desperately struggling to suck in air, but he might as well have been trying to inhale solid concrete.

"Garreth!"

He would suffocate in here! Half dragging Harry, half carried by him, Garreth bolted for the street.

Outside, the air turned from concrete to cold molasses. Garreth staggered up the street until the last foul taint of garlic disappeared. Only then did the air return to normal consistency. He leaned against a building, head thrown back, gulping air greedily.

"Garreth, what happened?" Harry demanded.

Garreth had no idea what to say. Would any mention of garlic start fatal thought trains? "I'm all right." As long as he avoided garlic. Put one more piece of the legend in the truth column. "It was nothing."

"Nothing! That wasn't *nothing*, partner. We'd better—"

From the direction of their car, a radio sputtered. "Inspectors 55."

Harry hurried back to the car to roger the call. Garreth followed with unsteady knees.

"Public service 555-6116," Dispatch said.

Harry's brows rose. "Sound familiar?"

Garreth shook his head.

They drove to the nearest phone booth and Harry dialed the number. Garreth could not hear Harry's end of the conversation, only see his lips moving through the glass wall of the booth, but as he talked, Harry became more animated. He came back to the car at a run and jumped behind the wheel.

"Hey, Mik-san, are we still interested in Wink O'Hare?"

Garreth sat up straight. "Are you kidding? Did someone find him?"

"A lady who says she's Rosella Hambright's sister knows where he is. Seems he got peeved at his girl and worked her over. The sister doesn't approve and wants Wink's hide for it."

"Let's go get him," Garreth said.

They collected two black-and-whites for backup on the way. Garreth surreptitiously checked the house, a decaying two-story building with poverty ground like dirt into its facade, before they moved in. Wink was supposed to be in the second-floor apartment. Narrow, bare stairs led up from a front hall that reeked of garbage and broken plumbing. Two windows overlooked the street. Built against its neighbor, it had no side windows. In back, rotting stairs in two flights rose to a narrow back porch with one window into the apartment and a back door whose upper half contained nine small panes of glass.

The wages of sin is the hell of hiding in stinking holes, Garreth thought while walking back up the hill and around the corner to where Harry and the black-and-whites waited.

Harry deployed everyone, a uniform to be behind a black-and-white out front, covering the front windows, another around the corner of a building covering the rear window. A third uniform would go in the front with Harry, and the fourth, up the back with Garreth.

"You're sure you're all right?" Harry asked.

Garreth removed his glasses and looked him straight in the eyes. "I'm fine. Let's go."

"We'll give him a chance to come out. If he doesn't, you break in the back door. I'll go through the front at the same time. Back door and hall door are at right angles to each other, so we shouldn't be in each other's cross fire, but for God's sake be careful about that."

Garreth and his uniformed partner, a barrel-chested veteran named Rhoades, made their way around to the back of the building and eased up the stairs, checking each tread to avoid telltale creaks. Keeping low, they crossed the porch, then flattened themselves against the building on each side of the door.

With his ear pressed against the side of the house, Garreth heard Harry knock at the front door and call, "Wink O'Hare, this is the police."

Nothing stirred in the apartment.

"Come out, Wink."

A board creaked inside. Listening carefully, Garreth made out the sound of stealthy footsteps. Garreth shifted his hand up on his gun so that he could use the handgrip to break the window. His eyes met Rhoades's. The uniformed officer nodded his readiness. Garreth, breaking the window, would go in high. Rhoades would dive in low.

"O'Hare, open up!"

The footsteps inside moved closer.

"Garreth! Get him!"

At Harry's yell, Garreth smashed the handgrip of the gun into the pane directly above the knob. The glass shattered, but with it a wave of pain like fire burned up his arm and out through his body at the same time a shot sounded explosively inside the kitchen and glass higher up shattered under the impact of a bullet.

Rhoades swore. Garreth tossed his gun into his left hand and pointed it around the edge of the doorjamb to shoot back at Wink, tilting his head just enough to expose one eye for aiming. But his finger could not move the trigger. The gun mechanism seemed frozen.

"Shoot!" Rhoades yelled.

Garreth could not. Fire seared him.

What the hell was wrong with his gun? He remembered then, in dismay, that he carried a new one, one he had never fired before. *Damn.* That did not account for the pain, though.

The thoughts raced through his head between one heartbeat and the next. Another followed, one that could explain both the pain and apparent failure of the gun, but he could not accept it. *No, that's just a legend! Besides, this is a hideout, not a dwelling . . . just a hideout!*

Wink disappeared from the kitchen doorway and two more shots sounded, this time followed by a man's agonized yell. Garreth could not tell whether the shots came from Wink's .45 or the hot-loaded Special that Harry carried. "Harry! *Harry.*"

"Don't just stand there!" Rhoades yelled.

The uniformed officer hurled himself at the door, shouldering Garreth aside. A third shot sounded. The aging door gave way under his weight. He hit the floor inside rolling, kept rolling back onto his feet, and vanished through the kitchen doorway.

With pain wrapping him in flame, Garreth pressed at the opening, willing himself through it. The hot metallic/salty reek of blood filled the apartment. *"Harry, are you all right?"*

"Get in here, Mikaelian," Rhoades's voice snapped.

The pain vanished instantly. Garreth stumbled forward, cold with fear. Fear justified. He found Harry sprawled groaning in the middle of the living room while the uniform who had come up the front with him tried to staunch the blood from a hole in the middle of Harry's chest. Garreth saw Wink, too, shoulder-wounded and screaming as Rhoades roughly cuffed his hands behind his back, but it was Harry he went to, dropping on his knees and pulling out his handkerchief to use as a compress on the wound.

A hand caught his collar and dragged him back. "What the hell were you doing out there?" Rhoades demanded. "If you'd fired when you had the chance, this wouldn't have happened. You froze, didn't you? This turkey shot at you and you lost your nerve!"

"I—" Garreth stared up at him. He could hardly admit his defense, that the apartment was a dwelling and that as a vampire, he could not enter it the first time without an invitation. It appeared that not even a bullet from his gun could violate the barrier around a dwelling.

Rhoades pushed him toward the telephone. "See if you can make yourself use that and call for an ambulance. If we get him to a hospital fast enough, maybe we can still save your partner's life."

Flushing from the lash of the sarcasm, Garreth picked up the phone.

The ambulance took a lifetime to arrive, and every minute of the wait, Garreth sat on the floor holding Harry's head in his lap, silently willing him to live. *Hang on, Harry! Dear God, don't let him die!* As though he, unholy creature, had a right to appeal to a power of Good for anything. Wink's complaints that he was bleeding to death, Rhoades's mutter as he read Wink his rights, the anger of the four uniformed officers directed at the one who failed them . . . all existed somewhere beyond Garreth, not touching him. Only Harry felt real, Harry and fury at himself. What a fool he was! *See the vampire, funny beast, trying to act like a human.* Foolish, certainly, not to have systematically checked out *every* legendary condition of vampire existence. In the jungle, death is the price of error, only this time Harry might pay the price for Garreth's error. *Hang on, Harry. Don't let me destroy you.*

He rode with Harry in the ambulance to the hospital and rooted himself in the trauma unit's waiting room, smelling blood everywhere and sickened by it. Lien was not home. He could only give Dispatch the license number of her car and hope that some patrol unit found her before she heard the news on the radio or TV.

"Mikaelian."

Serruto's voice. Garreth knew he could not meet the lieutenant's eyes, so he kept his gaze riveted on the door through which Harry had disappeared.

"What happened?" The question sounded concerned, not angry.

Garreth kept his voice expressionless. "They say I froze."

"Did you?"

He could say no. He could say his gun jammed. Or he could say yes, and blame it on psychological shock, on suffering from the effects of his own recent experiences, on having come back to work too soon, after all. But the first could be disproven by examining his gun and the second seemed too easy. He stared at the doorway and said, "It's my fault Harry was shot."

He heard Serruto sit down beside him . . . smelled his mixed scent of soap, after-shave, and, beneath them, blood. "I have this feeling of being ignored. I didn't know what to tell the captain. Somehow I thought these operations needed to be cleared through me first."

Why did Serruto confine himself to mild sarcasm? He ought to be yelling. Garreth and Harry knew procedure. Why had they failed to follow it? Had his, Garreth's, eagerness to collar Wink persuaded Harry in the same way the doctor and then Serruto had been persuaded to let him come back to work? Was *all* of it his fault? "I got carried away and forgot to call in."

"And Harry? He's the sergeant. Why didn't he call in?"

Garreth sat angrily upright. "Harry's in there maybe dying and you're trying to blame *him*?"

Serruto sighed. "I know how you feel, but—"

Garreth stood. "How can you possibly know how I feel?" He heard the despair in his voice, a despair sharpened by the realization of how true the question was. Serruto could not know. No one normal, no one human, no one who was as he used to be could ever know exactly how he felt.

And it was looking across that now-perceived, unbridgeable gulf between himself and everyone he knew that Garreth saw Lien come running white-faced into the waiting room.

She stopped in front of him. "How bad is it?"

A constriction in Garreth's throat made speech impossible. He could only shrug.

Serruto answered her. "We don't know."

"How did it happen?"

"I'm sorry." Garreth forced the words out. "I'm sorry I didn't take better care of him. It's all my fault.'"

She, too, disappointed him by looking sympathetic instead of angry.

The doctor came through the doors from the trauma unit. They spun to face him. Garreth felt as though even his heart stopped, waiting for what the doctor would say.

The doctor spread his hands. "He's still alive. The bullet missed his heart. However, there's massive trauma and hemorrhage, so although we have the bleeding stopped now and the damaged vessels repaired, we'll just have to wait to see how he snaps back."

Her face like a china mask, Lien asked, "May I see him?"

"I'm sorry; not yet."

Pain twisted in Garreth. If Harry lived, it would be through no credit to Garreth Doyle Mikaelian. And if Harry lived this time, what about the next? Because there would be a next time, inevitably, another dwelling, another impenetrable barrier Garreth would face and fail. He might as well accept a hard fact . . . he could not continue playing cop when his own personal set of rules differed so much from those applied to the rest of humanity.

Garreth felt in his inside pocket for his badge case. Pulling it out, he turned toward Serruto and extended it. "I shouldn't be carrying this." The words pierced like a knife in his gut.

Serruto frowned. "Mikaelian—"

The lieutenant did not reach for the badge case,

but Garreth let go of it anyway, before he lost his courage to give it up. It fell to the floor, flipping open.

Lien, Serruto, and the doctor stared startled at him. The badge seemed to stare, too . . . a seven-pointed star, the remaining half of his soul, shining up from the floor.

"Mikaelian."

"Oh, Garreth."

Their voices reached out for him, like nets or webs, seeking to snare him. Garreth fled the trap. He spun and bolted from the room. He fled down the corridor with their voices chasing him. An orderly reached for him but he jerked loose in one easy pull and escaped into the twilight.

Tears blinded him. He jerked his glasses off and wiped his eyes. What did he do now? Or should he do anything? He did not really want to live. He did not enjoy it, and his life, or undeath, had endangered the existence of people who could be integral, productive members of society.

He started walking, considering how he might kill himself. It must look like an accident, to spare his family. That made it harder than ever. He cursed the changes in him that did that to him. If Lane had used her strength to simply break his neck, it would have been over, finished with. *Damn you for not doing it!*

He stopped short in the middle of a street. Brakes screamed and horns blared unheard around him.

Because Lane had made him what he was, Harry was dying. Indirectly, she could be held responsible, too, for that fiasco in taking Wink.

An angry voice swore at him. Garreth finally heard and moved on across the street.

She had destroyed Garreth's life, killed his partner, taken away his job, and removed him from his friends. She had destroyed more lives than his, too, when he counted the families of Adair and Mossman. He had no way of knowing how many others she had killed in her lifetime. The tally must be high. All those lives over all those years, and she still went free, to kill and destroy again, laughing at law, sidestepping justice. Growing up with a cop father, working as a cop himself, Garreth believed strongly in law and justice as the foundation of civilization. Without them, nothing remained but barbarism and chaos.

Garreth took a deep breath. He knew now what he could do ... the same job he had been doing before. Before he ended his disliked unlife, he would hunt down the red-haired vampire. *It takes one to catch one* might be truer for this case than any. He would hunt her and he would bring her back to stand accountable for what she had done to Adair and Mossman and to Harry and him. If it took him to the end of the earth and time, he would find her.

Hunter

1

By lamplight, the liquid in the cut-glass tumbler had the rich, dark red of Burgundy. Since giving up regular food, Garreth had taken to gulping his meals, dispensing with the unpleasant necessity as quickly as possible. Tonight, however, he turned the tumbler in his hands, wondering sardonically what Marti's Aunt Elizabeth would think if she knew the end to which her crystal wedding gift had come. He sipped the blood almost idly, playing with it as a wine taster might. *This Rattus '83 is a bold vintage, speaking to the palate with lively authority, while ...*

Garreth ended the game abruptly by emptying the glass. He played not for amusement, he knew, but to delay, to avoid considering the problem he had set himself. How could he hope to hunt down Lane Barber alone when the combined facilities of the department were failing to find her? Refilling the tumbler, he wondered whether his melodramatic resignation had been premature.

No, he had no other choice, not when carrying the badge endangered fellow officers' lives. Besides, as a "free agent" he could spend his time exclusively on this one case, and since he knew what Lane was—his exclusive knowledge—he could think of leads that nonvampires would never consider. Perhaps he could learn how she thought, too.

The telephone rang, startling him. He stared across the room at it. Should he answer? He did not feel like learning that Harry had died or, if it was his parents, like admitting to his father how he had screwed up.

It went on ringing. After the ninth time, Garreth dived on the phone and unclipped the cord from it, then walked back to the table in the silence and sat down with his tumbler of blood again.

First question: Where could she go?

Unfortunately, probably anywhere. In forty-odd years of singing, she must have made many connections. She could no doubt travel to any large city in the country, or perhaps even around the world, and through those connections find a new job. Most of them would not be familiar with anyone named Lane Barber, either. She could change identity again; she must have that honed to a fine art.

Habits did not often change, though, the famous *modus operandi*. She drew her food supply from customers where she worked, small, intimate clubs which offered ample opportunity for meeting customers. The Barbary Now and several other clubs the agent named where Lane had worked were all that type. How many such bars and clubs existed within the United States? Thousands? Hundreds of thousands?

Garreth sighed. Finding her in North Beach had been simple compared with the task that faced him now. He had the time, of course—her bite had given him *that*, at least—but in another sense, he did not. He needed to find her before his

money ran out and he had to take a job somewhere. He knew something about her, but, unfortunately, not enough to narrow down her possible
avenues of escape.

Perhaps the place to start learning was the one
where she shed all facades ... home.

He finished off his supper, washed the glass
out, and left it draining on the sink while he
grabbed his trench coat and let himself out into
the evening.

One doubt troubled him on the drive to her
apartment. It was her dwelling. Would he be able
to enter?

He could not. Since he had no key, he tried to
pass through the door as he did through the gates
of the piers, but that same searing pain that had
held him paralyzed outside Wink's hideout burned
through him as he touched the door. Garreth
backed hastily away and leaned against the porch
railing while the flames cooled in him. The fact
that she was a vampire and that he had been
invited in before his transformation did not appear to cancel the prohibition. Now what?

He doubted he could talk Serruto into letting
him in. Being officially off the case, his interest
would probably be classed as interference, if not
vengeance-seeking. *Isn't it?* He needed to use
someone else.

He found a public telephone and called Lane's
landlady. "Mrs. Armour, this is Inspector Mikaelian." Resignations took time to process; officially he could still be considered a member of the
department. "We met at your home last week."

"Oh, yes. You were asking about Miss Barber."
She paused. "The other officers said—did she
really try to kill you?"

"I'm afraid so, ma'am. I—we need to look
through her apartment again. I'm sorry to bother

you this evening, but could you meet me there with the key?"

"I already gave a key to a very nice-looking lieutenant," she said in a puzzled voice.

"Yes, ma'am, but the lieutenant is out of touch this evening and the key is locked in his desk. It's an imposition, I know, but this is important."

Her sigh came over the wire. "All right."

Meeting him at the curb some time later, she said, "You detectives work long hours, don't you?" She handed him the key. "Will you try to return this as soon as possible? It's the only other key I have to the apartment."

He stared at the key and bit his lip. "I'd appreciate it if you could come through with me. You've seen the apartment before and I think you can help me.'"

She looked simultaneously interested and reluctant. "Will it take long?"

Try not to lie all the time, man. "It might."

She complained in a gentle way all the way up the steps, but she agreed to help. Unlocking the door, she moved through and began switching on lights.

Garreth waited on the porch, pain licking at him.

She looked back from the doorway of the living room. "Well, come on in; I don't have all night."

The pain vanished. Garreth followed her quickly. "Look around and tell me if you think anything is missing. What she's taken might give us some idea where she's gone."

Mrs. Armour stood in the middle of the living room and turned. "She has lovely things, doesn't she? She's collected them from all over the world."

And spent good money on them, too, Garreth judged, if his term in Burglary had taught him as much as he thought about estimating the worth of objects. Though no art expert, he recognized the quality of the paintings and some small pieces of sculpture. Old toys resting on the bookshelves between sections of books drew more of his attention, however . . . several old-looking dolls, a miniature tea set, a cast-iron toy stove. Hers, from her childhood? he wondered. He studied a tray hung on the wall, its sections turned into shelves holding an assortment of small objects that reminded him of the "treasures" he had collected in an old tin tackle box when he was a boy.

She had no broken pocketknife, but there was a top—wooden, not plastic—and some marbles more beautiful than any he had had, he noted with envy—a giant tooth, a tiny rodent skull, and various stones: colored, quartzlike, or containing shell and leaf fossils. He could not identify one group of objects, though. He took down the largest to study. Held by its flat base, its large central point and two flanking smaller ones reached jaggedly upward, like the silhouette of a mountain range. Its color was dark and glassy as obsidian. Except for size, each object in the group looked identical.

"Shark teeth," Mrs. Armour said.

He blinked at her. "What?"

"Miss Barber told me once that those are shark teeth."

Black? He shrugged. Very well. His tackle box had never held anything that exotic.

Garreth put back the tooth and turned his attention to the books. Nonfiction outnumbered the fiction, but of the several hundred volumes covering a wide range of subjects, including extraterrestrial visitors and medical texts on viruses, only music, dancing, and folklore were represented by any substantial number of books.

He glanced through the folklore. All the books contained sections on vampires.

The publication dates of the library as a whole went as far back as 1919. A couple of children's books—printed with large color plates tipped in and black-and-white drawings, not the large print and easy vocabulary of the books he bought to give Brian—bore inscriptions in the front: "To Mada, Christmas 1920, Mother and Daddy," and "To Mada, Happy Birthday, 1921, Mother and Daddy." The ornate penmanship looked vaguely familiar.

He went on to check for inscriptions in the front of other books. A few had them, written in varying hands with dates from the twenties to the midseventies: "To Maida," "To Della," "To Delaine," "To Mala." Some were also signed by the person giving the book, but never with more than a first name.

Mrs. Armour, peering over his shoulder, remarked, "It's odd that the books are inscribed to so many different people, isn't it?"

"Maybe she bought them in used-book stores," Garreth said. Now, why, he wondered almost immediately, had he covered for Lane? Guilt? Let no normal human have the chance to discover what Lane is, for by giving that away, he would give away himself, too?

He searched the desk. Not that he expected Harry or the lab boys to have overlooked anything useful, but he wanted to make sure. A slim chance existed that they might not recognize something as useful that he, with his special knowledge, would. But he found nothing except blank writing paper and some felt-tip pens . . . no checkbooks, canceled checks, credit card records, or copies of tax returns.

Moving on to the kitchen, he found it as bare as Harry and Serruto had described, nor did the bedroom yield him information aside from the fact that she bought her clothes all over the world and with discrimination. He pursed his lips thinking of the price tags that accompanied labels like those.

"Can you tell me what clothes might be missing?" he asked Mrs. Armour.

She frowned. "Now, how should I—well," she amended as he raised a brow, "I guess I did peek in once. I think there used to be a blue Dior suit and some English wool skirts and slacks hanging at the end there." She described those and some other items in detail.

The dresser had been cleaned out. So had the bedside table and the bathrom medicine cabinet.

"Can you think of anything usually in the apartment that you haven't seen here today?" he asked.

From the bathroom doorway, Mrs. Armour considered the question. "I don't know. I haven't been here all that often, you know."

"Keep looking around, will you, please?"

He could understand Lane destroying papers but he had trouble believing that she would just walk away from all her personal belongings, an accumulation that she had obviously brought with her through the sequential changes of identity. She must have a few items too loved or revealing to be left behind.

He headed back for the living room. It had more of her effects than any other room. It also had the desk. He stared at it, pulled by some magnetism he could not explain. A letter had been on that desk the first time he saw it. He wished he had seen more than the address on it before Lane turned out the light.

He tried to visualize the envelope in his mind, picturing the ornate lettering. He paused. *That* was where he had seen the writing that matched that on the flyleafs of the children's books.

A letter from Lane's mother! He ticked his tongue against his teeth in excitement.

"I remember something," Mrs. Armour said. "There used to be two photographs on that top shelf."

Photographs. He turned his full attention on her. "Do you remember what they were?"

"One was of her grandparents. She never said so, but I assumed it. It was very old, that brown color, you know, and the woman's hair and dress were World War I style. I have a wedding picture of my parents that looks very much like it. The other looked old, too . . . three little girls sitting on the running board of a car."

An outdoor picture? "What was the background behind the car like?"

"Background?" She blinked. "Why, just a street, I think. Maybe there was a house in it."

"What kind of house? Brick? Stone? Wood frame? Large or small?"

She stared at him. "Really, Inspector, I never paid that much attention. Is it important?"

"Perhaps." Little girls might well include Lane as a child. A close look at the background might have helped tell him where she came from . . . and where she came from could give him someone who knew where Lane was now.

2

"I never thought we'd see you again, Inspector," Nikki said. The Barbary Now barmaid set a glass of soda water in front of Garreth, eyeing him with avid curiosity. "The cops who came in the other night, your partner and the handsome one, said you'd been killed."

Garreth smiled thinly. "I was, but death was so boring I gave it up. Can you stand to answer a few more questions about Lane Barber?"

She sighed. "Shit. More? I've told every frigging detective in the city every damned thing I know . . . which is zip, *nada*. we never passed more than the time of day, little comments about music or fashions or some guy."

Garreth broadened his smile to a friendly, persuasive one. "People say more than you might think. You mention a toy you've bought for a nephew or child and they come back telling you about one they bought once. Did Lane ever do that? Or maybe she mentioned some game she liked as a kid, or a pet she had."

Nikki's fingers drummed on the bottom of her plastic tray. "No . . . nothing."

Garreth could hardly believe that. Even someone with the experience and control Lane had must relax once in a while. Why should she avoid talking about pets and toys as long as the reference did not give away her age?

Then he thought about how he had lied needlessly to Evelyn Kolb about his interest in her thermos. Fleeing where no one pursued.

He paid Nikki for the soda water and sat back sipping moodily. Maybe Lane always avoided making personally revealing remarks. That was not much different from what someone like Chiarelli did, being undercover twenty-four hours a day every day. After so many years, caution may have become a reflex. Had that always been true, though? Maybe clues to her past lay in previous identities. As a younger, less experienced person, she might have been more open.

Her picture, with a different name attached, must be in the past files of agents here and in Los Angeles. Finding those agents would involve time and patience, but he was used to legwork. Eventually he could learn previous names and where she had worked. That would lead him to people who had known her.

The trouble was, memories failed. The farther back into her past he went, the fewer people would even remember her, let alone recall specific conversations. The trail inevitably became colder and thinner. Except if someone had a good reason to remember her.

Such as an assault?

If he could find them after forty-odd years, the people involved in that assault back in '41 might give him the best chance he had at her past. The assault itself suggested a woman more hot-tempered and less cautious than the one he had met. She even gave her real name when booked. Perhaps she told people about herself back then, too.

He wished he had written down the facts and names in that complaint when he had the file in his hands. Now he would have to go to Bryant Street in the morning and hope that word of his resignation had not reached the Records people yet so that he could see the file again.

He also wished he had had a closer look at that envelope on Lane's desk. He closed his eyes, trying to visualize it. He saw the address with its ornate penmanship clearly enough, but what he needed was the return address, and no matter how he concentrated, he saw nothing but a blur, a vague, peripheral smudge. He tried visualizing the postmark, too. That had not registered at all on his memory.

Finally, sighing, he gave that up. Scratch the luck of a return address. What else did he have? Names?

He considered names. All those she had used for herself professionally could be considered derivations from "Madelaine." Not unusual. Typically an alias bore a resemblance to the righteous name. He could almost bet that all her false surnames resembled "Bieber" much as "Barber" did. However, the name on the registration of the car and driver's license, Alexandra Pfeifer, was another matter. He still saw a resemblance, but an ethnic one. What were "Bieber" and "Pfeifer," Germanic? Could it be she chose "Pfeifer" because she was familiar with names like that? Could she have come from an area populated by people of German descent?

As if an answer to that helped. There had to be hundreds of Germanic settlements across the country.

Finishing his soda water, Garreth left the club and headed back for his car. What he needed to do was consult experts and find out where large Germanic groups had settled. It might help him.

At his car he was fishing in his pocket for his keys when a voice said, "Thank God. I was afraid I'd be sitting here all night, Mikaelian."

Garreth spun around.

Rob Cohen stepped from behind a nearby car. "This is getting to be a habit, turning out the force to find you. At least you're considerate enough to drive a conspicuous car. The lieutenant wants you at Bryant Street to talk to the shooting team."

3

A schematic drawing covered the blackboard. Garreth kept his eyes fixed on it while he answered the questions the detectives on the shooting team asked over and over again. His throat felt desert dry and his muscles almost daylight weak. Maybe dawn was coming. It seemed he had been here all night, endlessly repeating his version of the afternoon's nightmare.

"The gun wouldn't fire?" one of the team asked for the dozenth time. "Is that what you say?"

"No, sir," Garreth replied one more time. "I said I couldn't fire it."

"You said the trigger felt frozen."

"Yes, sir." He carefully told the truth. The team would pounce on evasions or lies.

"Is this the gun?"

He looked at it. It was the one he had surrendered when Serruto brought him in. "Yes, sir."

The four uniformed officers with Harry and him had undergone similar grillings earlier, he knew, but the knowledge in no way eased his own discomfort.

Pointing the revolver at the floor, the detective pulled the trigger. The hammer clicked on an empty chamber. "It's operating now. Had you ever fired this particular gun before?"

"No, sir. It was issued to me this morning."

"To replace the one being used as evidence?"

"Yes, sir."

"This is your first day back on duty?"

It went on and on. Please, Inspector, repeat as nearly as you can the exact events from the time you received the radio message to call that phone number. How was it neither of you called in for clearance to go after O'Hare? How did you determine the positions of the various officers at the scene? How many shots were fired? By whom? When? Over and over it, ending always in the schematic of the living room, where an outline indicated Harry lying bleeding.

Weariness dragged at him. Through the slits of the blinds he caught glimpses of reddened sky. Dawn.

Serruto came into the room, face grim, and whispered to one of the shooting team. Fear flooded Garreth. Was it about Harry?

Serruto backed against the wall by the door. The detective turned to look down at Garreth. "Describe what happened to you in the restaurant where you and Sergeant Takananda went for lunch."

Garreth stared at him. How could anyone have learned about *that*? The obvious answer took long seconds to occur to him, but when it did, Garreth came out of his chair grinning. "Did *Harry* tell you about that? Can he *talk*?"

"He told us," Serruto said soothingly. "He's going to be all right."

Garreth wanted to cry in sheer happiness and relief.

"Tell us about the restaurant," the detective repeated.

So overjoyed about Harry that nothing else mattered, he told them, scrupulously detailing all his symptoms, omitting only his knowledge of the cause. That gave them a whole new set of questions to ask, of course, but eventually they ran out of even those, perhaps in sheer exhaustion, and let him go.

Serruto walked down the corridor with him. "Mikaelian, until further notice, keep in touch. No more APBs, okay?"

Garreth nodded, too tired to talk. He could feel daylight outside the building. It made his head ache. He pulled the dark glasses out of the coat over his arm and put them on.

"I have your badge in my office. If you change your mind, you can have it back."

Garreth bit his lip. "Thanks, but I can't take it."

Serruto eyed him. Garreth sensed an emotional jumble in the lieutenant, but when Serruto spoke, it was only to say dryly, "Resigning doesn't get you out of the paperwork for everything up to now."

They stopped at the elevator. Garreth punched for *down*. "I know. Let me get a few hours in the rack and I'll type the reports."

"Why don't you see Harry before you do either? When they let us in to see him a couple of hours ago, the first thing he did was ask about you. He blames himself for everything."

Garreth shook his head. "No. It's my fault. I—"

Serruto interrupted. "You don't have to fight for the blame. I'm willing to spread it between both of you. You're not a child, Mikaelian; no one should have had to tell you that that attack indicated you weren't fit for duty. You should have seen a doctor immediately. Harry should have made sure you went and that I was notified of what happened." He grimaced. "My guess is, before the shooting board is finished, all of us will be wearing some egg."

4

The Records section clerk regarded Garreth with some surprise. "Well, good evening, Inspector. I heard you gave up your badge."

The grapevine worked as efficiently as ever, he noticed. "I did, but I have a few reports to finish before it's official. Would you have time to find this for me?" He handed her the case and serial numbers on Madelaine Bieber's assault charge.

"I think so. How is Sergeant Takananda?"

"He's doing fine."

Except for insisting on blaming himself for the O'Hare screwup. "I'm senior partner," he had repeated several times during Garreth's visit, his voice thin and weak but emphatic. "I let us go hotdogging in there."

"Don't worry about it now," Lien had said, just as quietly and emphatically. "Neither of you died."

Garreth's and Harry's eyes met, mutually agreeing not to discuss the differences between her scale of priorities and that the shooting board would apply.

"What's this Lien tells me about you turning in your badge?" Harry asked. "You didn't have to do that. You just need more time to recuperate before you come back to work."

Lien's eyes begged Garreth not to discuss the issue. He gave her the barest nod in reply. Anything that might stress Harry should be avoided at all cost, and Garreth read serious anxiety in Harry over the resignation. "I see that now."

"Go ask for it back."

"I will," Garreth lied.

Harry relaxed. A moment later, a nurse appeared and chased them out of the room.

In the corridor, Lien had looked up at him and read the truth somewhere in his face. "Thank you for giving him peace. What will you do now?"

"I have some things to finish first. Then"—he shrugged—"maybe I'll go back to school and finish my degree."

The lies went on and on, he thought, leaning on the counter in Records. Did he think the web of them would help him bridge the gulf around him? Or were they building a protective fence to keep others from discovering that gulf and falling into it?

"I'm sorry, Inspector," the clerk said, returning. "That file is out."

Garreth sighed. Who else would want it after all these years? Unless ... "Did Sergeant Takananda check it out?"

"No. Lieutenant Serruto."

Thanking her, he went back to Homicide. He found the squad room nearly empty. The few detectives there crowded around him as he came in, asking about Harry. He repeated what he had told the clerk in Records.

Beyond the windows of his office, Serruto slumped tiredly at his desk, looking as though he had not slept in days. He glanced up and, seeing Garreth, beckoned to him.

"How do you feel?" he asked when Garreth reached the open door.

"Fine. I'll get started on the reports." He lingered in the doorway. "I wanted to check out this Madelaine Bieber whose prints were all over Barber's apartment. R and I says you have the file on her assault arrest."

"Yes." Serruto eyed him. "Why do you want to know about her?"

Garreth put on a faint smile. "Curiosity, I guess."

Serruto reached into his desk drawer and pulled out a badge case Garreth recognized. He laid it on top of the desk. "Mikaelian, if you want to play detective, you pick this up again; otherwise, forget about Madelaine Bieber and Lane Barber until you're called to testify at Barber's trial. They're police business." He yawned hugely and added almost as an afterthought, "I nail vigilante hides to the wall."

Garreth retreated to his typewriter.

Now what? he wondered, feeding a report form into the typewriter. He could wait out Serruto. He could sit here working all night until Serruto and the others left, then search for the file. His sharpened hearing could detect someone coming in time to avoid being caught burglarizing his lieutenant's office.

Is this how you uphold the law, an inner voice asked contemptuously, *breaking it for your own private ends?*

He bit his lip, suddenly ashamed. What was he thinking about? It might take a vampire to catch a vampire, but if he let himself become like her in the process, what right did he have to hunt her? *All right, no shortcuts,* he promised his conscience. *Somehow, even without a badge, I'll stay legal.* He rubbed aching temples.

"Why don't you forget that and go back home to bed?" Serruto asked from the doorway of his office. "On second thought, let's make that an order. Go home. You're on limited duty: desk duty only, daytime only."

"Yes, sir," Garreth replied, and obediently left.

Riding down in the elevator, however, he considered the problem of legally seeing the contents of the file. Could he ask Cohen or Kolb to look at it and pass on the information? They might expect him to say why he wanted to know. Worse, they might tell Serruto who asked them to look at it. Was there anywhere outside the file that he could find the same information?

He found the answer to that about the time he stepped out of the elevator on the ground floor. Then he had to run for his car to reach the library before it closed.

"I need the October 1941 editions of the *Chronicle*," he told the librarian on duty in the microfilm section. He wished he remembered the exact date of that assault. It meant searching the entire month of newspapers.

He spun the film through the viewer as fast as he could and still read it. He felt closing time coming and speeded up the viewer a bit more.

By concentrating so hard on small items, though, he almost missed what he wanted. Lane had earned herself two columns and a picture on the front page. There was no mistaking her, towering tall between the four police officers hauling her back from a woman who crouched with blood leaking through the fingers of the hand held over her left ear. "The Barbary Coast Still Lives," the headline proclaimed.

Garreth thanked Lady Luck for the lurid reporting of that day and pressed the button for a printed copy of the page. Maybe he had something here. This Madelaine with her face contorted in fury was a far cry indeed from the Lane Barber who stood him up against a wall forty years later and coolly proceeded to drink his lifeblood, then go back to work.

He read the story in the dome light of his car, writing down all names and addresses in his notebook. He smiled as he read, amused at both the gossipy style of the story, laden with adjectives, and what he saw between the lines, knowing Lane to be what she was.

A woman named Claudia Darling, described as "a pert, petite, blue-eyed brunette," was accosted in the Red Onion on the evening of Friday, October 17, by "a Junoesque" red-haired singer named Mala Babra—Lane could fill a phone book with her aliases—employed by the club. An argument ensued over a naval officer both had met in the same club the evening before, Miss Babra claiming that Miss Darling had caused the serviceman to break a date made previously with Miss Babra.

Garreth smiled. He could just imagine Lane's frustration ... supper all picked out and some other lady walking off with it.

When Miss Darling denied the allegation, the story went on, Miss Babra attacked. They had to be separated by police hastily summoned to the scene. Four officers were needed to subdue and hold Miss Babra. Miss Darling suffered severe bite wounds to one ear and scratches on the face, but *the popular habitué of the nightclub scene is reported to be in satisfactory condition at County General Hospital.*"

Garreth eyed the last sentence, ticking his tongue against his teeth. He sensed a sly innu-

endo, something readers of the time had been
meant to infer, but which he, a generation later,
failed to understand. He studied the photograph:
the four officers straining to hold Lane, obviously
surprised by her strength; Lane ablaze with fury;
and the Darling woman, showing what the photographer must have considered a highly satisfactory amount of leg as she crouched dazed and
bleeding on the floor. The bare leg caught Garreth's
attention, but the rest of the woman held it. Even
with the differences in hairstyle and fashions, he
recognized what she wore as just a bit flashier,
shorter, and tighter than the dresses on the
women in the background. Now he understood
the innuendo and chuckled. Even a generation
removed, she clearly signaled her profession to
him: hooker.

That was a break. If she was in the life, she had
probably been busted a time or two, and that
meant a record of her: names, addresses, compan-
ions. Tomorrow he would run her through R
and I.

Humming, he switched off the dome light and
started the car, heading out of the parking lot
toward home to pick up his thermos before
hunting supper.

5

Danger! Even in the oblivion of vampire sleep, Garreth sensed it. The heat of human warmth touched him, spiced by the scent of blood. Someone stood in the room with him ... stood over him! *Wake up, Garreth.* As though floating somewhere apart, he saw the young Englishman pick up a spade and bring it down toward the man lying in the coffin.

Fear dragged Garreth up from darkness, spurring him to open his eyes and roll away from the slashing spade, but sleep and daylight weighted him. His arms rose with painful slowness to ward off the blow.

"No, don't," he said.

A hand caught his arm and shook it. "Garreth, wake up. You're having a nightmare. It's all right."

The words reached his ears, but his brain made no immediate sense of them. His eyes, focusing, saw Lien's face above him and recognized that it did not belong to the spade-swinging man, but his mind spun in confusion, disoriented. Lien? Where was he? The pallet under him on the bed indicated that he must be home. So how—

Panic flooded through him. He sat bolt upright. Lien! She had caught him in his unorthodox sleeping arrangement! And naked, too, beneath the single sheet over him, he remembered, clutching the sheet and pulling it up to his chin.

173

"Lien, what are you doing here? How did you get in? What time is it?"

She sat on the edge of the bed. "It's past two in the afternoon. I came because your mother called me after church. She's been trying to reach you since Friday. When I saw your car out front, I knew you had to be home, but I pounded on the door for five minutes without any response, so I used your spare key to let myself in."

As of today, the practice of hiding a key outside stopped. What if an enemy had stood over him, like Jonathan Harker in his nightmare? He would have been helpless to protect himself.

"Why did you unplug your phone?" Lien asked.

Unplug his phone? Oh, yes . . . he remembered now. He had done it Friday. He sighed. "I forgot I did it."

"I've reconnected it. Now you'd better call your mother before she has a heart attack." Lien started to get up, but paused in the act. "Why do you have that air mattress on top of the bed? And how can you sleep with only a sheet? It's freezing in here."

He avoided the question. "I'll call . . . if you'll let me get up and dress."

She headed toward the bedroom door. "Don't take too long."

He pulled on the first shirt and pair of pants he found, which turned out to be jeans and a ski sweater. The jeans, always snug before, hung on him. He added a belt, taken up four holes tighter than usual, and slipped his off-duty gun into an ankle holster.

He was hurriedly shaving when he heard Lien call, "Garreth, how old is this food in your refrigerator?"

He dropped the razor and ran for the kitchen. Lien stood before the open refrigerator, unscrewing the top from his thermos. "I thought I'd fix you something to eat, but everything seems to be either moldy or mummified."

"Don't open that!" He snatched the thermos away from her, then, as she stared open-mouthed at him, stammered, "It's . . . the liquid protein that's part of my diet. It . . . needs constant refrigeration." Carefully tightening the lid again, he returned the thermos to the refrigerator.

Lien frowned at him. "You don't mean to tell me that's *all* you're eating?"

"Of course not," he lied. "It's just all I eat here at home."

He shut the refrigerator and herded her out of the kitchen, sweating. Had she seen too much? Would it make her suspicious? He wished he could think, but his mind only churned, screaming at him to run.

"You should eat more," Lien said. "Losing weight too fast isn't healthy, and you look positively gaunt."

As much as he adored her, he longed to throw her bodily out of the apartment. Her concern and solicitude terrified him. "Thanks for coming by."

"I want to hear you call your mother before I leave."

He did not sigh; that might tell her how anxious he was to have her leave. Instead, he made himself smile and pick up the phone.

And after all the fuss, his mother wanted nothing more than to see how he was. "Mother keeps insisting that you're dead," she said, "and you know how unnerving her Feelings can be for everyone else. Why don't you come home for a visit? Actually seeing you should reassure her."

"Maybe this weekend," he said, "if I have time."

"Judith needs to talk to you when you're here, too."

"Judith?" A new fear touched him. "Is something wrong with Brian?"

"He's fine. It's something else; she'll tell you."

"Do you know?"

She hedged and wandered off on a tangent, which told him she knew, all right.

"Tell me. Don't let her hit me cold with it."

"Well." He heard her take a breath. "She wants your permission to let Dennis adopt Brian."

That single sentence buried all his impatience to be rid of Lien and on his way to the office to check the Darling woman through R and I. "She *what*! You can tell her—no, I'll tell her myself!"

He stabbed down the phone button. Releasing it again, he punched Judith's phone number. No one answered. Punching for Information, he asked for Judith's parents' number. She often spent Sunday afternoons there.

"Hello, Garreth," Judith said cautiously when her mother put her on the line. "How are you?"

"What do you mean, you want permission for your husband to adopt Brian? What the hell makes you think I'll ever agree to that?"

Her breath caught. "So much for polite amenities. No, it's all right," she said to someone on the other end. "Just a minute, Garreth." He heard her moving and a door shutting, with a diminution of background sound. "Now. I thought maybe you'd agree because you love Brian and want what's best for him. Brian and Dennis are already good friends, and—"

"They can be friends, but I'm his father. I stay his father."

"He needs one full-time, Garreth, someone he can feel he belongs to. What are you? He's lucky if he sees you four or five times a year."

"You were the one who insisted on moving back to Davis. My job doesn't give me enough time off to—"

"Your job is exactly what you choose to let it be." Her bitterness came clearly over the wire to him. "It wouldn't have to be twenty-four hours a day every day, but you wanted it that way. You chose that job over Brian and me."

Oh, Lord; here we go . . . two minutes of conversation and down into the same worn rut. "Judith, I don't want to start that again."

"With Brian adopted, you wouldn't have to pay child support anymore."

She thought she could *buy* Brian for her precious Dennis? "Forget it!" he said furiously. "Brian is my son and I'm not giving him to anyone else!"

He slammed down the receiver, shaking, and turned to find Lien regarding him with sympathy. All the anxiety related to her presence here returned in an icy flood. *Don't let her think too much.*

"I have to be going. I have stacks of paperwork," he said. "Thanks again for coming by. I appreciate your concern."

"You'll visit Harry sometime today, won't you?"

He picked up a ski jacket and hurried her out the door. "Of course. May I have my spare key back? Thank you." He clattered down the steps ahead of her and out onto the street, calling over his shoulder. "I'll come by this evening."

Pulling away from the curb, he saw Lien in the rearview mirror, staring after the car. He shivered. She had caught him asleep! She had almost found the blood in the thermos. If he remained friends with Harry and her, sooner or later he would slip, would give away something fatal. He had to find Lane just as soon as possible, take care of her, and leave the city before he woke some morning to find someone standing over him with a pointed wooden stake.

6

According to R and I, Claudia Darling had been born Claudia Bologna. Her yellow sheet listed eight arrests for prostitution in the years between 1940 and 1945. After that her only offenses were those of many good citizens, speeding citations. One had been issued in 1948, one in 1952—by which time her name had become Mrs. William Drum, with a Twin Peaks address—and a final one in 1955.

He copied down the information and studied it as he rode up to Homicide.

Serruto's office sat empty, but otherwise the squad room looked like any day. Garreth felt almost like a civilian in his sweater, jeans, and ski jacket. He walked quickly to his desk, only nodding greetings to the other detectives there. He felt better after he began the reports. They were easy ... just typed from his notes and memory, no real involvement required, no emotion. His fingers danced across the keys with almost self-volition, translating the thoughts in his head to words on paper. The rhythm soothed, draining away tension and anxiety, even when the report dealt with a dead-end lead or Wink's screwed-up capture. He typed steadily most of the afternoon, oblivious to the other activity in the room, only occasionally pausing to greet someone or let another thought creep in.

While proofreading, though, his mind slipped back to his conversation with his ex-wife. He fumed just thinking of it. Let Dennis have Brian? No way! Yet he recognized that Judith had a valid argument. Maybe that was what he found so infuriating. He had to admit that he had not been much of a father . . . and what kind could he ever be now? *Come on, son; let's go out for a bite. You have a hamburger and I'll take the waitress.*

He tapped the reports into a neat stack and carried them into Serruto's office. That was enough for today. Now, to Miss Claudia Bologna Darling Drum. He closed the door of the office and sat down behind the desk with the phone book.

Three William Drums lived in San Francisco, none in the Twin Peaks area. Dialing the number of William C. Drum, he found a Mrs. Drum at the other end, but a young woman and not a Claudia. She had never heard of Claudia Drum.

No one answered William R. Drum's phone.

He dialed William R. Drum, Jr. A child answered. Hearing the high-pitched voice, Garreth grimaced. This did not sound promising. "May I speak to Mrs. Drum, please?"

"Who?"

Garreth tried another tack. "Is your mommie there?"

"Mommie?"

Garreth felt like an idiot, talking baby talk to make himself understood. But to his great relief, a woman's voice came on the line a few moments later.

"This is Inspector Mikaelian of the San Francisco police," he explained. "I'm attempting to locate a Mrs. Claudia Drum."

"I'm afraid I don't know anyone by that name."

"She's an older woman. Your mother-in-law isn't named Claudia?"

"No, Marianna. Wait a minute." Her voice became muffled as she called to someone with her, "Bill, what's your mother's name?"

Several voices murmured, unintelligible to Garreth, then the voice of an older man came on. "This is William Drum, Sr. You're looking for a woman named Claudia? I may know her. Can you describe her for me?"

"She's short, blue-eyed, brunette. Her maiden name was Bologna and in 1955 she lived in the Twin Peaks area."

"And you say you're with the police?"

Garreth gave Drum his phone number and invited him to call back. Drum did, then explained that Claudia Drum was his first wife. "We divorced in 1956."

"Do you know where she is now and what name she's using?"

Drum hesitated. "I'm curious, Inspector, what you want with her. If all you know is that name, this must concern something very old."

"We're looking for information on a woman who assaulted her in 1941."

A long silence greeted that remark. Garreth pictured Drum staring nonplussed at the receiver, wondering why the police cared about a forty-year-old assault. Finally, with a shrug and a dry note in his voice, Drum said, "Her name is Mrs. James Emerson Thouvenelle and she lives on the wall." He gave a Presidio Heights address and phone number.

Garreth wrote them down, impressed. Claudia had done well for herself, rising from hooker to the mansions overlooking the Presidio. He wondered if Drum's dry tone indicated he knew he

had been a mere stepping-stone to that mansion.
Garreth made sure he thanked William R.
Stepping-stone Drum warmly before hanging up
and dialing the Thouvenelle number.

How would his request to see her be received?
As a rude reminder of her past?

When he mentioned Mala Babra, however, the
rich voice on the other end of the line laughed.
"That crazy singer? Are things so slow for you
boys that you're digging into the basement files?
Yes, I'll talk to you."

Garreth saw one problem: identification. It was
all very well to tell her over the phone that he
was from the police. She could call back and
verify that. What did he do when she asked to see
identification at her house?

His eyes dropped to the drawer where Serruto
had put his badge case. His hand reached out for
the drawer pull, then jerked back. *You were going
to keep clean, remember?*

"Will this evening be convenient for you?" He
would bluff his way in somehow.

"If you come before seven."

Garreth parked at the curb at a quarter till the
hour. The heavy front door bore an ornate lion's
head knocker in the middle. He reached out for it,
but the door swung open even before he touched
the knocker. A plump pouter pigeon of a woman
looking the epitome of grandmother and matron
studied him from the level of his shoulders.

"You're the young man who called? Mikaelian?"
she asked.

"Yes. You're—"

"Claudia Thouvenelle. Well." She looked him
over, relieved about something. "Please come in.
Do you have a first name?"

"Garreth." He followed her to a set of double
doors down the hallway.

She pulled open one of the doors and leaned into the library behind. "James," she said to the man sitting in a leather chair, "this is Garreth Mikaelian, the son of my old girlfriend Katherine Kane. You remember me telling you about her, don't you? Gary and I will be across the hall chatting if you need me."

She led an astonished Garreth across the hall to a living room and settled herself on a sofa. She met his eyes with her own, unnaturally blue— contact lenses?—and cool as ice. "I see no need to reveal the long-dead past to my husband, though understand that I'm not ashamed of it. I even find the idea of talking about those days after all these years a bit nostalgic. What do you want to know about that madwoman?"

"Everything you can tell me: who she was, where she came from, who her friends were."

She blinked, in disappointment, Garreth would have sworn. "I don't know anything except that she nearly disfigured me. She was crazy. It wasn't my fault if the naval officer preferred me to her. Who wouldn't prefer a woman-sized woman to that great gallumphing elephant?"

Garreth silently compared the matron with her blue-gray hair and sagging jowls to the slim, taut-bodied redhead who had her choice of men to bed and bleed. He could imagine that a woman so tall in those days might find the pickings a bit lean. Lane had the last laugh on her generation now, though.

"May I ask what your interest in her is after all these years?"

"We're trying to locate her. We think she has information we need on a current investigation."

"Have you checked the state mental institutions? She was quite unbalanced and should have been confined."

Garreth wrinkled his forehead. "Then why did you drop the charges?"

"As a favor for a friend, Don Lukert, the manager of the Red Onion. He was afraid that the owners might be upset by the bad publicity, so I agreed to drop the charges if he'd fire her and use his influence to see that she couldn't find another job in North Beach. He did and I did."

Vindictive bitch, Garreth thought. Aloud he said, "This manager. Is his name Donald Lukert?"

"No. Eldon."

"Do you know where he is today?" Mr. Lukert might have known something about his singer.

The woman shook her head. "I made enough during the war so that with some wise investments, I retired after Armistice and dropped out of my old circles. I went by the Red Onion a few years later but it had burned and another club built in its place. Don wasn't there. If he's still in the city, he's probably in a nursing home. He was in his late forties back then."

"Did Mr. Lukert ever talk to you about Miss Babra?"

"Oh, a couple of times perhaps. We had some laughs over how ridiculous and grotesque she was."

Garreth decided he did not care much for Claudia Bologna Darling Drum Thouvenelle.

"She tried to make him think she was a Balkan princess. She carried the blood of ancient nobility in her veins, is how she put it. She gave him some fantastic story about having escaped from eastern Europe just ahead of Hitler's storm troopers. But she wasn't European. That Bela Lugosi accent she used disappeared the moment she started shrieking at me and before that, a client of mine I met at the club heard her speaking what she *claimed* was her language and he said it was nothing but a preposterous hodgepodge of German and Russian."

Garreth blinked. German matched Lane's choice of names, but where did the Russian fit in? *Possible German and Russian community?* he wrote. They would have to be groups insular enough to be speaking their own languages in addition to English.

After asking questions for another ten minutes without learning anything more that seemed useful, he closed the notebook and stood. "I think that's all I need. Thank you for your time."

She escorted him to the door, speaking in a voice pitched to carry. "I'm so glad to hear about Kate. I'd lost track of her and thought I'd never hear of her again. Give your mother a big hug for me, will you?"

Garreth sighed in relief as the door closed behind him. What luck. She had never come close to asking for his ID. *Lucky cop. Thank you, Lady Luck. Keep smiling, Lady.*

7

The final, formal steps of resignation took less time and hurt more than Garreth anticipated. Checking in all equipment issued to him by the department felt like the division of property in a divorce. Gun, theirs; holster, his. Badge and ID card, theirs; badge case, his. Call box and other assorted keys, theirs; receipt for items currently being kept as evidence, his. So it went, down to his signature on all the necessary papers and the receipt of his final check.

He put that away carefully in his billfold. How long would it last? Until he found Lane?

"Good luck, Mr. Mikaelian," the clerk said impersonally.

Mister. Civilian. Garreth turned away, biting his lip.

Cleaning out his desk felt like divorce, too ... packing up what he felt like taking, giving or throwing away the rest. Some of it amazed him; had he really kept so much candy squirreled away in his desk? No wonder he had not been able to lose weight. And where had the Valium come from? For the most part, however, he worked numbly, feeling a chill like an arctic wind blowing through him ... that despite the heat he had taken the past twelve hours. *See the heat getting the heat.*

First it had been Harry last night—someone Harry refused to identify had told him about the finality of Garreth's resignation—and then the shooting board this morning.

The officer going in the front with Harry had sighed in relief as the board ruled his shooting of Wink righteous, but no one else found any comfort. The board gave Harry and Garreth what amounted to the Starsky and Hutch Award for Hot Dog of the Month, but also named the four uniformed officers as accessories. Failure to clear the operation with Serruto headed the list of sins, followed by criticisms of the execution that left no doubt the board felt only divine intervention prevented any loss of life.

They had reserved an entire section of their opinion just for Garreth. "Under the best of circumstances, even if all other procedure had been correctly observed, this operation would have been handicapped, if not compromised, by the presence of Inspector Mikaelian. From the evidence of his own statements and those made by Sergeant Takananda, it is clear that this officer should not have been on duty. The board questions the judgment of Dr. Charles in certifying him fit. We question the judgment of Lieutenant Serruto in accepting that certification. And in light of the particularly savage attack on Inspector Mikaelian such a short time before, its bizarre aftermath in the morgue, and the inspector's forcible departure from the hospital and refusal to return for proper medical observation and treatment, this board wonders why a psychological evaluation of this officer was not required before returning him to duty."

Behind his glasses, Garreth had glanced over to where Serruto sat with his handsome face grimly deadpan. Garreth burned in an agony of guilt. The lieutenant would be bearing the brunt of that last criticism. Under questioning, Serruto had stated that he planned to send Garreth to the department shrink, but could not explain why he had failed to do so. Of course he would not remember that the thought had disappeared the moment Garreth looked him in the eyes and declared himself fit.

In Homicide afterward, checking to be sure Garreth had all the necessary reports turned in, Serruto had said, "We can't make you see the shrink now, but you should go. Whatever brought on that attack in the restaurant and made you freeze at O'Hare's place is a time bomb ticking away inside you. You ought to have it defused."

"I'm fine," Garreth had said, declining, keenly aware that the advice and its refusal would probably be noted in his personnel jacket . . . the final comments on his service.

He tried not to think of that now, as he went through his desk.

"Tea, Mikaelian?"

He looked up to see Evelyn Kolb offering him her thermos. He nodded. Maybe it would help ease the cold inside him.

She pumped him a cupful. Sipping it, he reflected on Mr. Eldon Lukert. The phone book gave no listing for him, though a call to the phone company revealed that he had had one until five years ago. The county tax rolls still carried him. Garreth had managed to learn that much before the shooting board sat in judgment. Claudia Bologna etc. might be correct in her opinion that he was in a nursing home. Garreth planned to call them all to see.

Almost before he knew it, the tea was gone and the desk cleared. The box of belongings sat filled, ready to be removed. Reluctantly, Garreth put on his coat.

Serruto came out of his office, a hand extended. "Good luck, Mikaelian."

Garreth shook the hand. "Thank you." He thought about going around the room shaking everyone's, but a lump in his throat warned him that he might be in tears by the time he finished, so he shook just Kolb's and waved at the other detectives. "So long."

Their eyes reflected a common thought: *That could be me.* They said, "Good luck."

Garreth felt as though he stood on a ship pulling away fast from shore, watching the distance between himself and them growing ever wider. He ambled out of the room with the box, wanting to run, silently swearing at Lane. *These were brothers, lady. These were my family, and you took them away from me. Why didn't you just kill me straight out? Why couldn't you let me die clean?*

He drove home thinking: *Mr. Eldon Lukert, be good to me. Lead me to her. Please.*

He started with the A's in the nursing home section of the yellow pages and worked his way through the listings, one phone call at a time. If necessary, he was prepared to call every home in the Bay Area, including San Mateo, Alameda, and Marin counties.

Halfway through the San Francisco listings, the woman answering said, "Eldon Lukert? No, we don't have a patient by that name now. It sounds familiar, though. Just a minute." She went off the line.

Garreth crossed his fingers.

She came back. "We did have an Eldon Lukert until last month . . . Mr. Eldon Wayne Lukert."

"That's the gentleman I need. Can you tell me where he went?"

She paused. "I'm sorry. He didn't actually go anywhere. He died."

8

Garreth stood at the window, staring out at the twilight-reddened sky. Lukert died last month. *The bitch Luck strikes again.* Dead end . . . literally. Finis. He rubbed his forehead. Now what?

Out of the churning in his mind, one thought rose: Lane's apartment. It still drew him. She had lived there, called it home. Pieces of her, collected and kept over the long years and many changes of identity, filled it. Those pieces must indicate what she was and where she had come from, if only he could put them together right.

Driving to the apartment, he approached the door with caution. He had been invited in once. Would it still hold good, as the legend said? Or would the fiery pain bar him again?

At the door, his body still felt cool and comfortable. He leaned against the door, willing himself to the other side. Still no pain touched him. There was only the wrenching that he had come to associate with moving through barriers, uncomfortable but not painful, and in a moment he stood in the hallway.

How dark it had looked that first time he walked down it behind Lane Barber. No more. Now he saw it as gray twilight. For once he felt grateful for his vampire vision; he could move around the apartment and study it all he needed without lights to arouse the curiosity and suspicion of neighbors.

He stepped into the living room . . . and stopped cold still. It had been stripped clean! The furniture remained, but the paintings, the sculpture, the books and objects on the shelves were all gone.

Garreth ran for the bedroom and jerked open the closet. Her clothes still hung inside. In the kitchen he found the few items in the cupboards untouched, too.

He went back to the living room to stare at the empty shelves. When had she come back? Sometime in the last few days, obviously. She had come back and taken the items important to her. How did she know the apartment was not being watched?

Perhaps because she herself had been watching? He sat down in a handy chair. Could it be she had never left the city at all? He bit his lip. Never left the city. Why had they not thought of that?

Perhaps Serruto had and simply neglected to mention it to Garreth; after all, Garreth had not been deeply involved in the investigation since his injury. He found it easy to imagine how they missed finding her. After ridding herself of the car or hiding it, she probably checked into a hotel in some kind of disguise. With her height, she could even pass as a man.

She had stayed, and watched, and when it was safe, had picked up her belongings. This was one very cool lady. What was it her agent had said about her? All ice and steel inside. Really!

A shiver moved down his spine. *The maiden is powerful.* Beware of such a maiden. Made of ice and steel and with over forty years head start on him in vampirism and living experience, did he really stand a chance of finding her? What might she do if she suspected he was after her?

Then he shook his head. Personal danger should be the least of his worries. His life was already gone. All she could take away from him now was existence. On the other hand, she had the capacity to harm a great many more people if allowed to continue unchecked.

Very well, then ... he must keep going. He needed a direction, though. Any help he might have gained from her belongings had disappeared. He had to proceed on what he already knew.

What *did* he know?

The writing paper still remained in the desk. He took out a sheet and itemized his knowledge. She came, probably, from a Germanic background. She sometimes used Germanic names. She spoke German and Russian.

He made a note to find out through one of the local universities the location of German and

Russian groups near each other in the United States around World War I when she was born.

Could any of her belongings regionalize her? Too bad he did not know rocks well enough to describe those in the type tray to a geologist. If all of them were childhood "treasures" as other objects in the tray seemed to suggest, and if two or more came from a single geographic area, it might have been a lead. All he remembered, though, was the black shark tooth. Was that something he could use?

The apartment had given him as much as it was ever going to. He left, checking out the window beside the door to make sure the street was clear before passing through to the porch, then drove down to Fisherman's Wharf.

A few of the shops in the area remained open, catching late tourist trade. He wandered into one. "Do you have shark teeth?" he asked the girl behind the counter.

She took him to a section where the wall displayed small circles of jawbone lined with rows of wicked teeth. He studied the teeth. They looked the same shape as the teeth he had seen, but were all white, not black.

"Do you have any black shark teeth?"

She blinked. "Black? I've never seen black ones before."

He tried a similar shop farther down the street with the same results. The two clerks and a customer there had never seen or heard of black shark teeth, either.

The time had come, he decided, to seek expert advice. In the morning he would call one of the universities and ask them where black shark teeth came from.

Morning. He chafed at that. Why did it always have to be during the day when he could accomplish anything? He crossed Jefferson and began wandering through the arcades of the Cannery, peering into its shop windows fuming in impatience. Nothing was open when he felt most like working. Lane had taken convenience from him, too.

Then, in the window of a jewelry shop, he saw them . . . earrings, hooped for pierced ears, with small black teeth dangling from them! The shop had closed, of course, but a light still burned and he could see someone moving around inside. Garreth rapped on the window.

A man came out of a back room. He shook his head, pointing at the sign in the window stating business hours.

"I just want to ask a question," Garreth called.

I'm closed, the man's mouth said.

"I just want to know where those earrings come from!"

Come back tomorrow.

Garreth groped in his jacket pocket, then swore when he remembered there was no longer a badge to pull out and dangle before the window.

"Sir," he called, "this is very important. I *must—*"

But the man shook his head a final time and walked out of the room, leaving Garreth swearing in frustration. The question would have taken only a minute to ask and answer. The shopkeeper would have opened up fast enough for a badge. So why did he refuse Garreth that minute?

Because I don't have a badge; I'm only a civilian now.

And as the implications of that beyond the present inconvenience sank in, Garreth saw how truly alone he stood against his quarry, and he shivered in the cold wind blowing down his unprotected back.

9

The TV morning news warned citizens to drive cautiously. Fog had rolled in overnight and blanketed the entire city so heavily that it lay in a dim, shadowless twilight. Foghorns sounded from Mile Rocks east to Fleming Point and from Point San Pablo south to Hunters Point. Traffic accident investigation units ran fifteen calls behind. Garreth, though, welcomed the fog. He still felt the sun above it, weighting and weakening him, but for once he could enjoy opening the shades and letting such daylight as there was fill the apartment. He could sit by the window wearing his trooper glasses, feet upon the sill, phone in hand, and look out at the billowing grayness while he dialed the number of the biology department at the University of San Francisco.

"My name is Garreth Mikaelian. I need to talk to someone who can tell me where certain kinds of shark teeth are found."

He would have thought that was a simple request, but the phone went on hold for what seemed to be an eternity before a reedy male voice said, "This is Dr. Edmund Faith. You're the gentleman who needs to know where to find certain breeds of sharks?"

"I need to know where their *teeth* are found. Let me explain."

"By all means, Mr.—"

"Mikaelian. I found a shark tooth in a shop on

193

Fisherman's Wharf the other day. It's unusual because it's black. I'd like to find another and have a pair of earrings made for my wife. However, the girl in the shop had no idea where the tooth came from and neither did anyone else I asked."

"A *black* shark's tooth?"

"Yes. Do you know where in the world they come from?"

"Mr. Mikaelian, if you're interested in black shark teeth, you don't want me; you want a paleontologist. I'm not sure of all the areas they're found, but I do know that the black ones are fossils."

"Fossils?" Garreth sat upright.

"Maybe I can give you a name," Dr. Faith went on. "Let's see." Over the line came the rustle of paper. "Yes. Try Dr. Henry Ilford in the geology department." He gave Garreth a phone number.

Garreth jotted the number down, then jiggled the phone button and dialed the new number.

Dr. Ilford, a secretary informed Garreth, was in class. Garreth remembered from his college days how difficult it could be finding a particular professor when one needed him, and with a sigh, said, "I need information on locating fossil shark teeth. I'll talk to anyone who can help me."

"I'll see if the graduate students are in their office," the secretary said.

The phone went on hold again. Garreth drummed his fingers. As much as he preferred phoning to running around in daylight, perhaps he should have driven to the campus. Listening to a phone in limbo, he found it too easy to imagine the secretary finishing a letter then going on coffee break, forgetting about him.

Before long, though, another voice came on the line, pleasantly female, inquiring if she could be of

help. Garreth patiently repeated his question.
"Can you tell me the areas where black shark
teeth are found?"

"Well." She drew out the word. "Fossil shark
teeth can be found in about seventy-five percent
of the country. It's almost all been under water at
one time or another."

Garreth sighed. Seventy-five percent? So much
for the tooth as a lead to Lane's background.

"But," the young woman went on, "most of the
teeth are white. The only places I know to find
the black ones are on the eastern seaboard and in
western Kansas."

Garreth scribbled in his notebook. "Just those
two places? How easy are the teeth to find
there?"

"I think you have to dig back east, but they're
on the surface and accessible in Kansas."

Accessible. "Could a kid find one without much
trouble?"

"I'm sure he could. I've been told it's possible
to pick them up just walking across a plowed
field or in the cuts along roads and streams."

Which should be how she acquired it, if the
tooth in the type tray were a "treasure." He
recalled the other fossils in the type tray. "Are
there many kinds of fossils available in the
Kansas area, say in limestone?"

"It's wonderful fossil country."

He thanked her and hung up, then sat staring
at his scribbled notes. Kansas. The postmark the
lab brought up on the burned envelope had a 6
and 7 in it. Harry had said that the Kansas ZIPs
used those numbers. He ticked his tongue against
his teeth. Did the trail smell warmer?

He went through the phone book again, this
time for the number of the sociology department.
"I need to talk to someone who can tell me where

immigrant German and Russian groups settled in this country."

That brought him more interminable time on hold while the secretary hunted for a likely prospect. She came back suggesting he call in two hours, when a Dr. Iseko would be in his office.

Hanging up, Garreth sat looking out the window. A partial ZIP code and—when he reached this Dr. Iseko—areas of German and Russian settlements would still not pinpoint Lane's home exactly. He needed a town. Three partial letters had also been visible on that postmark. What were they? An O or U preceded by A, K, R, or X and followed by any letter beginning with a vertical stroke. He hunted through the bookcase, but had nothing like an atlas, nothing with a detailed map of Kansas in it. It appeared he would have to go out, after all.

He drove down to what had become his best source of information lately, the public library. There he spent an hour with the ZIP directory, finding towns with 67 as the first or second two numbers and whose names contained letters in the right combination to match the postmark.

Halfway through the list of towns, a name leaped out of the book at him: *Pfeifer*. Pfeifer! Eagerly, he raced through the rest of the names. Ten fit. He looked up their locations in an atlas. Of the ten, two possibles lay in the immediate vicinity of Pfeifer, Dixon to the southwest and Baumen to the northeast.

Then he went looking for a telephone to call back the university. This time he found Dr. Iseko in his office.

"I'm a writer doing research for a book," Garreth told him. "I need to know if Kansas has communities of German immigrants living in close proximity to Russian immigrants, and if so, where."

"I'm afraid there are none quite like that in Kansas," the anthropologist replied.

Garreth's stomach dropped. He swore silently in disappointment. "But what about towns like Pfeifer?"

"That's the Ellis County area? Pfeifer and the communities around it like Schoenchen and Munjor don't have German *and* Russian immigrants; they were settled by the so-called Volga Germans, Germans who immigrated to Russia and lived along the Volga before immigrating to this country in the latter quarter of the nineteenth century."

Something electric sizzled through Garreth. He felt all his hair stand on end. "They're a kind of mixed German and Russian, then? Does their language have both German and Russian in it?"

"It most certainly does. It's a very unique language. An acquaintance of mine wrote his dissertation on it."

Claudia etc. had said: *It was nothing but a hodgepodge of German and Russian.*

"How large an area did these Volga Germans settle?"

"The Catholic group is mainly around Ellis County. However, there was a Protestant German-Russian group who settled in Bellamy and Barton counties, and some of them extend into Rush and Ness."

Garreth wrote it all down. After thanking the doctor and hanging up, he went back to the library and the atlas. Dixon lay in Rush County; Baumen, in Bellamy County.

Back to the telephone, calling Information in Kansas, calling Information in Dixon and Baumen.

Did they have listings for Biebers? Yes. Both had Biebers.

Excitement rose in Garreth. He might be completely wrong, Lane might come from the East, but Kansas looked good. Very good. He had a feeling about it. A Grandma Doyle-quality Feeling? Or perhaps blood called to blood. After all, in a sense, he was Lane's son; she had made him.

However strongly he felt the key to her lay in those two small towns, though, he would never know for certain without further investigation. He could not do it by phone, either. If she were in touch with people there, they might warn her she had been traced. To be effective needed subtlety.

He would have to go there.

10

The country did not have the dinner-plate flatness Garreth expected, but its gold-brown hills, so unlike either the yellow ones of California or those in San Francisco, stepped with streets and houses, rolled to an almost unimaginably distant horizon, only sparsely dotted with trees and human constructs. The sky arched overhead, a cobalt bowl of infinity broken only here and there by wisps of cloud. The sun burned Garreth's eyes even behind his glasses. Driving south toward Dixon out of Hays, he felt overwhelmed, a mote crushed between the immensity of earth and sky. He wondered whether it might have been wiser to drive during the day instead of only at night, sleeping in his little tent at public campsites by day. Then he could have gradually accustomed himself to the broadened horizon instead of being suddenly hit by it on this drive.

To take his mind off his unexpected agoraphobia, Garreth thought ahead to Dixon, rehearsing his cover story. He wanted to hunt his relatives. When his grandmother died last year, she had left a letter revealing that she was not the real mother of Garreth's father. Phillip Mikaelian, the letter said, had really been born to a young girl who roomed with them and became pregnant out of wedlock. After the birth, the girl ran away, abandoning the baby, and rather than send it to an orphanage, Garreth's grandmother had raised the boy as her own. She had no idea where the real mother was, but she had a photograph and remembered that the girl used to write letters to a town in the Ellis County area of Kansas. As he was currently between jobs, he had decided to trace his real grandmother's family. He looked young enough to pass as the grandson of a woman born around 1916.

The photograph he carried was actually of Grandma Doyle, taken in the late twenties when she was seventeen and fresh from Ireland. The hard cardboard square stiffened the inside pocket of his coat. Feeling it, Garreth remembered two weekends ago, when he asked for it.

Handing it to him, his grandmother had said, "May it bring you she who killed you, and then a peaceful sleep."

She had known what he was from the moment he walked in the house. She said nothing, but beyond his parents, he saw her reach for the silver Maltese cross she always wore around her neck.

"Garreth," his mother had exclaimed in horror, "you're becoming skin and bones!"

His father said, "What the hell is this I read in the paper about your partner being shot and you quitting the department?"

But his eyes and attention were on Grandma Doyle. "Grandma?" He reached out to hug her but she hurriedly backed away and left the room. Garreth stared stricken after her. "Grandma!"

His mother touched him on the arm. "Please forgive her. I think she's getting old. Ever since you were attacked, she's insisted you're dead. I think she just needs time to accept that, for once, her Feeling was wrong."

Garreth had given silent thanks that his mother misinterpreted the reason for his distress. "I understand." Which did nothing, however, to lessen the pain of having someone in his family fear him.

"What's been going on out there with you?" his father asked.

Garreth's jaw tightened in resentment. Could they have at least a little of: *How are you, son?* and: *It's good to see you home in one piece*, rather than immediately moving into: *Up against the wall. Spread those feet. You* don't *have the right to remain silent, and anything you say or don't say will be used against you.*

Explaining was not only going to be difficult; it would be impossible. Nevertheless, Garreth tried.

His mother went white, listening. "Will you go back to college now?"

He heard the relief in her voice. Of course she was glad to have him out; now she did not have to fear phone calls about him.

But his father said, "Shane never gives up. They've operated on that knee four times and sometimes he has to play filled with painkillers, but he always plays. He never quits because he's been hurt a little. He's never walked out of a game because he was going to be penalized, either."

That stung. Garreth protested, "I didn't resign because of what the shooting board might say or do!"

"Are you going to see a psychiatrist like they suggested?" his mother asked.

His father snorted. "He doesn't need a shrink; he just needs to quit feeling sorry for himself." He leveled a hard stare at Garreth. "You ought to ask for reinstatement, take your lumps from the shooting board like a man, and get back to work."

Garreth had not argued. "Yes, sir," he said, and escaped from the house into the backyard. Even sunlight was preferable to further conversation with his father.

Why did this have to happen? He loved his father dearly. If only the man could ask a question without making it sound like interrogation and offer an opinion that did not seem to be an order. The worst part was, Garreth could not help wondering if his father was right.

The earth welcomed him as he sat down in the shade of the big cottonwood where he and Shane had built a tree house years ago. The platform still sat in the fork, a little more weathered each year but sound enough yet for Brian and for Shane's kids to play on it when they visited.

Garreth had lain back against the trunk, rubbing his forehead as he thought about Brian. As soon as he visited the boy the question of adoption was bound to come up again. He closed his eyes wearily. What should he do about it this time?

Feet whispered down the back steps and across

the lawn toward him, but he left his eyes closed. The scent of lavender overwhelming that of blood told him who it was.

The feet stopped a short distance away. "*Deargdue*. Undead," his grandmother's voice said quietly. Fighting his eyes open, he saw her lower herself into a lawn chair. "Why is it you're walking?"

He sat up. "Grandma, I'm not dead! Look at me. I walk; I breathe; my heart beats. I reflect in mirrors. I can touch your cross, too."

"But what do you eat? Do you still love the sun?" She pointed at his glasses.

He could not answer that. Instead, after a hesitation, he said, "Whatever else I am, I'm still your grandson. I won't hurt you."

She regarded him uncertainly, then, with a quick touch on the cross around her neck, patted the side of the chair. "Come to me."

She sat in the sun, but he moved to the ground beside her.

She reached out hesitantly to touch his cheek. "Is it to avenge yourself on she who did this to you that you can't sleep?"

He considered several answers before sighing and giving the one she appeared most ready to accept. "Yes."

She stroked his hair. "Poor unquiet spirit."

His inner self protested, denying that he was walking dead, but he swallowed it as useless to say—she would expect the refusal to believe—and leaned his head against her knee. "I need your help."

"To find *her*?"

Garreth nodded.

"What will you be wanting me to do?"

At the fierce tone of her voice, he looked up and had to laugh. She looked so righteously angry, so ready to go into battle against the fiend who had done this to her grandson, that Garreth regretted needing only the photograph from her. Coming up onto his knees, he hugged her.

She hugged him back and then, to his dismay, began sobbing. He knew he was hearing her cry over his grave.

He held her until she quieted, wondering ... could she be right? Was he nothing but a temporarily animated instrument of revenge?

It made a hell of a thought to take with him when he visited Brian. Thinking it, he stood at a distance from himself and the boy. He noticed for the first time a certain formality in the boy's attitude toward him, a reservation not exhibited toward his stepfather. Logic told Garreth that was natural; Brian saw Dennis every day, whereas, for six years, since the boy was two years old, Garreth had been no more than a visitor. How much less would Garreth be from now on?

"Judith," he said, "I've been thinking about the adoption."

She looked quickly at him. "I'm sorry I brought it up when I did; I didn't realize the kind of stress you were under."

He shrugged. "It doesn't matter. If you and Dennis want to go ahead—"

She shook her head, cutting him off. "Of course we want to, but can you be sure *you* really want us to? Why don't we let it ride for a bit, until you have things straightened out for yourself?"

He had regarded her with surprise, but nodded, and for once, a visit had ended amicably.

He wished he could have said as much for the rest of the weekend, which became a test in ingenuity in avoiding meals and dodging questions about how he had changed and what he planned to do now. Altogether, returning to San Francisco had been a great relief.

A relief which, unfortunately, had not lasted long. Harry, feeling better every day, began nagging him during Garreth's daily visits. "Kansas? What in the world are you going to Kansas for? Come on, Mik-san; why don't you see the shrink and come back to the department where you belong?"

Only Lien kept silent on the subject, quietly helping him sublet the apartment, sell what he no longer wanted, store what he chose not to take with him, and buy a few new clothes to replace the ones that no longer fit. She had said nothing until the day she helped him pack his car. Then, as he closed the back, she said, "I don't know what's happened to you. I wish I knew how to help. I asked *I Ching* for advice to give you. Do you mind listening to it one last time?"

He leaned against the car, smiling fondly at her. "What did the sage have to say?"

"The hexagram was number twelve, *Standstill*. It says that heaven and earth are out of communion and that all things are benumbed."

He bit his lip. That was certainly true enough for him.

"Inferior people are in ascendancy but don't allow yourself to be turned from your principles. There are change lines in the second and fourth places, advising that a great man will suffer the consequences of a standstill and by his willingness to suffer, ensure the success of his principles. However, acting to re-create order must be done with proper authority. Setting one's self up to alter things according to one's own judgment can end in mistake and failure."

Garreth listened soberly. "What else? The change lines make a new hexagram."

"The second one is number fifty-nine, *Dispersion*." She smiled. "It suggests success, especially after journeying and, of course, perseverance. Persevere, Garreth, and be true to yourself. And don't forget about us."

He had hugged her hard, promising to keep in touch. Lien, Harry, San Francisco, and his family seemed so far away from these Kansas plains he drove across now that they might have belonged to another lifetime, but *I Ching* lingered with him. Persevere. Yes, he would, to the end of the earth and time ... whatever it took to find Lane. That threat of failure if he set himself up as judge bothered him, however. It smacked too closely of the warning regarding powerful maidens. He was not making himself judge, was he? He only intended to find her and take her back to San Francisco.

The highway entered Dixon. After asking directions, Garreth found the high school. Climbing out of the car outside the small building, the warm wind struck him. It had some of the same qualities as a sea breeze, a pushiness, an aggressive wildness, a singing contempt for the land and that which crawled there. It buffeted him, bringing the scents of fresh-watered grass and dusty earth, and pushed him up the steps into the building.

He located the office, an expanded broom closet bearing the word **OFFICE** on the frosted glass panel of the door, and the principal, a Mr. Charles Yoder. Yoder listened to his story with interest.

"People are more and more interested in their roots these days. I'll be happy to help you if I can."

What he did was take Garreth to the Board of Education building and down a steep set of stairs to a dim basement. There they hunted through file envelopes stacked together on metal shelves and through ancient metal and wooden filing cabinets. A secretary joined them eventually. "Graduation pictures? I know I've seen them somewhere . . . a whole stack of them."

They finally located the pictures on a top shelf, all still framed, the glass so dusty as to render the sepia-toned photographs behind all but invisible. The principal went back to the high school, leaving Garreth and the secretary to bring the pictures up into the light and clean them. But when all that had been done, and Garreth compared the pictures of the girls in the 1930 to 1940 classes with his mental image of Lane Barber, he found no match.

The secretary wiped at a smudge on her nose. "I'm sorry," she said.

Garreth shrugged. "It would be almost unbelievable to find the right town first off, wouldn't it?"

Still, he would have liked that much luck. Now he had to check all the high schools in the area, both to maintain his cover and on the slim chance that even if the letter came from Dixon, Lane's family lived somewhere else in the area.

"I met a Bieber in San Francisco," he said to the secretary. "Madelaine Bieber. She was a singer. I wonder if she came from somewhere around here, too."

"Madelaine? The name doesn't sound familiar."

He dropped back by the high school to thank the principal and managed to work in the remark about the singer with him, too . . . but with no more luck. The name meant nothing to Yoder.

Back in his car, Garreth spread the Kansas map on the steering wheel and studied the area around Dixon. He had time yet today to visit another town. Or maybe two? Was it possible to cover three a day? A whole cluster of towns sat at no more than ten-mile intervals and he needed to work as fast as possible. Every day depleted his dwindling cash reserves still further.

He started the car and headed down the road west toward the next town.

A name on a map did not necessarily mean a town there, Garreth discovered. It could indicate no more than a gas station and a grain elevator—a row of huge, melded columns which he found an odd but fascinating structure. There had once been a real town, but it had dried up over the decades until just the elevator remained, a massive tombstone to mark its passing. The former town had once boasted a high school, too, in that bygone era, but the records had disappeared into limbo. The best a withered old man tending the gas station could suggest was for him to check the county seat.

"They might've moved the town records there."

Garreth visited the county courthouse—and the local high school, as long as he was in town—but the county clerk knew nothing about any school records transferred from the defunct town. She advised checking back the next day.

The high school had its records, but they were not immediately available, either. They, too, suggested that he come back the following day.

Tomorrow. Garreth sighed. Why always tomorrow? Lane's mother had to be elderly, and if he did not find her soon, he might be in the same position he had when looking for the manager of the Red Onion, with only a grave to question.

Gloomily, he wondered at the real chances of finding Lane this way. Between dead towns and lost records, he could so easily miss the traces of her. And then what would he do? Question every Bieber in the area? Word would certainly find its way back to her then, and knowing a hunter had come this close, she might stop communicating with her family and disappear forever.

On that depressing note, he headed the car back toward Hays.

11

One nice thing about bad days, Garreth reflected ironically, was that something else always came along to offer an alternative worry . . . in this case, hunger. The four quarts of blood collected to keep him fed on the way east were gone. Tonight he needed to find a new source of food.

Rinsing out his thermos in the washbowl of his motel room, he considered the possibilities. He had already concluded that rats would not be as common in a small town as along the Embarcadero, a fact he faced with mixed emotions. As much as he detested being dependent on rats to live, at least he knew where and how to hunt them. He knew nothing about jackrabbits and prairie dogs, the two comparable species he most associated with the plains, and after driving across this country today, he wondered whether the creatures *could* be considered a viable alternative. Not one rabbit had appeared anywhere near the road during the drive, nor had he seen a single sign of a prairie dog town. The sound of distant and not-so-distant barking told him the town supported a canine population, but he still found himself reluctant to use dogs. People cared about them.

Outside, the sky blazed scarlet, then darkened. A series of violent cramps doubled him, goading him into action. Garreth headed for his car. He had learned to hunt rats, after all, by hunting them. Why should rabbits be any different?

The highway took him out of town almost immediately. Somewhere north a few miles, he turned off the highway onto a graveled road and pulled over. On both sides of the road lay rolling fields. He studied them, alert for any signs of life, but nothing moved. Still, it must be there. The night wind brought him a faint scent of something warmly blood-filled.

Garreth considered the fence around the pasture on his side of the road. Instead of planks, four taut strands of barbed wire enclosed the pasture. He tested the ends of the bars with a cautious finger. Sharp. Crawling through the fence could ruin his new jeans, not to mention putting holes in his hide. Then it occurred to him that a fence presented less of a barrier than a gate across a pier entrance. With a sigh for his mental slowness, he moved through the fence.

Once inside and walking across the pasture, he found plenty of life, mostly too small to do him good, mice and quail. He literally stumbled over the quail. They leaped skyward around him with startled cries and a storm of wings. Ahead, though, a rabbit leaped out of the brush and bounded up a rise, frightened into flight by the panicking quail.

Garreth followed cautiously, just close and fast enough to keep the rabbit in sight while he waited for it to halt. Once when it zigged across in front of him, he dropped to a crouch and waited motionless until the rabbit turned away again. The stalk gave him a vague sense of déjà vu, which turned to amusement when he identified the reason for the feeling. He laughed silently. *See the ex-cop shadowing the rabbit. Isn't it nice he can put his training to good use?*

Moments later Garreth gave thanks he had not gone flat out in a footrace after the rabbit. It disappeared over the crest of the rise, and when he followed it, he found himself face-to-face with a cow that loomed huge as an elephant and pale as a ghost in the twilight brightness of his vision. If he had been moving fast, he would have run head-on into it.

The cow snorted in surprise.

Garreth backed away. He had better get the hell out of here.

Then he stopped, nostrils flared, nose filled with the blood scent that the wind had brought him at the pasture fence. He stared at the cow. Cattle had blood, too . . . in great quantity. If Lane could drink from a man and not kill him, would a cow even miss a quart or two?

On the other hand, could he control a cow as he did rats? This one seemed docile, but he knew nothing about cows, had, in fact, never been this close to one before. Did they often grow so terrifyingly large?

Another doubt assailed him, too. Could he find a vein? That neck was far thicker than Velvet's had been.

The cow snorted again and lowered its head. Garreth sensed that he must either act or retreat. He licked his lips and wiped suddenly sweaty palms on his jeans. Moving enough to catch the cow's eye, he focused on it. "Hello, friend. Listen to me. Stand still for me. Don't move."

The animal's eyes widened, showing white rims that glistened in the night. Its ears wagged.

"I need a little of your blood, enough to feed me. It won't hurt." He kept his voice low and even.

The cow relaxed visibly.

So did Garreth. "Lie down for me. Lie down."

The white rims still showed around the cow's eyes, but its legs began to sag, the forelegs folding first, followed by the hind ones. Its nose dropped to touch the earth.

Still talking, Garreth moved toward the cow. He reached out and gingerly touched the massive head. The hair felt warm, soft, and curly under his fingers. The cow did not flinch or resist. Murmuring soothingly, Garreth knelt and moved his hand back along the head past the ear, toward the throat. He probed the neck behind the jaw, searching for a pulse.

He found it, beating strong and slow. Keeping the fingers of one hand on it, he pushed at the thick shoulders with the other. "Roll," he said softly. "Lie flat."

With a sigh, the cow did so. Garreth, still on his knees, bent over the outstretched neck and, extending his fangs, bit where his fingers touched.

But found only flesh and the barest taste of blood. *Not again!* He wanted to scream in frustration.

The cow twitched. Panic boiled up. Garreth needed all his willpower to control it. He thought frantically. The pulse throbbed under his fingers; he smelled the blood running hot under the pale hide. It had to be in there somewhere. He made himself try again, biting in a slightly different position.

This time blood spurted. The twin gushers filled his mouth. After his usual refrigerated diet, its heat startled him. He nearly let go. But the driving hunger in him quickly overcame surprise, followed, however, by more frustration. Despite its heat and volume, the blood *still* did not satisfy him, only filled his stomach. He sat back, holding thumbs over the punctures with longing snarling in him. Tears of fury gathered in his eyes. *No. It isn't fair! Blood is blood. Why isn't this enough? Why do I never stop wanting human blood?*

The cow lay quiescent, its eyes closed, snoring. Garreth removed his thumbs. The punctures had stopped seeping blood. A handful of earth rubbed into the hide covered the marks. Then Garreth stood.

The cow opened its eyes and rolled onto its chest, but made no further attempt to stand, just closed its eyes again. Still, Garreth eyed it as he backed away. It was a very large animal. He did not turn until he was over the hill, then, once out of sight, he ran . . . partially to put distance between himself and the huge animal, partly in a vain attempt to run away from the longings racking him. But there was enjoyment, too, in the nighttime strength and energy clamoring for release.

He ran, his lungs and heart pumping. The ground streamed beneath his feet as power surged through him. Soon exhilaration drowned all other thoughts and he gave himself up to the unthinking joy of motion. He had never been able to run this fast before!

The fence stretched ahead. Should he stop for it? *Hell, no.* He hit it without even slowing down—*wrench*—passing through like the night wind.

At the car he stopped and to his delighted astonishment, found his heart and breathing barely above normal. He whooped. At this rate, he could run for miles without even trying. What a kick.

Headlights found him there beside the car.

He froze in their glare, throwing up an arm to shield his eyes. The action came reflexively but even as his forearm rose between his eyes and the lights, Garreth realized it served another purpose as well, to keep the driver of the car from seeing his eyes reflecting red.

The lights halted as the car stopped. A door opened.

Not being able to see who climbed out of the car, Garreth assumed the worst—a drunk or bully who thought a man alone on a country road made easy pickings—and prepared to fight. Since resigning, he had had to stop carrying a gun, but tonight's run had given him some hint of the strength his vampire change had brought him, and between that and police hand-to-hand combat training, surely he could tie any assailant in knots.

"Howdy," a voice said from behind the lights.

Garreth heard the hard edge of authority beneath the amiable greeting. He lowered his arm enough to peer over it at the shape of a light bar on top of the car. Relief swept through him. No drunk or bully but a local cop. Then, remembering times on patrol with a few partners before Harry, he wondered if he might not have been better off with a drunk or bully.

"Good evening, Officer," he said.

"Deputy sheriff," the voice corrected him. "What's your name?"

"Garreth Mikaelian. My driver's license is in my pocket. Would you like to see it?"

"Yes." As Garreth fishcd his billfold out of his hip pocket and extracted the license, the deputy said, "You have California plates. You a student at the college, son?"

College? Yes, he did seem to remember some

sign naming a college in Hays. He debated his answer and chose honesty. "No."

The deputy moved into the headlights to take the license. "Visiting someone in town?"

"I'm here on personal business . . . staying at the Holiday Inn."

"What are you doing way out here?"

What answer would the deputy accept? What would *he* accept if their positions were reversed? The easiest solution was to look the man in the eyes and persuade him to find nothing suspicious in Garreth being out here. Conscience stopped him, however. The last few times he had persuaded people, he could not help but remember, it brought nothing but trouble to people he cared about. In any case, who could be sure of the long-term effects? If nothing else, the deputy had surely called in before leaving his car and an inconsistent report would raise questions Garreth might not care to answer. No, somehow he had to satisfy the deputy here and now in a straightforward way.

"I'm a night person and your town goes to sleep before I do. Since there was nothing else to do, I took a drive. This is a spectacular sky."

"I saw you in that pasture."

Garreth kept his voice casual. "I wanted to see what the countryside looked like from the top of that hill. I did, and then I came back to the car."

"Running in the dark? What was your hurry?"

He could hardly tell the deputy how well he saw in the dark. "Look, Deputy, maybe I trespassed, but I didn't hurt anything. I'll take you where I went and you can see for yourself. There's nothing but a cow asleep on the other side of the hill."

"Cow?" The deputy laughed shortly. "The Good Lord looks after fools, I guess. Son, that 'cow' is

Vale's Chablis of Postrock, Postrock ranch's prize Charolais show bull, or he was until he got too mean to handle."

Garreth swallowed. "Mean?"

"He's put three men in the hospital. You could have paid for that walk with your life." The deputy handed back the driver's license. "Suppose you forget about looking at the night sky and go on back to town."

Garreth went, shaking in retrospective fear. But gradually, new feelings replaced the fear. He had found a plentiful source of blood, and he had controlled the bull. Best yet, he had not had to kill for his meal. He had better find a cover for his nocturnal hunting trips, though. The next deputy might not believe that he was driving for lack of anything better to do.

He would take up "jogging." Everyone ran these days. Tomorrow, before he set out south to look at more school records, he would buy a pair of running shoes and a warm-up suit to lend his story credence. But maybe he should be a bit more careful, too, about what cattle he fed on.

12

One day ... two ... a week. Garreth combed the records of the towns around Hays, places with exotic names like Antonino, Schoenchen, Liebenthal, Munjor, Bazine, Galatia, and, of course, Pfeifer. He could hardly afford to overlook Pfeifer. But in all of them, he drew a blank. Deciding that mentioning Lane's name in any connection might leak back to alarm her, he revised his questions to ask about any Bieber girl who had left home late in her teens during the thirties, possibly to go to Europe or one of the coasts. That should sound innocent and expected in light of his cover story to directly question as many Biebers as possible.

The question brought some response. A number of older people said, "I remember that. She went to the college in Hays and ran off with one of her professors. Caused a big scandal." They spoke with a curious accent, hissing final *s*'s, turning *w*'s to *v*'s and *v*'s to *f*'s.

"Do you remember her name and where she lived?" Garreth asked.

One old woman said, "She was one of Axel Bieber's granddaughters, I think. Axel was my mother's half brother's cousin. They lived in Trubel up in Bellamy County."

Trubel? Garreth checked the letters. No, the B would not fit the postmark. Still . . . Heart pounding in hope, he headed for Trubel.

It proved to be another dead town . . . six houses, a general store-cum-gas station and post office, and the inevitable grain elevator. The high school had burned near the close of World War II, destroying all its records, and never been rebuilt.

Garreth tried to swallow his disappointment. "There used to be a family here headed by a man named Axel Bieber. Are any of them still around?" he asked the man at the general store.

"There's Rance and Ed Bieber farming south of here about six miles," was the reply.

Garreth lost his way twice before finding the farm. Rance Bieber turned out to be a man in his thirties, a great-grandson of Axel Bieber. He knew nothing about one of his father's cousins running away with a college professor. His father, Edward, was off in the state capital at a meeting protesting grain prices. His mother had been dead for twenty years.

"Where can I find one of your father's brothers or sisters who might know this cousin I'm looking for?"

"Well, the closest are an uncle in Eden and an aunt in Bellamy."

Garreth took the names and addresses and went to see them. Both said essentially the same thing, that they knew *of* the cousin—the scandal had set the family on ear—but they did not know the woman personally.

The aunt in Bellamy said, "My Grandpa Bieber wouldn't have anything to do with Uncle Ben—that was her father. My grandfather was a Lutheran, you see, and Uncle Ben married a Catholic woman and joined her church. Grandpa never forgave him for becoming a Papist."

"Where does your uncle live, do you know?"

"He's dead now, I think."

Graves and more graves. Disappointment settled in a cold lump in Garreth's stomach. "Where did he *used* to live, then?"

"Oh, up in Baumen in the northern part of the county."

The lump in Garreth's stomach dissolved. Baumen was one of the towns on his list from which the letter to Lane might have been mailed.

That day he paid off his motel bill and moved his base of operations to Baumen. After checking the cash he had left, Garreth bypassed the single motel to check into the Driscoll Hotel downtown. Fortunately, while old, it was clean, but even at its low prices, he could not afford to stay there long . . . not unless he found a job soon.

He swore unhappily, resenting the time that

working would steal from his hunt. Still, what else could he do? He had to have money for gas and his room. He would check the local high school, he decided. Maybe that would end his hunt for Lane here and he would not have to stay any longer.

13

For a change, the records for the Baumen High School were stored in an attic instead of a basement. Like the basements, the attic was dusty, but unlike a basement, it was also hot and stuffy. The school principal, a man named Schaeffer, had not been able to find the graduation pictures for the years 1930 to 1936 and Lane had not been in the '37 to '40 pictures, so he took Garreth up to the files. "There's a picture in their school records. That cabinet should hold all the Biebers."

Garreth stood at the cabinet, bending down to go through its second drawer and praying for the principal to leave. As long as the man breathed down his neck, he had to check each and every file instead of being able to go straight to where Lane's file would be located.

"How can you see up here with those glasses on?" Schaeffer asked.

Eyes. Garreth thought carefully about that, then took off the glasses and hung them on his shirt pocket. He twisted around, blinking in the light, to look straight at Schaeffer. "Don't you think it's hot and dusty up here? I know you'd be more comfortable in your office. You don't have to stay with me."

Schaeffer's face went blank for a moment, then he mopped at his brow. "It's a shame we can't afford air conditioning for this building. Mr. Mikaelian, if you don't mind being left alone, I think I'll go back to my office."

"I'll be fine."

He watched Schaeffer leave, and the moment the door closed behind the principal's figure, he slammed the drawer shut and pulled open one on the bottom. He flipped through the files, past the Aarons, Calebs, Carolyns, and Eldoras. His hand paused at Garrett Bieber out of simple reaction to the similarity to his own name, and then went on, through the letters of the alphabet to the M's.

The folder there came to his fingers like iron to a magnet. *BIEBER, Madelaine.* He pulled it out of the drawer and spread it open on the floor. First the picture. He studied it. Though obviously of a young girl and brown with age, it was recognizably Lane. A sigh of satisfaction came up from his soul. He had found her origin. From here, hopefully, he could reach out to capture her. He paged through the record of her four years in the school, looking for anything more he might learn about her from it.

She had been a good student, he saw, earning straight A's. She had graduated first academically in her class of ten, but had not been valedictorian at graduation. The grades he somehow expected, but the lack of honor surprised him; that is, it did until he noticed the long list of disciplinary actions against her. She had, various teachers stated, an uncontrolled temper and frequently became involved in fights—the knock-down, tooth-and-claw variety—with both other girls and an occasional boy. Garreth saw the young woman who had attacked a prostitute for stealing her supper ... but a very different person from Lane Barber. Could any of those teachers still be alive to appreciate how well Lane had learned to control her temper?

The record also gave her parents' names, Benjamin and Anna, and her home address, 513 Pine Street. Garreth made a note of it, though he doubted that it remained valid after all these years.

When he had all out of the file that he thought he could use, he returned it to the drawer, then he had only to sit in the stifling, dusty heat to wait until enough time had elapsed for searching the files before leaving the attic.

He headed for a phone. The phone book listed five Biebers, one of them an Anna living at 513 Pine. Smiling at the clerk in the high school office, he copied down the addresses of all the Biebers. "I guess I'll talk to a few people. Thanks for the help."

He started, of course, with Anna Bieber at 513 Pine, just a few blocks from the high school. A middle-aged woman answered the door. Her face bore similarities to Lane's. "Mrs. Bieber?" he asked. If she was not Lane's mother, perhaps she was a sister.

"Come on in," the woman said. "I'll get Mother."

Mrs. Bieber turned out to be a tiny, frail-looking wisp, nothing like the strapping woman Garreth would have expected to spawn an amazon like Lane. Like her daughter, though, she looked younger than her years. Though she moved slowly, she still walked straight, without the bend of age, and her eyes met Garreth's face directly, undimmed. For a moment, the similarity to his own grandmother seemed so strong, panic fluttered in him, wondering if she, too, possibly recognized him for what he was.

But her hand did not touch the crucifix around her neck and she cordially invited him to sit down. At the end of listening to his story, she looked him over with searching eyes. "My daughter Mada ran away at the age of eighteen with a professor from Fort Hays. May I see the picture you have?" She spoke with the distinctive accent he had heard so often these past days.

"It isn't your daughter," he said, handing over the photograph of Grandma Doyle. "I've been to the high school, and your daughter's school picture doesn't match mine. But I thought maybe you would remember a relative who looked like the girl in my picture."

She studied it. "I'm sorry, no." She handed it back.

Now what? How did he bring up Lane without asking questions that would arouse suspicion, and without appearing to pry?

Garreth pretended to examine his photograph. "I wonder how anyone can just leave home and never go back. I hope you hear from your daughter?"

The old woman beamed. "Mada calls every week, no matter where she is. She's a singer and she travels a good deal, even to Mexico and Canada and Japan. I'd be satisfied with a letter; calling must be terribly expensive, but she says she enjoys hearing my voice."

His breath caught. Jackpot! He did not have to pretend delight. "Every week? How lucky you are."

"I know." She launched into stories about friends who had children who hardly ever called or wrote.

Garreth only half listened. Called every week.

Could he reasonably ask where Lane had called from the last time? Knowing even just a city— Belatedly he realized Mrs. Bieber had said Lane's name again. "I'm sorry. What was that?"

"I said, for someone so huge and awkward as a girl, Mada became a very attractive woman. She's still handsome."

He blinked. "You see her often, too?" Could she be somewhere near?

"Every Thanksgiving or Christmas," Mrs. Bieber said with pride. "She always comes home for one of the holidays."

Garreth wanted to yell with happiness and hug the old woman. Lane *came home. Lady Luck, you're a darling!* Instead of running around the world looking for her, all he had to do was wait . . . find a job here, make friends with Mrs. Bieber so he would know when to expect Lane . . . and let the fugitive come to him.

Spider Game

1

The help-wanted section of the local paper had little to offer Garreth. The jobs advertised all appeared to be day positions. "Is there night work available anywhere in town?" he asked the Driscoll Hotel's desk clerk.

She pushed her glasses to her nose. "Well, there's the drive-ins, but high school kids usually work there. I suppose you could try the Pioneer Café up the street and the Main Street Grill across from us. They stay open late, until nine o'clock, and until eleven weekends."

That late? Gee whiz. Aloud, he said, "Thanks." And left the hotel.

In the street outside he stood orienting himself. Baumen was a far cry from San Francisco. He had never seen a main street with railroad tracks down the middle. With two lanes of traffic and two strips of diagonal parking on each side, the far side of the street looked almost as distant as the far end of Baumen's three blocks of stores. Like the grain elevators, though, the buildings intrigued him. Everything here seemed to be built of that buff sandstone: barns, houses and stores, high schools, courthouses, even fence posts. He rather liked it, both for the easy color and the way it gave human habitation an appearance of having grown organically from the prairie around it.

Heading up the street toward the Pioneer Café first, he found himself almost alone in the late afternoon. With the stores closed for almost half an hour now, the street lay empty of all but a scattering of parked cars. A placard in the ticket window of the Driscoll Theater next to the hotel announced show times on Friday, Saturday, and Sunday. Garreth eyed it in passing. A weekend theater? What did these people *do* nights?

Three quarters of the way up the block, all thoughts of entertainment were wiped from his mind. The breeze carried a foul taint, a smell that turned the air turgid in his lungs. Garlic! He spun away. So much for the Pioneer. But would the Main Street be any better?

He crossed his fingers.

Across the tracks and down the other side of the street, he stopped at the drugstore, which also served as the local newsstand, but they carried no papers from San Francisco or anywhere in California. A few doors farther down, a display in Weaver's Office Supplies included *I Ching* along with other books, Bibles, religious jewelry, and stationery. The book brought a stabbing pang of homesickness.

Give it up, a voice in him urged. *Go home and tell Serruto where to find Lane. Let him handle it. You don't belong here.*

The very logical, sensible suggestion tempted him, but he shook his head. *Get thee behind me, angel. It's my case; she's my collar.*

At the doorway of the Main Street, he paused, cautiously sniffing. The air smelled of grease but no garlic. He went in. The menu, stuck in a holder in the middle of the table, offered a range of meals from breakfasts and hamburgers to chicken-fried steak, but nothing even vaguely Italian.

"Take your order?" the single waitress asked.

"I'd like to speak with the manager, please."

"You mean the owner? Verl," she called to a man at the grill, "someone to see you."

Garreth came up to the counter and introduced himself.

"Verl Hamilton," the stocky, balding man replied. "Aren't you the kid looking for his relatives?"

Word had spread. He nodded. "And I need a job in order to afford the search. Do you have anything open?"

Hamilton eyed him. "I like to see a man's eyes when I'm talking to him."

Garreth took off the trooper glasses.

"You know how to cook?"

He considered lying, then shook his head. "Frozen dinners and hot dogs and marshmallows over an open fire is about all."

Hamilton sighed. "I could sure use an evening cook."

"I'm a fast learner. I was a police officer for eight years and a couple of times had to learn new skills in a hurry for an undercover assignment. And I really do need a job," he finished earnestly.

The waitress said, "Verl, I've subbed on the grill. Let him wait tables and I'll cook."

Hamilton pursed his lips and tugged an ear, then nodded. "We'll give it a try."

Garreth grinned. "When can I start?"

"Tomorrow. Come in at three o'clock."

"Verl, tomorrow's Thursday," the waitress said.

"Damn." Hamilton frowned. "How about starting right now? It'll only be a few hours but you can see what's going on. Tomorrow you can give me your Social Security number."

"What's wrong with Thursday?" Garreth asked.

The waitress replied, "The stores stay open late. Everyone comes in to town to shop and they stop here for coffee and dessert. It's no time to break in."

So Garreth quickly found himself in his shirt sleeves, sitting at a table with Sharon Hagedorn, the waitress, nodding while she explained the table numbering and how to write up orders. They went through it twice, then she turned him loose.

The job seemed easy enough, barring the tiring drag of daylight on him. Sunset helped that. The plates lightened and his step quickened. The novelty soon wore off, though. He saw that it would be a job, something to earn money. Nothing more.

Shortly before closing time, a cop walked in to a chorus of: "Hi, Nat," from Hamilton and Sharon. Garreth had seen the car park outside, a tan and dark brown compact with a sleek Aerodynic light bar on top. The uniform of the stocky cop had the same colors as the car, a tan shirt with shoulder tabs and pocket flaps of dark brown to match the trousers.

The cop, whose name tag said "Toews," slid onto a stool at the counter, eyeing Garreth. "You're new."

Garreth nodded. "Coffee?"

"With cream. Throw on my usual, Sharon," he called toward the waitress at the grill, then he set his radio on the counter with the volume adjusted to make it just audible. He smoothed his mustache—red like his sideburns though his hair was dark—and looked Garreth over some more.

"Is that your ZX with California plates in front of the Driscoll? You're the one looking for your relatives."

Garreth nodded and poured the coffee. He longed to sit down and talk. Seeing the officer was like meeting a cousin in a foreign country, but the brusqueness of Toews's voice warned him away.

Hamilton rang up the ticket of the last customer and locked the door behind the man. "This is Garreth Mikaelian, Nat. He used to be a cop out there."

Garreth winced. Now he felt as though he had just badged an officer who stopped him in a strange town, to keep from being ticketed.

But Toews immediately thawed. "You were? I'm Nathan Toews." He pronounced it *Taves*. "Where did you work?"

"San Francisco. Homicide."

Toews raised a brow. The unspoken question was obvious: *Why did you quit?*

Garreth felt compelled to answer it. "My partner got shot up pretty bad and it was mostly my fault. It shook me up."

"Order up," Sharon said.

Garreth picked up the cheeseburger and fries. Toews poured catsup over the fries. "Too bad you're transient. We've lost an officer and God knows how long it'll be before we find a replacement."

Hamilton snorted from where he sat counting receipts. "Latta's no loss. He deserved to be canned for a stunt like blowing out the window of the patrol car with the shotgun and claiming someone took a shot at him."

Garreth stared at Toews for a long time before shaking himself. *Forget it, man.* He thought about the officer's remark, though. A permanent job

would give him an excuse for staying past the
end of his alleged search, and being official would
help when arresting Lane.

"What's the job like?"

Toews shrugged. "Door rattling, traffic, ref-
ereeing domestic disturbances, and picking up
drunks weekends, mostly."

Which did not really answer the big question:
Could Garreth handle the job? How much would
his limitations handicap, if not outright endanger, other officers? And in view of the circumstances under which he had quit at home, why
should these people even want him?

Still, he continued to think about it all the way
back to the hotel and while pulling on his
running suit for "exercise."

He followed the main street north. From four
lanes it narrowed to two on the west side of the
railroad tracks, passed the railroad station and
stock pens with a sale barn and fairground east
beyond them, then crossed the Saline River and
angled west as Country Road 16. The countryside,
which had dropped from the plateau Bellamy sat
on into the river valley around Baumen, rose
again to rolling plateau, pastureland brightly
lighted by the waxing moon and broken only
occasionally by a stretch of barbed-wire fence.
Cattle dotted every section, block-square beef
cattle, sleek black or curly red and white. All, he
noticed, appeared smaller than the white behemoth he drank from that first night, but like the
Charolais bull, the black steer he finally approached yielded to him, and he fed, wishing he
had some way to refrigerate his thermos so he
could bring it along and fill it up.

Patting the cow's head in thanks as he stood,
Garreth became aware of something else near
him. He turned to face another pair of glowing

eyes. The animal looked like a small, thin German shepherd. A coyote?

The creature eyed him, and the supine cow beyond. Garreth shook his head. "No. Don't bother it."

The coyote's eyes burned into his. Garreth held them until the cow scrambled to its feet.

Leaving, he found to his surprise that the coyote followed, trotting about ten feet off to the side. When Garreth broke into a run, so did the coyote. It followed like a shadow, not threateningly, he decided, reading curiosity in the cock of the carnivore's ears. Puzzled by his not-quite-human scent? Whyever, he enjoyed the company.

The coyote paced him most of the way back to town, until Garreth passed through the fence onto the country road just north of the river. Then it dropped back and faded into the darkness of the prairie. Garreth jogged on into town alone.

He heard a car coasting in behind him as he passed the railroad station. Glancing over his shoulder, he identified the light bar of a patrol car and stuck up a hand in greeting.

The engine revved. The car shot past him to swing across his path and came to a tire-screeching halt. A spotlight flashed in his face. Garreth threw an arm up in front of his eyes.

"In a hurry to go somewhere?" a voice asked from behind the light.

Damn! "I'm jogging." Garreth plucked at his jogging suit.

"In the middle of the night? Sure. Come over here. Put your hands on the car and spread your feet!"

What? Garreth opened his mouth to protest, and snapped it closed again. Resisting would only make trouble. Angrily, he spread-eagled against the car.

The spotlight went out. Moving up behind Garreth, the cop began frisking him. Garreth glimpsed an equipment belt polished to a mirror shine. The cloying sweetness of after-shave masked any scent of blood. "You do this like someone with lots of experience at it, friend," the cop said.

Which was more than Garreth would say for the cop. Almost any of the scumbags on the street back home could have turned and taken the man in a moment. The cop's idea of a frisk missed half the places a weapon might be hidden, too.

Keeping his voice polite, Garreth explained who he was.

"Oh, the ex-cop Nat met. No wonder you know the routine." The cop stepped back. "I'm Ed Duncan. Sorry about the frisk, but you understand we can't be too careful with strangers. There's a lot of drug traffic through the state. No hard feelings?"

Garreth understood that Duncan had probably been bored out of his skull and used the first opportunity to create some activity. He resented being the subject of it. "No hard feelings."

Turning, he discovered that Duncan bore a faint resemblance to Robert Redford. From the way the cop walked and wore his uniform, Duncan knew it, too.

The car radio sputtered. Duncan leaned in through the window for the mike. "505 here as always, doll. What do you need?"

Someone had reported a prowler.

Duncan rolled his eyes. "It's probably just the Haas dog again but I'll check it out."

Watching Duncan drive away singing a country-western song, Garreth thought again about Toews's remark. If someone as cavalierly careless as Duncan could survive here, maybe Garreth's limitations would not cause trouble. In the morning, he decided, he would drop by the station and check out the job more closely.

2

In his forties Chief Kenneth Danzig had the build of an ex-football player, and though his waistline was trying to match his shoulders for width, he still looked capable of battering through a defensive line or a felon's door. His blood smelled warm and strong. Seated behind his desk in the office he shared with the padlocked evidence locker, he made the room seem even smaller than its actual limited dimensions. He fingered Garreth's application. "I take it you regret resigning?"

"Yes, sir." Garreth had stated the checkable facts of the resignation frankly. He wished he could read the chief, but small-town cop though he was, Danzig wore a city cop's professional mask. "Law enforcement is my life. It's the only kind of job I know or want."

Danzig's face never moved. "Why apply here, though? Why not ask for reinstatement in San Francisco?"

Garreth had been expecting that question. He had a half-true answer ready. "I need a change and this is nice country. I like it more every day I'm here."

Danzig leaned back in his chair. "Do you think working in a small town means a soft job? Or that you'll never face a 'shoot/don't shoot' choice again? Remember the Clutter murders in *In Cold Blood*? Those were here in Kansas. York and Latham were another pair of turkeys on a murder spree who came through here. We tried them just over in Russell. We're on the drug traffic pipeline and almost every year there's a hi-po trooper killed making a routine stop on I-70. You get into trouble out here and you're often on your own, with no backup close enough to do you any good."

He made the job sound as dangerous as any city. Garreth drew a deep breath. "I don't expect a soft job. Of course I hope I'll never have to draw my gun again—who doesn't—but I'm not running away from the possibility." *I'm just running away from kicking in doors.*

"We work semipermanent shifts. As a new man, you'd have to work nights, and you'd be stuck there until we have a daytime opening and you have enough seniority to claim it. Any objections?"

"No, sir." None at all! "I prefer nights."

Danzig leaned forward. "Considering your history, I wish I could send you to a shrink for a psychiatric evaluation, but the taxpayers of this town can't afford luxuries like that. We're lucky to find officers willing to work here at all. But I don't hire anyone without at least a physical exam. I'll set up an appointment for you with Dr. Staab at the medical center."

He had been expecting that, but cold still slid down Garreth's spine. A doctor he could probably handle, but ... what about bloodwork? Using his powers, he had talked the doctor in San Francisco out of running bloodwork on that checkup before sending him back to work. The same trick could not work where it was required as part of the physical. He would have to think of something else. *Are you crazy, man? Be safe; give it up.*

He sat frozen in the chair while Danzig made the phone call and handed Garreth a memo sheet with the appointment time. "We'll contact San Francisco for your records while you're taking care of this. Now let's fingerprint you to make sure you're who you say you are."

Walking out of City Hall later, Garreth toyed with the memo slip and debated whether to forget the whole thing. *Now you see why Lane keeps her head down. She's smart. You're courting disaster, Garreth Doyle Mikaelian.* But perhaps he wanted to be found out, he mused, to be destroyed finally and for always.

He stared at the appointment slip for a long time, thoughts churning, before folding it and putting it in his pocket. He might be a total fool, but he wanted the job, and not just to kill time waiting for Lane. He wanted it for himself, wanted a badge again. He wanted to come home.

3

The Lord watched out for fools, even damned ones, Garreth reflected. A week after he stewed over it so much, his stuck-out neck not only remained unchopped but here he stood in a suit and tie, carrying copies of the Kansas Criminal Code and Vehicle Code to study, beginning six months probation. Even the physical had gone smoothly, the bloodwork problem solved by catching the lab tech's eyes and instructing her to destroy the samples she took from him, replace them with samples from herself, and forget she had made a substitution.

The chief introduced him to the day office staff, a tiny wisp of secretary named Nancy Sue Schaefer and a pretty but broad-beamed dispatcher, Geri Weaver. Then Danzig led him over to a slim, dark-haired young woman in uniform at a type-writer. "And this is Margaret Lebekov, our after-noon officer and expert with juveniles and domestic disputes. Maggie, this is Garreth Mikaelian."

Garreth held out a hand, smiling. "Glad to meet you."

She looked up, stared at his hand, and returned to typing. "Yes."

Garreth examined his fingers for frostbite. Ter-rific. Six officers in the department and one of them hated him on sight. In a sudden spasm of fear he wondered if she, like Grandma Doyle, sensed his unhumanity.

"When you go on your own, you'll be on nights, from eight, taking over from Lebekov, until four A.M.," Danzig went on. "That overlaps Toews's and Duncan's shifts. Until your uniforms come and you know the town, though, I want you to ride with Sergeant Toews."

"Yes, sir."

"You'll need a Kansas driver's license. The examiner is in Bellamy on Thursdays. Drive down then and take the test."

"Yes, sir."

A look at the three cells and drunk tank upstairs completed the station tour, by which time Lebekov had left, Toews was coming out of the combination interview/locker room buckling on his equipment belt, and a voice on the radio announced that 102 would shortly be 10–19, coming into the office.

Garreth sucked in a deep breath. Shift change. Despite the vast differences in place, the rhythm of it felt as familiar as the beat of his heart ... Day watch coming in—one Lieutenant Byron Kaufmann, a beefy veteran with fading red hair—a briefing for Garreth and Toews that differed only in size from every other Garreth had ever attended; checking equipment and the car; pulling out onto the street. It *was* like coming home.

Toews eyed Garreth sidelong as they rolled down Oak toward Kansas Avenue. "Have you found your grandmother yet?"

"No." He had made daily trips to surrounding towns, keeping up the cover. Perhaps the time had come that he could quit. "I'm beginning to doubt I will."

"But you still want to stick around here?"

Garreth shrugged. "There's no reason to go back to California."

Toews peered in his outside mirror at a battered pickup which passed them going the other direction. "That gives us two city boys. Danzig used to be on the Wichita P.D."

The radio mumbled sporadically, but little of the traffic had local call numbers. Garreth quickly gathered that all the area law enforcement agencies used the same frequency. The loudest voice kept drawling, "Bellamy S.O.," the sheriff's office.

Toews saw Garreth listening. "That's Lou Pfeifer, the sheriff. He's usually patrolling somewhere in this end of the county so he can look in on his ranch and his wife and daughters."

"206 Baumen," a woman's voice said. "Requesting a 10–28 on local K-king, five-five-three."

Toews shook his head. "That's the fourth registration I've heard Maggie run since we came on. She's on a rip tonight."

"She didn't seem in a very good mood when Danzig introduced me to her at the station," Garreth said.

"Oh." Toews shifted in his seat. He watched a driver slow but roll through a stop sign across the street. He honked the horn as the car came at them, and when he caught the driver's eye, shook his head. "It says stop, Walt," he called. To Garreth he said, "That's because you have the shift she wants."

Garreth winced. "Damn."

"It isn't your fault. Danzig will never give it to her because he doesn't believe in women patrolling at night. Do you ride?"

The change of subject left Garreth. He blinked. "Ride what?"

Toews stared. "Horses, of course. I have a great little mare out of Skipper W that I use for calf roping. I'll take you by to see her in a little while. What *do* you do when you're not on duty, then?"

The game of get acquainted had begun, a friendly mutual interrogation that they sandwiched between calls . . . an elderly woman whose daughter in Hays had been unable to reach her by phone all day proved to be healthy, only working in the yard with her hearing aid turned off . . . a motorcycle stopped for speeding had a driver operating on an expired license . . . checking businesses along Highway 282 at the east edge of town they found the Gfeller Lumber gate unlocked. The search for mutual interests went on while they waited for the owner to come out and lock up.

To Garreth's disappointment, they shared almost nothing in common but law enforcement. Between that and the obvious enmity of Maggie

Lebekov, Baumen P.D. did not look quite like home, after all. On the other hand, it made a decent bivouac and would keep him busy enough not to brood over the uncertain, perhaps nonexistent, future beyond collaring Lane.

4

The house was two stories and large by Baumen standards, white-painted brick with a driveway running under a portico on the side. Large old trees shaded it, oaks and maples whose leaves, turned lemon yellow and scarlet, glowed almost incandescent in the autumn afternoon sunlight.

Flame touched Garreth, too, but it was inside, licking at him as they stood before the door.

Toews pushed the bell. A small, elderly, white-haired woman answered the door. Toews touched the visor of his cap. "Hello, Mrs. Schoning. Is Helen home?"

The woman nodded. "I'll get her. Please come in."

They followed her into a wide hallway flooded with rainbow light from a stained-glass window at the turn of the stairs. Mrs. Schoning left them there to disappear into the rear of the house.

"You ought to have a good chance," Toews said. "I don't know who else in town she'd have to rent to."

Garreth crossed his fingers.

He needed somewhere besides the hotel to live, somewhere free of the fear of a maid coming in to find his earth pallet on the bed or in the closet and gossiping about it. A town this size had no apartments, though, just houses. Except maybe one over the garage of Helen Schoning, clerk of the Municipal Court.

Miss Schoning appeared, a slender woman in her late forties with only a trace of gray in short chestnut hair. Blood smell eddied warmly from her. Garreth fought a sudden surge of hunger.

She smiled at them. "What brings you here, Nat?"

"This is our new officer Garreth Mikaelian. He's interested in the apartment."

"Ah, yes, the Frisco Kid." She studied him keenly for a minute, then extended her hand. If the coolness of his skin surprised her, she did not show it. "Welcome to Baumen. The garage is this way."

Out a side door into the portico and back along the drive to a large two-car garage. She led the way up a set of steps on the side to the second floor.

"It's small. I take it you don't have a family."

"No, ma'am."

Unlocking the door, she stood back to let him enter first. "Call me Helen, please. Here you are."

Half the area had been furnished as a den, with wood paneling, built-in bookcases, and a large leather couch and chair. A rear corner was partitioned for the bathroom. Between it and a set of French doors leading out onto a deck above the garage doors stretched the cabinets and small appliances of an apartment kitchen.

Helen opened the couch out into a bed. "I can provide sheets and blankets. The phone is an extension from the house. You can use that and pay part of the bill or put in a private line. Half the garage is yours to use, too. It's seventy-five a month."

"Baumen 303," the radio on Toews's hip muttered. "See Mrs. Linda Mostert at 415 South Eighth about a missing person."

"En route," Toews said. "It sounds like Mr. Halverson is out again, partner. Come on."

Following him out, Garreth called back, "I'll take it. May I move in tonight?"

"Just knock on the side door and I'll give you the key."

He waved thanks.

Mr. Amos Halverson turned out to be Mrs. Mostert's father, a healthy but sometimes confused old man who regularly took walks and forgot his way home. By talking to people in yards along the street, they learned the old man had headed north. Twenty minutes later they located him working on his third beer in the Cowboy Palace and drove him home.

Returning to patrol, Garreth said, "I wonder if he's all that confused. Do you realize we just paid for his beer and gave him transportation home?"

Toews grinned. "He's earned it. He ran a grocery store when I was a kid and I remember a lot of times he gave me and my sisters free candy. Where do you want to eat tonight?"

Not that they had a great deal of choice. Garreth said, "The Main Street."

"We ate there last night. How about the Pioneer?"

Garreth's lungs clogged just remembering the garlic reek from it. He thought fast. "I . . . got sick once in an Italian restaurant and since then I haven't been able to stand the smell of garlic."

Toews grinned. "So how long have you been a vampire?"

Every nerve in Garreth overloaded. He gaped at

Toews, feeling the bomb explode in him . . . unable to move, scarcely able to think. "A . . . what?" *He guessed; he knows! What an idiot you are, Mikaelian, to ever have opened your mouth about garlic.*

The other's grin broadened. "You're a little slow on the uptake, city boy. Vampires can't stand garlic, so if *you* can't, you must be one, right? Tell me, how do you manage to shave without a mirror?"

Garreth groped in confusion for almost a minute before he realized Toews was joking. Then he cursed himself. *A guilty conscience obstructeth logic* . . . not to mention strangled the sense of humor. He had better say something quickly, though, before the lack of reply betrayed that he had taken Toews seriously. "I use an electric razor."

Toews chuckled. "The benefits of technology. Okay, it's the Main Street again."

Garreth drank tea and pretended to study the Criminal Code. Inside he still shook. That had been a near call.

Toews wolfed down a cheeseburger. "You better eat something more than tea, partner. Friday and Saturday are our busy nights."

Garreth quickly learned what he meant. As dark approached, every parking space along Kansas Avenue and up the side streets filled with locals coming downtown to the bars and private clubs, the latter the only place dry Kansas allowed hard liquor. Garreth and Toews wrote up two accident reports for fender benders resulting from trying to park more cars than intended in the diagonal spaces along the tracks.

Every teenager in the area also appeared to be downtown, but since they could not drink, the ones not attending the movie theater drove, making a loop that went north on Kansas to the Sonic Drive-In, across the tracks, south seven blocks to the A&W, and back across the tracks to go north again, endlessly. They drove cars, pick-ups, and vans, and carried on conversations by driving alongside each other and leaning out the windows to shout across the space between.

Toews ticketed only flagrant violations, the most flagrant being a blue van weaving wildly through the traffic, and broke up a couple of impending fights. They also checked businesses along Kansas. Later came drunk-and-disorderly calls, and an accident in the parking lot outside the VFW. Taking a report from one driver while Toews talked to the other, watching a couple pass none too steadily toward their own car, Garreth shook his head. This was a *dry* state?

5

Garreth had intended just to pick up the key, but Helen Schoning insisted on coming out with him. She raised one of the garage doors. "This is your side. If you want to work on your car, feel free to use my tools. Just ask first and put them back afterward."

He stared around the garage. She looked as though she could open her own auto repair shop. "You use these?"

She smiled and went over to stroke the fender of the car in the other half of the garage. "Some-one has to keep this running."

He felt his jaw drop. It was a gleaming old Rolls-Royce.

"My father bought it in 1955 when his first wells came in. He was so proud of it. It was the only car like it in Bellamy County. Still is." She paused, chin down, looking at him through her lashes. "Mr. Mikaelian, I do have one favor to ask. If you should come home some night and find a car in your side, will you please park in the drive behind my side so the other car can get out? And say nothing about it to anyone?"

He felt himself staring again and closed his mouth with a snap. "No problem."

She smiled. "I hoped you'd understand. I enjoy my solitude—which is not the same as loneliness despite what most people around here think—and am single by choice, but I also like companionship from time to time. Discreetly, of course. This is a small town and some of my friends are married."

Garreth regarded her with amazement. She was not what he would have expected to find here. "You don't miss the stability of a long-term relationship?"

She laughed. "What stability? Nothing ever stays the same. People, either. Each of my relationships has suited my needs at the time. What more can I ask? Good night."

Moving in did not take long, just luggage and his pallet. Then he sat back in the deep leather chair and sighed happily. Privacy. Better than that, a refrigerator. He would take his thermos with him on the run tonight and fill it.

Helen had made up the couch. Laid under the bottom sheet, the pallet would fold conveniently, safely out of sight, with the bed.

All that remained was to buy some health foods, even if he had to go to Bellamy or Hays for them . . . stage dressing so his cupboard would not look as oddly empty as Lane's. Then like a spider in the center of his web, he would sit and wait for his red-haired vampire fly to appear.

6

Mrs. Bieber greeted Garreth with delight and invited him in. "How nice to see you again. Have you found your grandmother yet?"

He shook his head. "No, but I think I've found a home." While they drank tea he told her about the apartment and job. Overcast outside made the room enjoyably dim. After a while he asked casually, "How are you? What do you hear from your singer daughter?"

"Mada's in Mexico. Following the herds south for the winter is how she put it." Mrs. Bieber looked apologetic and embarrassed. "People, she means. I'm afraid she's not always very polite."

"Do you know which holiday she's coming home?"

"No." The bright eyes probed him. "Why do you ask?"

Garreth shrugged. "No particular reason."

Mrs. Bieber frowned. "You don't have to lie to me, young man."

He froze. *Damn*. What had he done to give himself away? "I don't know what you mean."

She leaned toward him over her teacup with a sly smile. "Deep down don't you think she's your grandmother?"

Amazing. The cup remained steady in his hand despite a surge of relief that left him feeling limp. "How can I? The pictures are nowhere alike."

"Maybe your picture is wrong. I can ask Mada a few questions the next time she calls."

"Good God, no!" Garreth lowered his voice as her eyes widened in surprise at his passion. "Please don't. That would be so embarrassing to both of us." Not to mention fatal to his hopes of trapping Lane here. "Please don't say anything about me to her."

Her eyes danced but she agreed and he changed the subject to casual conversation about his job. What he wanted most to talk about, though, he could not . . . his run the previous night.

He had taken the thermos with him. Filling it involved more than he anticipated . . . biting a large hole in the cow's carotid artery, then spending the extra time necessary holding off the place until the blood clotted. By that time he had collected an audience of three coyotes, who stayed back at his orders but later accompanied him most of the way back to town. Memory of the run still exhilarated him . . . the stars brilliant in the black velvet of the moonless sky, his breath white on the night air, the coyotes running like ghosts around him. He would so love to be able to discuss it with someone. How could Helen think solitude was not lonely?

He stood finally. "I'd better go. I'm due at the station for roll call in a few minutes."

She saw him to the door. "Thank you for coming. Visit again if you like."

Hell and garlic could not keep him away.

7

The thick layer of clouds, drooping in dark, waterlogged folds, prevented Garreth from seeing the sun, but he felt it set, felt the welcome cessation of pressure and the renewed flood of energy through him. In the distance, thunder rumbled. He stretched, drawing a deep, contented breath. "Nice evening."

Nat rolled his eyes. "Californians have strange taste. It ain't nice at all for someone who wants to rope calves tomorrow afternoon, partner. Say, why don't you come over for Sunday dinner? You can meet my wife and kids and then watch Skipper Flint Jubilee and me work."

Before he stopped eating food, Garreth had never realized how much social activity revolved around it. He hunted a diplomatic refusal. "Thanks, but I intend to sleep in late. Give me a time and I'll meet you at the fairgrounds for the roping, though."

They moved down the street trying the doors on the Light House electrical shop and Sherwin-Williams paint store. The Saturday night parade of cars rolled past in a bright string. The blue van they had cited the evening before slowed down opposite them long enough for the adolescent boy driving to lean sideways and flip them off. They pretended not to see him.

"I got a guy for that once," Garreth said.

Nat tried the door of Rivers Hardware. "How?"

"I wrote him up for an illegal signal. He was using his left arm and indicated a right turn which he then failed to make." Garreth grinned. "And the judge fined him."

Nat's radio said, "Baumen 303. 717 Landon. Tom Loxton."

Nat rogered the call and sighed as they hurried up the street to where they had parked the car. "Damn. He's right on schedule."

"With what?"

"Tom's half Indian. Every time he gets liquored up, about twice a month, he sits on his front porch taking potshots at passing cars. He's never hit anything yet, but there's always a first time."

They parked the car across the intersection at one end of the block and walked down to the house. "You wave off traffic at the other end of the block while I talk to him," Nat said.

A reed-thin man with long hair and a red bandanna around his head lounged in a porch swing at 717, pointing a rifle at them. Garreth eyed him. "Maybe I ought to stay with you."

"I'll be all right. You just stop cars from coming past here."

Garreth went reluctantly, itching to reach for the .38 on his belt under his coat. He kept Nat and Loxton under observation while he watched for cars.

Nat leaned on the gate and called casually, "Hi, Tom. Why don't you put the gun down?"

"Not till I get me some white-eyes." Loxton's voice slurred.

The silhouette of a woman appeared in the doorway from the porch. Loxton yelled at her.

"Tom, let's talk about it," Nat called, and started to open the gate.

"Guard, Cochise!" Loxton yelled.

A huge black and tan dog hurtled around the

corner of the house to plant himself barking and snarling in the middle of the sidewalk.

Nat jumped back, slamming the gate.

The woman said something Garreth could not hear. Loxton swore at her and she slammed the door.

Along the block, neighbors came out onto porches to watch. Garreth grabbed the nearest man and stationed him in the intersection, then cautiously moved back to join Nat.

"Tom, call off the dog and put down the rifle," Nat said.

"Go to hell!"

The dog snarled.

"What do you usually do with the dog?" Garreth asked.

"He's never been loose before. Tom must really be loaded tonight."

Garreth thought about the coyotes. He side-stepped and when the dog swung toward the motion, caught its eyes. He said, "Cochise, sit down and be quiet."

Whining, the dog backed a step.

Loxton yelled, "Guard, Cochise!"

Garreth held its eyes. "Sit."

The dog whined again, but sat. Loxton leaped to his feet in rage. "You damn mutt! Guard!"

"Your dog respects the law, Mr. Loxton," Garreth said. How close did he need to be to exert influence? He considered what he wanted to do, tried to decide if there could be consequences as negative as the ones of influencing the doctor and Serruto to let him come back on duty. He saw no obvious ones. Pushing through the gate past the dog, he focused all his attention on the drunken man. "Why don't you just put down the rifle and show us you respect the law, too, sir?"

Loxton stared back at Garreth, expression

smoothing from rage to blank, then slowly laid the rifle on the swing.

Climbing back into the patrol car later, Nat said in awe, "No one but Tom and Millie has ever been able to control that dog before."

Cold chased up Garreth's spine. Had he been a fool to draw attention to himself with one of his vampire talents? Or could he joke it away as they had the other night? He made himself grin at Nat. "The Dolittle Animal Talk course was one of the electives offered when I went through the Academy."

Lightning arced across the clouds overhead, followed a few seconds later by a crack of thunder. More lightning followed, and thunder so loud it shook the car.

"Shit," Nat sighed. "There goes the calf roping."

More and more lightning chased through the clouds. Garreth's skin crawled. The awesome show went on for ten more minutes before the rain started. That came first as a light rattle of drops on the roof of the car, then in blinding sheets.

The rain did not noticeably thin the traffic downtown, though, just transformed it into a glittering light show, headlights and reflections of lights off wet cars and rain-slicked paving.

Over the radio came weather reports from surrounding sheriffs' offices. In some places high wind was bringing down tree limbs and electric lines. Maggie Lebekov announced she was coming in to the station. "Tell 303 the town is all theirs."

Minutes later, though, her voice came over the radio again, high with excitement. "206 Baumen. 10–48, Kansas and Pine. One victim is trapped. I need an ambulance and the fire department's extracting equipment."

Nat switched on the light bar and siren and

threaded the car through the traffic. "This is bad weather for traffic accidents. We'd better help."

At Kansas and Pine three vehicles sat jammed together, two pickups with a Volkswagen accordioned between them. A yellow-slickered Lebekov and a tall boy in a cowboy hat yanked at the driver's door of the Volkswagen. Inside the car a girl screamed and pleaded for help. Garreth smelled blood and leaking gasoline even as he came piling out of the car.

"It's jammed," Lebekov yelled above the thunder. "The steering wheel is pinning her, too."

The blood smell flowed thick and hot around Garreth, stirring a storm of hunger. The girl must be bleeding. Peering into the car, he saw what the dark-blind eyes of the others could not, bone protruding from the flesh of one leg under the dash and blood running from around it.

He fought down a cramp of craving. They had to free the girl before she bled to death! Could the fire department's equipment arrive soon enough? Minutes might be too long.

"Turn your face away," he called into the car.

The girl did not seem to hear. She went on screaming and pounding on the steering wheel. Garreth wrapped the tail of his suit coat around one hand and drove the fist through the window. Breaking out enough glass to give him a hold on the frame of the door, he braced a foot against the side of the car and pulled.

"Garreth!" Nat yelled, "you can't—"

The door tore loose in a scream of metal. Garreth reached in and levered up the steering column, then scooped out the girl. Some part of him saw a crowd of people staring dumbfounded, but his main attention remained on the girl. She bled profusely.

He laid her on the paving out of fire range, in

case the cars went up, and whipped off his tie. "Loan me a baton."

Lebekov handed him hers, and used her slicker to keep rain off the girl's face while Garreth made a tourniquet. "Nice work, Mikaelian."

Nat said dryly, "I see the Hulk Course of Accident Assistance was one of your electives, too."

Garreth gave him a fleeting smile. He had acted without thinking. Would it set people to wondering? "Amazing what adrenaline will do, isn't it?" Not that it mattered. Whatever the cost, he had had to do it. He could not let the girl die.

She began sobbing hysterically. He reached down to catch her chin and force her eyes to his. "You're going to be all right, miss. Just relax. If you breathe deeply, the pain will ease up. Come on, try it. Take a few deep breaths for me, will you?"

She took one, then another.

"See. That's better, isn't it?"

She nodded. In the shelter of Lebekov's slicker, her face relaxed in relief.

Garreth felt his own tension loosen. He savored the clean wetness of the rain streaming down his face, drowning the blood smell. So this vampire ability to control others could be used for more than personal gain. It might actually serve others. So could his strength. In the sound and fury of the storm, that brought a little comfort to his personal corner of hell.

8

"That's Mada in the middle," Mrs. Bieber said.

The photograph showed three little girls sitting on the running board of a twenties-style touring car in front of a house that looked like this one minus an addition and part of the porch. The description Mrs. Armour had given of the photograph in Lane's bookcase made it sound like a copy of this one.

"The other two are my daughter Mary Ellen, who's a year younger than Mada, and their cousin Victoria. Mada and Victoria were about seven then." She cocked her head, smiling at him. "Are you sure you don't have anything more exciting to do with your evenings off than visit an old woman who isn't even a relative?"

Not when he needed to learn everything possible about his quarry. It meant using this friendly old woman, though, which filled him with guilt even as he smiled at her. "You're a friend, aren't you?" He bent over the photo album. "She's about the same size as the others."

"She didn't start growing so tall until later. Here's a picture of her at ten."

There was no mistaking her now, towering over her younger siblings. With the October night chilly and windy outside, Garreth leafed through the album and easily picked Lane out in the subsequent photographs, head and shoulders above any other child she was with.

"She's the brightest of my children. Let me show you something." Mrs. Bieber led him into the dining room and pointed proudly to rows of plaques on one wall, each announcing a first place in spelling, debate, or archery. "Mada won all those, but she would have given up every one in a moment to be six inches shorter. My heart ached for her so often. She used to come home crying because the other children taunted her about her height. I never knew what to say. Maybe if I'd been older and wiser, but I was barely more than a girl myself, just sixteen when she was born. Later she stopped crying. She developed a terrible temper, flying into a rage at the least remark. She was always fighting someone. That only made matters worse, of course."

Of course. Children, and even adults, turned like animals on someone who looked or acted different. Lane must have made an easy target, too.

Mrs. Bieber said, "'I hate them,' she would sob to me, with such savagery in her voice. 'Someday they'll be sorry. I'll show them they don't own the world.' I tried to teach her to forgive, to be kind to her enemies, but it was many years before she could."

Garreth doubted that Lane ever did. She simply gave up threatening. After all, she *had* her revenge . . . living off their lifeblood, reducing them to cattle, leaving some of them nothing but dead, dry husks. When she was bitten by the vampire who made her, whoever it had been, wherever it had happened, how had she felt? Had she cursed, or wept in confusion and dismay, loathing her body for what it became? Looking at the pictures in the album, imagining the world through the eyes of the tortured child she had been, he thought not. He suspected that she had seen instantly what the change would bring her and embraced hell willingly, even happily, greedily. In her place, perhaps he would, too.

In sudden uncertainty, he snapped the album closed and thrust it back at Mrs. Bieber. Maybe this visit was a mistake. He wanted to know Lane, not sympathize with her, understand how her mind worked, not feel echoes of her pain in him.

"Is something the matter?" Mrs. Bieber asked in concern.

He gave her a quick smile. "I was just thinking about your daughter's childhood. No wonder she ran away."

She laid her hand on his arm. "It wasn't all that bad. We had happy times here at home. It's still good when everyone gets home together. There's a tenseness and . . . distance in Mada when she first comes that makes me wonder if she's really any happier in all the glitter of those exotic places she goes, but at least she's content and happy here."

He carried the last remark away with him, echoing through his head, chewing at him. She enjoyed coming home. Only this time, instead of a happy family reunion and carefree holiday, she would find a cop waiting, a date with retribution and justice. Mrs. Bieber would be hurt, too, when he arrested Lane.

Unbidden, Lien's quotation from *I Ching* the day he left San Francisco came back: *Acting to re-create order must be done with proper authority. Setting one's self up to alter things according to one's own judgment can end in mistake and failure.*

Driving home through the windy night, Garreth felt a nagging doubt and wondered unhappily about the rightness of what he was doing.

9

Handing the patrol car keys over to Garreth, Maggie sighed. "Are you sure there isn't any way I can talk you into going on afternoons? What if I give you my body?"

He grinned. "Danzig is the one to sell yourself to if you want nights. What's the matter—rough shift today?"

She grimaced. "Aside from breaking up another major assault between Phil and Eldora Schumacher, there was a ten-minute lecture from Mrs. Mary Jane Dreiling on how we're harassing her precious little Scott and I am single-handedly dooming the sanctity of the American family by not sitting home breeding babies like a normal woman! My teeth still ache from smiling at her."

"What did you ticket little Scott for this time?"

"Playing Ditch'em at fifty miles an hour in that hopped-up van of his. I wish you'd had the watch. Nat's told me that every time some turkey starts giving you a bad time you just peel off your glasses and say, 'It's a nice day, isn't it?' and suddenly you're dealing with a pussycat. What's your secret? Come on, share with a needy fellow officer."

Did he really use his hypnotic ability that much? Frowning, Garreth hefted his equipment belt, readjusting it. The worst part of being back in uniform was becoming reaccustomed to all the weight around his hips. He made himself smile.

256

"It can't be told. The trick is me Irish blood, Maggie darlin'." *Dearg-due* blood. "It's the gift o' blarney."

She sighed. "I might have known. Well, have fun tonight. You're all alone. With Nat off, Pfannenstiel's working and you know he'll be on his butt somewhere all night working nothing but his mouth." She disappeared through the station door of City Hall.

Garreth checked the equipment in the car and trunk before sliding into the driver's seat, still warm from Maggie's body and smelling of her blood. He did not dread the shift. Bill Pfannenstiel, who worked evening and morning relief, liked to talk and could be maddeningly slow, but he had twenty-five years of experience and knew every inch of the town. And unlike some of the older generation of officers Garreth had met, he was always willing to try talking through a situation before resorting to force. Garreth suspected that Maggie's dislike stemmed from Pfannenstiel's tendency to call her *Maggie-girl honey*.

Maggie's remarks about persuasive ability echoed around in his head while he patrolled. *Did* he use the vampire ability too often and without thinking? He tried not to, no more than necessary. He preferred to act like normal people.

He moved through the business district, checking doors and keeping an eye on the Friday night traffic. He spotted the Dreiling boy's blue van in the thick of it as usual. The kid saw him, too, and leaned out to give him the finger before pulling away.

Later as his and Pfannenstiel's cars parked together in the Schaller Ford lot while they watched traffic, Garreth asked, "What is it with the Dreiling kid? He's inviting someone to come down on him."

Pfannenstiel grunted. "Daring us is more like it. He doesn't think we can touch him. After all, his folks are plank owners."

Garreth blinked. "What?"

"One of the founding families. The town belongs to them."

Garreth eyed the passing cars. "We'll see. The first chance that comes along, I'm writing him up good. It'll cost him his license."

Pfannenstiel sighed. "That badge is a pretty big stick, but you want to be careful you don't trip over it."

While Garreth digested that bit of philosophy the radio came to life, putting them back to work. He checked on a barking dog, then rounded up three juveniles who had ripped off two six-packs from a local liquor store. Their parents met him at the station. With the beer paid for, the liquor store owner dropped charges, but watching the boys being dragged away by enraged parents, Garreth wondered if juvenile proceedings might not have been gentler and more humane than what waited for them at home.

"Like some cookies?" Sue Pfeifer asked. "They're fresh chocolate chips."

He shook his head.

The evening dispatcher looked down at her plump self and sighed. "I envy your willpower." The phone rang. "Baumen police." Her expression went grim listening. "We'll be right there." She slammed the receiver down. "That was the Brown Bottle. Bill Pfannenstiel went over to break up a fight and someone hit him. He's unconscious."

Garreth raced for the door.

He found a crowd at the sidewalk outside the Brown Bottle and sounds of breakage coming from inside.

Each crash made the bartender wince. "Mr. Driscoll will be mad as hell about this. Get that lunatic out of there."

"Where's Officer Pfannenstiel?" Garreth demanded.

"Still inside."

Garreth eased around the door, keeping low, baton in hand. He spotted Pfannenstiel immediately, sprawled against the bar with blood running down his face. Anger blazed up in Garreth. He would nail the bastard who did this.

A few patrons still remained . . . but flattened against the walls, too frightened to move toward the door.

With good reason. In the middle of the barroom floor, methodically reducing tables and chairs to kindling, stood a colossus of a man. Garreth guessed his height at near seven feet. His biceps looked bigger around than Garreth's thighs.

"Who is he?" Garreth whispered back at the bartender.

"I don't know. Part of the road crew repairing 282 south of here. His buddies smoked out when he hit Bill with a chair."

Sometimes talking was *not* the answer. This was one of them.

"You, Hercules!" Garreth barked. "You're under arrest. Down on your knees!"

The big man whirled. "Another goddamn pig." He sneered drunkenly. "A wimp kid pig. Here, oinker." Picking up a table, he threw it.

Garreth smiled grimly. *Two can play that game, turkey.* Dropping his baton into its ring on his equipment belt, he caught the table and threw it back.

The gasp from the bartender behind him matched the big man's openmouthed astonishment. Staring at Garreth, the man almost forgot to duck as the table went by ... and Garreth used the opportunity to trap the man's eyes with his.

"I said, you're under arrest." He felt the other resist him, saw denial in the big man's eyes. He met the drunken hatred with his own anger-driven will, however, and held him. "You *will do* as I say. Now, stop where you are!"

The man froze, clenched fists half raised, as though he had suddenly become a statue or store-window mannequin.

"Down on your knees!" Garreth snapped. "Hands together on top of your head! Cross your ankles! *Now*!"

The man went down so hard the floor shook. Fierce satisfaction flared in Garreth. He felt resistance beneath the compliance, but the man's body still obeyed. Garreth controlled this behemoth. He could make him do anything.

Garreth handcuffed him. "Up." He pointed him at a remaining chair. "Sit . . . and stay."

The prisoner did so.

Garreth was heading for Pfannenstiel, who had pulled himself up to sit with his back against the bar and was fingering the gash on top of his head, when one of the patrons against the walls called, "Hey, that's a good trick. Can you make him heel, too? Or roll over and play dead?"

The words brought Garreth up short. Suddenly he heard himself as those in the bar must have, giving commands in the same tone used on a dog. More, he saw the expressions on the faces. One waited with glee to see what might be next in the show but others bore varying states of fear. He did not need to read minds to know what they feared . . . him; someone in his position who would treat one man that way could do it to anyone else.

He carried, he realized, a bigger stick than a

badge. He carried the biggest stick of all, the power of absolute control, bestowed and limited by no regulatory body. The responsibility for it rested in just one person, Garreth Mikaelian. The thought awed and frightened him. He felt the stick between his ankles, tripping him.

To lighten his step, Garreth said dryly, "The gentleman is through entertaining tonight. Now, I'll need all of you to remain until I can take your names." He crossed to Pfannenstiel and squatted on his heels beside the older officer. "How do you feel?"

Pfannenstiel grunted. "Stupid. I should have known to duck."

Garreth smiled in relief. The officer did not appear seriously injured. "You take it easy. The ambulance will be here as soon as Sue rousts out the driver."

Standing again, he worked his way around the room taking names. And while he did, he slid glances at his prisoner. The big man remained motionless in the chair, staring straight ahead. The biggest stick. *Walk softly*, a voice whispered in his head. *Walk very softly.*

10

"How I envy you young people sometimes." Mrs. Bieber pointed at Garreth's windbreaker. "It feels like winter today but I see the children out around the high school in nothing more than that. You're so thin, too; aren't you cold?"

"Not as long as I keep moving," he lied.

She pulled a shawl tighter around her shoulders and moved into the living room. "The older I get, the more I hate winter. Mada keeps talking about moving me somewhere like Arizona or Florida."

"It's an idea."

She sighed. "But this is my home. All my children were born in the bed upstairs. The few friends of mine still living are all in this town. Mada called last night and offered to give me a vacation in Mexico as a Christmas present. I wouldn't mind *visiting* there for a while."

Garreth's stomach plunged. "You mean, go to *her* this year instead of her coming here?"

She nodded. "Mada said Acapulco is touristy but warm. I'd like that, though of course I would miss not spending Christmas with my grandchildren. Maybe I could go after Christmas."

Garreth's mind churned. Could he get to Acapulco? He tried to think of all he would need . . . a passport and a plane ticket, which might be hard to come by with no money. *Dracula, where are my bat wings when I need them?*

Maybe he could find money for driving down, or sell the car and fly. Enough people had eyed the ZX longingly that he should be able to find a buyer. As a place to arrest Lane, aside from the problem of being a foreign country, Acapulco had its attractions . . . principally that it would save Mrs. Bieber the distress of having her daughter taken in her own home by someone the old woman thought was a friend.

"Acapulco sounds nice," he said. "Let me know if you're going and where you'll be staying." He made himself smile. "I'll send you postcards from the shivering north."

She laughed. "I will."

Silently, he swore. Of all the lousy luck, just when he had himself settled in his web. He had better start planning for the trip now so he could leave the moment he knew where to find Lane.

11

Given the tendency of cops to hang out with other cops and the fact that he and Maggie were the only single officers in the department, Garreth supposed it was inevitable that they should start dating. It also provided a good chance to get out of Baumen. Not that seeing *Sudden Impact* in Bellamy was very much of an escape, but at least the movie theater there ran seven nights a week

Once in the theater, though, Garreth wondered if the movie was a mistake. He felt as though he were drowning in a sea of blood. The reek of it surrounded him, leaving him fighting cramps and shaking in longing. Someone had been eating Italian food, too; a taint of garlic eddied intermittently, each whiff bringing a moment of suffocation.

Maggie peered anxiously at him. "Are you all right?"

"Fine." But even saying it he knew the tremor in his voice betrayed the lie. "I . . . get a little claustrophobic sometimes." Not the best excuse in the world with the theater just half full this Monday night, but it would have to do.

Maggie appeared to believe him. "Do you want to leave?"

He shook his head and put an arm around her. "I'll tough it out."

Somehow he did, though the effort cost him the satisfaction he usually felt watching Dirty Harry blow away bad guy after bad guy with blithe disregard for civil rights, due process, and public safety. It was a relief to escape to the car. There he could at least roll down the window and let the wind dilute the warm blood smell coming from Maggie.

She snapped her seat belt and settled back. "A little gratuitous violence is good for the soul, don't you think? Have you ever wanted to act like Harry?"

He shrugged. "Sure, especially after spending two weeks tracking down some punk who cuts up girls or old ladies only to learn that he's back on the street before I've finished the paperwork on the arrest."

A nasty whisper in the back of his head asked him if he might not be doing a Callahan now with this self-appointed hunt of his. *Setting one's self up to alter things according to one's own judgment can end in mistake and failure.* He shook his head inwardly. No. After all, he was not looking to kill Lane, just arrest her, all perfectly legitimate since there was a warrant out on her.

"Did you ever find yourself sympathizing with someone playing vigilante, like Harry did that girl hunting down the men who'd raped her and her sister?"

He shook his head. "I might sympathize, but I'd never let them go like he did. If someone chooses to kill another person, no matter how strong or justified the motive, he should be willing to accept the consequences of his act."

Lord, that sounded self-righteous. Would he

apply it to himself, too? There was probably no way to know until it happened.

They passed the city limits. Garreth floored the accelerator. The car leaped forward like a wild thing unleashed.

Maggie whooped in delight. "This thing really moves. Just don't overrun your lights too far. Cows sometimes get out on the highway along here."

"No problem." Even on this moonless, overcast night the highway stretched in a shining gray ribbon, clearly visible far beyond the edge of the headlights.

He sighed. Night sight. Vampires. Lane. What was Mrs. Bieber going to do? Here it was nearly Thanksgiving and no word yet about whether she was going to Acapulco or not. Belatedly he realized Maggie had asked him a question. "What?"

"I said, what are you doing Thursday?"

He bit his lip. Was she going to invite him to Thanksgiving dinner? "Nothing in particular. Sleep."

"Not going to pollute your body with delicious, fattening carbohydrates and preservatives and additive-filled plastic side dishes?"

A flood of Thanksgiving memories rose in him, bringing a wave of homesickness. He could never enjoy another feast like those again. Would he even see another holiday? A nagging suspicion had haunted his dreams lately that once he had settled with Lane he would simply cease to exist. "I'm not going to feast, no."

"Then could I talk you into talking Danzig into letting us trade shifts just this once, O golden-tongued one? Dad and I have been invited to Aunt Ruth's in Victoria and I'd love to be able to spend the whole day there."

Garreth did not know whether to be relieved or

disappointed that she was not inviting him to dinner. "I'll talk to Danzig." Without his glasses on.

"Great!" She leaned over and kissed his cheek. Sitting back, she glanced out the window and said, "Look, it's starting to snow."

What? He pulled the car over to the side of the road and switched off the lights. Fat, feathery flakes drifted down around them, and with them the darkness lightened, as though each snowflake brought a bit of moonlight with it. Garreth leaned out the window to stare up, fascinated.

Maggie grinned. "I don't suppose you've seen much of this before. The ground's too warm yet for it to stick, but isn't it pretty?"

"You know what I'd like to do? Run in it. Want to? Just a couple of miles to that rise over there and back."

"Garreth!" She laughed. "Run? Just a couple of miles? Look at my shoes. I can't run anywhere in them. Even if I could, we'd break our legs running in the dark. Let's go on to your place. We can sit out on the deck in the snow there, if you like, and think of some way to warm up afterward."

Pleasure at the snow faded. He put the car in motion again and sighed inwardly. Sitting on the deck would be all right, but . . . he wanted to run. It seemed he and Maggie could date and talk about everyday things. It sounded like she was inviting him to make love later, too. But they could not talk about the things deep in him, could not even share some of the physical activities he had come to take for granted. She could not run through the magic of falling snow with him. Tonight he would just sell his soul for someone who could.

12

Baumen felt like a ghost town. Garreth saw almost no one. Kansas Avenue lay completely deserted. Which did not disturb him a great deal. With luck nothing would happen on the shift. Even beneath an overcast sky threatening snow that might manage to stick in today's near-freezing temperature, and wearing his trooper glasses, the light still gave him a headache. Somewhere above the clouds the sun pressed down on him, draining his energy. *I hope you appreciate what I'm doing for you, Maggie. I wouldn't take on the sun for just anyone.*

He tried not to think what she was doing at the moment, for fear it might bring on more memories and homesickness. But those came anyway. Would calling home after the shift help or just make the pain more unbearable?

"Baumen 407," the radio murmured. "Public service a Mrs. Anna Bieber at 555–7107."

Mrs. Bieber? Garreth drove to the telephone outside the A&W and dialed the number. Background voices almost drowned out conversation with the woman who answered. Garreth had to shout to make her understand whom he wanted to talk to.

But finally Mrs. Bieber came on the line. "I tried calling you at home but Emily Schoning said Helen said you were working. Can you come to the house after you're off? I have the address of the hotel in Acapulco where I'll be joining Mada after Christmas."

He sighed. So it was decided. At least he had several weeks to sell the car and make other arrangements. "It may be eight-thirty before I'm through. Is that too late for you?"

"I'll be expecting you."

He hung up the phone and leaned against the side of the booth, staring out at the patrol car. Guilt stabbed him at the thought of walking out on Danzig and the department. He could give them a story about critical illness in his family, but it was still unfair to everyone. Doubt at the correctness of his chosen course nagged him again. It spread pain from one temple across his forehead to the other, a headache which not even sunset cured.

At the watch change, Maggie took the car keys from him and said, "You look terrible. I think you're right about being a night person. Would you like it if I come over after I get off and show my appreciation for the favor?"

Monday night seemed to have started something. Would she be amused or insulted if he told her he had a headache? No, headache or not, he wanted her to come. He needed someone, however wide the gulf between them. "The bed and I will be waiting."

He raced through his reports and drove straight to Mrs. Bieber's, still in uniform except for the equipment belt left in his locker at the station.

The old woman answered the door. "My, you look nice. I've never seen you in uniform before. Come on in the living room." She led the way.

He smiled at her despite the lump in his stomach. "I hope you had a good Thanksgiving."

"Oh, yes. My daughter Kathryn hosted this year. It was noisy, of course, but I loved every chaotic minute." She stopped and turned to face him. "I'm afraid I have a confession to make."

A chill of unease moved down his spine. "Confession?"

"I have a hotel address, but that was just an excuse to get you here. Come on." She moved on into the living room.

He followed, only to stop in the doorway. A woman sitting on the couch stood up.

Mrs. Bieber grinned. "I wanted to surprise you. Garreth, this is my daughter Mada."

Mada! His stomach plunged. But this was not Lane! The woman had the right height, legs that seemed to stretch forever and looked even longer with the high heels on her black boots and snug fit of dark green slacks. Mahogany hair swept the shoulders of a scarlet turtleneck, but ... gray streaked the red and her skin had the coarseness and creases of middle age.

He felt numb with shock. All these weeks he'd been lying in wait for the wrong woman? But— his mind stumbled trying to think—the postmark, the school picture, Mrs. Bieber's description of her daughter as a singer; how could all that match so well and yet be so totally *wrong*!

"I . . . am very glad to meet you," he managed to force out. He must not betray his disappointment.

"And I you," Mada said in an amused voice.

He stiffened. It was Lane's voice.

Looking at her again more closely, this time he saw her eyes. His heart jumped. The eyes were hers, too. They reflected the light, vampire eyes, and they glinted cold and blood-red, recognizing him . . . measuring him.

Duel

1

A jumble of emotions and thoughts jostled Garreth's head:

Admiration ... *That's a really convincing makeup job.*

Relief ... *I don't have to go to Acapulco, after all.*

Anxiety ... *Oh, Lord, we're in the middle of her mother's living room; I can't arrest her here.*

Concern ... *This is going to make the department short for the weekend.*

Dismay ... *So soon? I thought I wouldn't be dealing with her until after Christmas. I don't want to leave here yet.*

Apprehension ... *What will happen to me now, when she's in custody and my reason for living is gone?*

From somewhere beyond the mindstorm, Mrs. Bieber's delighted voice reached him. "Isn't this nice? Mada got tired of Acapulco and decided to come home. We picked her up at the airport in Hays this morning."

"Not tired, Mama," Lane said. "I was there with a friend who had a terrible accident and I just couldn't enjoy it any longer." The middle-aged mask smiled at Garreth. "Mama says you're from San Francisco. Are you the same Garreth Mikaelian the papers were calling Lazarus?"

"Accident? You didn't say anything about that before," Mrs. Bieber said.

"I didn't want to spoil Thanksgiving, Mama. My mother has been telling me something about you, Mr. Mikaelian," Lane said lightly. "It's a very interesting story, but also a little puzzling. Baumen is a long way from San Francisco. How did you happen to come here?"

He took off his glasses and met her eyes. "Good police work."

"What kind of accident?" Mrs. Bieber asked.

Lane shrugged. "He was found at the bottom of the cliff with his neck broken and throat torn out. The police said he must have been attacked by some dogs and fallen over the cliff trying to escape from them."

Garreth reached automatically for his own throat, for the now almost-imperceptible lines of scarring.

"He?" Mrs. Bieber's forehead furrowed in distress. "You were there with a—I'm sorry," she said as Lane started to frown. "I just can't imagine you as part of this modern morality. I'm so sorry about your friend. Are you all right?"

Satiated, Garreth thought angrily. *Replete*. She had come home to wait for Acapulco to cool.

"I'm fine, Mama. He wasn't a close friend, and there was no impropriety." She smiled at her mother without taking her eyes from Garreth. "Men don't have wild affairs with women my age. I shared a room with his teenage grand-daughter in order to help him chaperon her. So you've decided to settle here because it's a pleasant change from the city, my mother tells me. But you're still a policeman."

The mockery underlying the pleasant tone irritated Garreth. He said evenly, "It's what I know how to do best, enforce the law." See what she made of that.

Her eyes flared red.

Mrs. Bieber glanced from him to her daughter, forehead furrowed, obviously sensing the tension between them but unable to understand the reason for it. In a determinedly cheerful tone, she said, "Why don't you two sit down and get acquainted while I go make tea. Garreth doesn't drink coffee, either."

She left the room.

Garreth took off his jacket but continued to stand, eyeing Lane.

She broke the silence first, laughing. With the sound of it he seemed to see through the mask to the ever-young face beneath. "You amaze and delight me, Inspector. I've been looking forward to our next meeting, but I confess I never expected it to be here. Tell me, how *did* you find your way?"

He blinked, nonplussed. She looked forward to their next meeting? What made her think there would be one? "I'll tell you all about it on the way back to San Francisco."

Lane turned away, walking in a wide arc toward a window, where she stood peering out into the night, toying with the jaw-high collar of her turtleneck. "Ah. So that's the reason for your remark just now about enforcing the law. You came to arrest me."

The arc took her well around a crucifix on the wall, Garreth noticed. "Hunting killers is my job and you killed Mossman and Adair. You tried to kill me."

She whirled. "No, no, Inspector; I did *not* try to kill you. If I'd wanted you dead, rest assured you would have been found with your neck broken."

So it had not been mere oversight. "Why didn't—" he began.

"Tell me, how do you propose to take me back?"

He frowned. How did she think? "There's a warrant for your arrest. Extradition will be arranged and you'll—"

She hissed, interrupting him. "Are you really so dense? I mean, *how* will you take me back? By what means do you propose to force me to accompany you and remain confined: Rose-stem handcuffs? A cell with garlic on the bars? May I remind you that anything used against me hurts you equally, if you can even convince your law enforcement colleagues to agree to such nonsense."

The words echoed uncomfortably through his head. It had not even occurred to him there would be problems with taking her back and jailing her. Even given his concentration on finding her, how could he have been so blind, so unforesighted. *Dumb, tunnel-visioned flatfoot.* There must be a way to handle her, though. He could not just let her walk away.

The crucifix caught his eyes. "Maybe I can drape a rosary around your wrists."

Lane's pupils dilated. "Superstition," she said smoothly.

But Garreth watched her breathing quicken and pupils dilate. Superstition, yes, since crosses and holy water did not bother him, but superstition still affected those who believed in it . . . and the look of this house told him she had been brought up in the bosom of the Roman Catholic Church. "Then why did you tear the Christian fish symbol off Mossman's neck?"

"I detest tacky jewelry." She came back to him, again swinging wide around the crucifix. "Open your eyes, Inspector. It's useless to arrest or try me. Our kind are beyond the reach of mere human laws."

"No." He shook his head. No one could be beyond the law. Without law there was only chaos. "I don't believe—"

He broke off as Mrs. Bieber came in with tea and slices of pumpkin pie. "Mada, you didn't eat a bite at Kathryn's. You must be starved by now. Have some pie. You, too, Garreth."

Garreth and Lane exchanged quick glances. He laughed wryly inside at the irony of finding himself on the same side of a problem as his quarry.

"If you don't think I ate, you didn't see me snacking out in the kitchen while we were cooking," Lane said. "You know I don't have a big appetite anyway, and I never eat dessert."

Garreth smiled but shook his head, patting his belt. "Sweets have been my downfall for years. Now that I've finally gotten the weight off, I don't dare relapse. Thank you for the tea, though."

Shaking her head, Mrs. Bieber poured the tea. "In my day, a good appetite was considered healthy. These days it seems everyone wants to starve to death. Well, have you two been getting acquainted?"

"Yes," they both lied, and, sitting down, accepted tea from her.

"I'm so glad. And I'm glad you came home, after all, Mada. Will you be able to stay through Christmas?"

Lane glanced at Garreth. "I plan to stay until I take you back to Acapulco."

Daring him to make her a liar? Garreth sucked in his lower lip. What *could* he do about her?

Sipping his tea, he listened to Lane tell anecdotes about people in Acapulco. Opposing feelings warred in him ... his belief in due process and justice against the obvious impossibility of following proper established procedure. He must violate the latter to accomplish the former, and that itself violated what his badge said he stood for. *I Ching* insisted that one must act with proper authority or end up in mistake and failure.

The delicate blood smell drifting from Mrs. Bieber set hunger gnawing at him. Before he did anything, he would eat and think the problem over. If he appeared to be retreating, Lane might not feel it necessary to bolt. Garreth stood and reached for his jacket. "I'd better go. Thank you for asking me over, Mrs. Bieber. And it's nice to meet you, Miss Bieber." He pulled on the jacket. "I hope we'll see each other again."

Lane arched a brow. "The night isn't over yet. Mama, I'm going to impose on this nice young man of yours to drive me around for some fresh air. I'll be back before too long."

He stared at her.

She kissed her mother on the cheek and smiled at Garreth. "Shall we go, Mr. Mikaelian?" She led the way into the hall, where she picked a coat off the huge mirrored coat and umbrella rack, then fairly pushed Garreth out the front door before surprise gave him time to think or react. "We got sidetracked from our conversation about the nature of reality and I'd really like to finish it."

2

The door closed behind them. Garreth said, "There's nothing more to say except to read you your rights."

"Oh, I think there's a great deal to say yet. That ZX is your car? Of course it is; I saw it outside my apartment." She took his arm. "Let's go for a drive."

I Ching had also said: *The maiden is powerful. Beware of that which seems weak and innocent.*

"I don't think so."

She scowled. "How paranoid cops are. What can I do to you? Anyway, do you really think I'd be careless enough to try something in my hometown, where everyone sees everything? Where my mother would see it? I won't foul her nest. I don't even hunt here, one reason I never stay too long."

Somehow he found himself propelled toward the car. "How do you eat?"

"Even during the holidays there are young men around the college campus in Hays. They're always willing to pick up an attractive young woman and demonstrate what superstuds they are. I hunt in disguise, of course . . . in my own face." She slid into the passenger side of the car and closed her door. "When I was a girl the most popular spots for couples to park were behind the Coop elevators across 282, around the fairgrounds and sale barn, and in Pioneer Park. I think these

days you police hang out behind the elevators
waiting for speeders, so let's go to the park."

Thinking about it, what *could* she do to him?
Garreth wondered. He was strong enough to
resist a physical attack and in the reverse of what
she had said to him, anything she could use that
would hurt him must also hurt her. He walked
around the car, climbed in, and started it.

Lane leaned back in the seat. "I have always
loved beautiful cars, though I've never dared own
one. They're too conspicuous. Though I was once
seriously tempted by the Bugatti Royale a friend
of mine in Europe had years ago, and lately I've
thought about Porsches. My favorite lovers have
always been men with fine taste in cars. Yours is
passable. Is this stock, Inspector?"

Now, why did he feel ashamed to admit it was?
"You didn't come to talk about cars." Hunger
gnawed at him. His stomach twinged in the
threat of a cramp. *Damn!* If only he had taken
time to eat before going over to Mrs. Bieber's.
"We're here to talk about law."

Lane sighed. "I told you, human law doesn't
apply to us, but ... I don't intend to talk about
anything more just yet, except maybe the weather."
She leaned her head out her open window and
blew. Like steam from a locomotive, her breath
blew back past her in clouds of billowing white.
"Fairy wreaths. I hope it snows. I love snow now.
I didn't used to because I hated being cold. Isn't
it a relief not having to care whether it's hot or
cold out anymore?"

The sudden shift from world-wise woman to
child left Garreth groping in mental confusion.
Like a child, too, she leaped from the car at the
park and raced from the parking lot up a path
toward the swinging bridge. The bridge connected to an artificial island made by digging a

channel looping from the Saline River around a
large oval of land and back.

She danced across the bridge in a rapid tap of
bootheels, pausing only to laugh over her shoulder at him. "In case you haven't already discovered it, yes, vampires can cross running water.
It's amazing the superstitions humans have
dreamed up to convince themselves they're pro-
tected from their nightmares."

In the center of the island lay an open stone
pavilion with a raised bandstand in the center.
Garreth caught up with her there, and found her
peeling off the middle-aged face she wore, so that
he truly confronted Lane Barber again, youthful
face shining pale in the twilight of his night sight.
She laughed at him. "No lights and yet not a
misstep anywhere. Isn't it wonderful being able
to see in the dark?"

What was she trying to do? "It has its uses,
yes."

She stuffed the latex bits of her mask in a
pocket, grimacing. "How solemn you are. Too
bad I couldn't have brought you here in the
spring, with tulips and crocus and daffodils everywhere, and peonies later in the summer. They
used to have a band on Friday and Saturday
nights. Lights lit up the pavilion so you could see
it from miles away. Everyone in town came.
Mama and Papa would polka and waltz until
they were almost too tired to walk home."

The ghosts of those dancers haunted the pavilion. He could see them in the leaves the wind
whirled across the paving. The ghosts and the
sudden wistfulness on the girl-woman face sent a
pang through him. Maybe there were things she
could do to him that had nothing to do with
physical assault. He regretted having come. "When-
ever you're ready to talk, let me know."

She sat down on the steps of the bandstand. "All right; let's talk." It was the woman's voice again. "You can't beat me, so why try? It isn't worth it for a couple of arrogant, self-centered humans. There's no reason for you to care about them. There's no reason for you to care what happens to any humans any longer."

He sat down at the other end of the steps from her. "The way you don't care about your family?"

She flung up her head, eyes flashing, and in the motion he saw another ghost . . . of the girl in the photo album and the singer who attacked Claudia Darling in 1941. Then she laughed. *Touché*. But . . . family is one thing, the rest of humanity another."

"Not to me. I'm sworn to protect them, and all my friends are human, of course."

Lane snorted. "Friends are someone you can do things together with and bare your soul to. Do you have anyone who fits that description, anyone you can sit and talk with as openly as we're talking? Is there anyone you'd trust to tell what you are and not be afraid that the next time you saw him he'd be carrying a sharp wooden stake?"

That stung. He remembered the morning he woke up to find Lien above him and had wondered about that very thing.

She leaned toward him. "Reality, Inspector . . . humans are only one thing to us: a source of food."

He sat up straight. "Not to me. I've never drunk a drop of human blood."

Her eyes narrowed. "You drink only animal blood?" She shook her head mockingly. "No wonder you're so thin. You really ought to eat properly, Inspector."

His jaw tightened. "I refuse to prey on people!"

"Oh, really." Her lip curled. "How righteous.

But I notice you have no scruples against using my mother as an informer and tricking her into thinking you're a friend to get to me."

That stung even harder. He felt faint heat crawling up his neck and face. "I'm sorry about that. I didn't like doing it. I like your mother."

Her voice flattened to a hiss. "I could kill you for that. It almost makes me sorry I didn't break your neck when I had the chance."

"I keep wondering why you didn't."

For a minute he wondered if she was going to answer. She leaned back against the steps and looked away. But after a bit, she said, "I intended to, but . . . you bit me."

He blinked. She sounded as though she expected that to explain everything. "So?"

Lane sighed. "The drawback to immortality is that while we go on, nothing else does. I hold on to my possessions because I lose the people. They die or are left behind when I take a new identity. I'm enjoying my family while I can because when they're dead, I won't have anyone left in the world I give a damn about. Everything I know best, the world I was born into, will be gone forever. It'll happen to you, too."

Without wanting to, Garreth saw it . . . his parents dying, even his son passing him in age. Eventually, he could become the contemporary of his grandchildren and great-grandchildren, except they would be alien to him, looking at the world through different eyes and even speaking a different language. Look at how the little slang Lane permitted herself—like calling him a mick—dated her.

"Immortality and vampirism are very lonely, Garreth."

The words echoed through him. Almost desperately, he thought of Helen Schoning. "It doesn't have to be. There's nothing wrong with serial relationships. Every time period ought to offer at least several people who can meet some of our emotional needs."

"And what if you could find someone like that, someone just right, like your late wife, say?"

That hit like a knife in the ribs. Garreth shot onto his feet with the pain. "How do you know about Marti?"

Lane smiled. "I asked around about you. Your neighbors were only too happy to talk to a reporter about the Man Who Came Back from the Dead. They told me you and Marti had a very special relationship. Her death must have been extremely hard for you."

His throat closed tight, trapping the pain suddenly filling his chest. "Leave my wife out of this."

"But that's just the point." Lane leaned toward him. "What if you found someone else like that? You'd know from the beginning that you were going to lose her eventually. And what if you found another soulmate, then another, always to lose her? How long could you endure that kind of pain?"

Agony racked him now just thinking about it. He clenched his fists and whispered hoarsely, "Goddamn you!" Then he laughed bitterly. "Except you already are, and me, too."

She raised her brows. "Surely you don't believe that nonsense. Damnation has nothing to do with us. We're neither demonic nor undead. We're as alive as humans, only in a different, superior way. What mechanism do you think actually produces a vampire?"

The question surprised him. He thought about it for a minute and had to shrug. "I never thought about it."

"Well, I have, and I've studied. I'm convinced there's a vampire virus."

He remembered the medical books on her shelves. "Like rabies."

She laughed. "Close enough. It's carried in blood and saliva like rabies. A person bitten receives a small inoculation of the virus. In a normal, healthy person the immune system destroys it. If there are repeated inoculations, though, some viruses survive to set up housekeeping in the host's cells, and when the body becomes very weak—dies—they take over, modify the host to suit their needs, and reanimate it." Lane's eyes gleamed as she warmed to her subject. "It would appear to take very little to just reanimate the body. The amount of virus from several bites or one long drinking session ending in death is sufficient for that, but apparently there has to be a large colony to affect the brain enough to restore higher intellectual functions."

He stared at her, suddenly understanding. "Blood would carry the most, and I received your blood by biting you."

She nodded. "I knew you would reanimate with higher functions intact, unlike Mossman or Adair." She stood and came over to reach toward the scars on his neck. "Flesh of my flesh. Blood of my blood."

The light spicy-musky scent of her perfume curled around him. He jerked away. "I don't believe you, lady. I'm a cop and you're a killer and you thought you'd make me your companion? How in hell did you ever think I'd agree? Didn't it occur to you that once I realized what had happened to me I might tell everyone what you were and destroy you?"

Her smile was knowing. "You didn't, did you?

You haven't told anyone anything, just come after me on your own."

Something he had done once before, he remembered with a sudden chill, and had died for the error. He bounded up the steps into the bandstand. "But not to become your companion. I'm taking you back, even if I have to tell everyone everything."

She followed him up. "And destroy yourself, too?"

He turned his back to the rail and leaned against it for support. "Why not?" he said steadily. "I detest what you've made me. You destroyed my life; you almost destroyed my partner's. You've brought misery to the lives of Mossman's and Adair's families. All I care about is seeing you face judgment for that, then I want to die . . . finally and for always."

Lane's breath wrapped white around her and melted away into the night air. "Do you? When there's so much you've never seen or experienced?" The musical cadence of her whisper filled the bandstand. "You lived on the bay for years, but did you ever once climb aboard one of the ships that dock there every day and sail away with her? Do you really want to die before you've seen wonders like the Himalayas above Katmandu or climbed to the temples of Tibet? Or walked the Great Wall of China and explored the ancient ruins of Karnak and Zimbabwe? Poling through the Okavango Delta in Africa at flood time there is such beauty and richness of life that it makes your throat ache, and there's nothing more awesome than the migrations in the Serengeti, when the plains stretch like a sea of grass and there are wildebeest and zebra as far as the eye can see. There's a city in northern China with a winter festival every year that fills the city with ice sculpture, not just snowmen but pure, clear ice chiseled into a wonderland of heroes and mythical animals and castles, and ice arbors with ice benches to sit on."

The whisper sang on, naming cities, describing mountains and rivers and caves, most he had never heard of but all sounding awesomely breathtaking ... sang on and on until Garreth's head swam and he ached in longing. He had looked at the ships along the bay, yes, and thought about the places they sailed, but he could never afford to board one. "Most people don't ever see those places," he said. "There isn't time for them all in a life."

Garreth did not recall seeing her move, but Lane suddenly stood beside him. The scent of her perfume filled his head. "Not a human life, no, but we have all the time in the world. We can explore every wonder completely before moving on to the next."

Yes, he thought with a slow wonder. "You can afford a trip like that?"

She slipped an arm through his and laughed, a low, rich sound. "My dear, a woman with hypnotic powers can learn a great many investment tips from the business giants she beds." She sighed happily. "It will be the grand tour of grand tours. Vienna and Rome and Copenhagen. They aren't like they were before the war, but they're still beautiful, and Peking, Mecca, and Sri Lanka. Carrara, where the best marble in the world is quarried, and Venice, where all the greatest glass craftsmen work. And there are pleasures I'll show you that are beyond your imagining, pleasures no human can appreciate. I'll teach you survival techniques it's taken me decades to learn. Garreth, my love, we will bestride the world like a colossus."

The bandstand felt like a carousel, with the night spinning dazzlingly past them. But uneasiness still stirred beneath his growing excitement and anticipation. What? Something he had forgotten? No matter; he would remember it later.

He shook his head. "I'm surprised you've waited this long to go. Wasn't the vampire who made you interested?"

Lane sighed. "We were going to. All the signs indicated Europe was about to fall apart, though, and we couldn't leave until the Polish property was secured or sold off. Another week and we'd have been clear, but Hitler pushed in so much faster and brutally than anyone ever anticipated." She shuddered. "*Blitzkrieg* isn't just a word when you've lived through it. Warsaw was in chaos. Irina and I got separated and I never saw her again, not even when I went back looking for her after the war."

Garreth blinked. "Irina? Her? A *woman* made you?"

"Don't sound so scandalized, love." Lane squeezed his arm. "Human blood is human blood; we don't have to drink from the opposite sex. That's usually the choice, and Irina normally fed only on men, but I begged her to take from me and let me drink from her. She called herself Irina Rodek and she had a Polish passport."

He felt his brows hop. "Polish."

Lane giggled. "All vampires aren't Transylvanian, you know. Not that she was really Polish. She once told me she was nearly five hundred years old. She'd been Russian for a while, an aristocrat, but had to flee during the Revolution. We met in Vienna." Her voice went dreamy. She leaned her head down on his shoulder. "July 1934. Vienna really wasn't the place to be that month with Hitler's *Putsch* and Dollfuss's killing, but Matthew was stubborn. What were politics to us, he said, as long as the cafés and museums stayed open? That was when he had his reservations and that was when we would use them."

"Matthew? That's the professor you ran away with?" Garreth said.

"Matthew Carlson, yes, but it's more accurate to say I ran *after* him. I'd had him for history that spring and knew he'd be going to Europe on his sabbatical, and I wanted so much to get the hell away from Baumen and Kansas. I threw myself at him. He was middle-aged with a middle-aged wife, so the idea of some coed, even an oversize, clumsy one, finding him sexy turned him to putty. He left his wife and took me with him instead. We were sitting in a café and I noticed his eyes going past me. I turned around to see what he was looking at. It was a who, a woman at the next table." Lane laughed. "I hated her on sight. She was so exquisite, like a Dresden figurine, small, perfect cream complexion, hair like sable, and violet, violet eyes. And she was looking at Matthew, flirting with him. Worse, he looked back, all goggle-eyed. Suddenly I was furious. I threw myself at her, fully intending to ruin her beauty for life."

Garreth remembered the photograph in the *Chronicle*. "You have tended to react violently to other women interfering with your meal ticket, haven't you?"

She grinned. "Oh, yes. And this would have been another nasty scene except she looked straight at me and said very calmly, in the most charming accent, 'Please don't be angry. Sit down. It would delight me to have you join me for tea.' And suddenly I wasn't angry any longer, and Matthew and I did join her."

The scene played in Garreth's head. He glanced

sideways at Lane, fascinated. "How did you come to find out she was a vampire and ask her to make you one, too?"

"I found out by observation, watching her with men, always a different one, including Matthew once, and seeing the man afterward. She sort of took me under her wing after that afternoon. 'I sense you are a very unhappy young woman,' she told me several days later. 'You think you are ugly.' She taught me to dress and walk. 'You cannot be small and cuddly so don't waste your youth longing to be. Think of yourself as a goddess, a queen, and move like one.' Irina was the one who showed me that I had a singing talent. She even paid for coaches to train my voice. But that was later. At first she was just kind, and when I saw how much men fawned over her, I wanted to be just like her, so I watched her closely in order to imitate her." Lane frowned. "*Why* I realized she was a vampire, I don't know. Even though I had always been fascinated by werewolves and vampires and ogres, dreaming of being one and wreaking revenge on all my tormentors, I didn't believe in them. If I'd been back in Kansas, the idea would never have occurred to me; it would have seemed preposterous. But I was in Vienna, where it seemed all the fairy tales in the world might be true. I'd found myself a kind of fairy godmother, hadn't I? I figured it out and when it came time for Matthew and me to leave, I refused to go with him. I went running to Irina, weeping, claiming he'd been overcome with remorse and guilt about the way he'd treated his wife and had abandoned me. I begged to stay with her, as her maid if nothing else."

"And she let you."

A complacent smile lifted the corners of Lane's

mouth. "Yes, but as a companion, not maid. I was useful to her, you see. She quickly realized I knew what she was and didn't care. She also saw that as I gained self-confidence, I attracted men ... meals for her. After a couple of years, I begged to join her in her life. She refused at first, saying how hard and lonely a life it is, but when I pointed out that she wouldn't have to be lonely anymore, she agreed. I think she was sorry. She kept scolding me and threatening to leave me on my own if I killed another man. 'It is excessive; it is dangerous. You must learn control,' she would say."

The uneasiness, the feeling that he should be remembering something, stirred again in Garreth. "Irina was right," he said.

Lane snorted. She flung away from him, pacing across the bandstand. "Not if it's done right, like a wild animal did it, or a fanatic cult. I knew what I was doing. Irina came from a superstitious age, when people believed in vampires, and was careful out of habit. Even so, sometimes ..." She turned back to face him. "Sometimes I wonder if she comprehended how much power we have. We can do whatever we like with no fear of reprisal."

The chill inside exploded outward, shattering the warm spell her plans had woven around him, reminding him why he was here and what he had to do. "No. We can't. We still have to be accountable."

Her frown told him she saw she was losing him again. Lane hesitated, mind churning visibly, then shook her head with an indulgent smile. "Ah, we're back to that again, are we?"

"I'm sorry, yes."

She shrugged. "I'm sorry, too, but I suppose it's too much to forget what you were so soon. You have to grow out of it. Then let me start you on your way by dispensing with this foolish illusion you have of returning me to San Francisco. It can't be done. Rosary handcuffs and a garlic cell might hold me, but you'll never get me from here to them. I'll kill you first, even though I adore you and long to show the world to you. Now lay down these wisps of humanity you cling to and come with me. Enjoy the power that is ours."

Cold and dread sunk into his spine, bones, and gut. Dread? Or maybe just uncertainty. What she said carried a ring of truth. "Power? Something I've learned as a cop, and maybe as a vampire, too, is that power always carries responsibility, and the greater the power, the greater the responsibility for not abusing it."

Lane snorted. "A human notion. For us there is no responsibility because there is no one with more power who can punish us."

The dread grew. The latter was certainly true. Garreth felt leaden, as though daylight pressed down on him. Very soon, he feared, he would see what the dread was, and he did not want to. That she was right? That he must forget Lien and Harry, Maggie and Nat, everyone he cared about, and look on them as no more than walking bottles of blood?

"And we certainly have no responsibility to humans," Lane continued coldly. "They are only food. We prey on them. We must. It's our nature."

The words cut like a knife, but to his surprise, the knife did not stab him. Rather, it sliced through his uncertainty, suddenly releasing him. He straightened like a drowning man finding a bottom under his feet and his head out of the water. "Bullshit! It's the vampire nature to need blood and prefer darkness and sleep on the earth, and that is *all*! The rest we choose: our source of blood, killing or not in obtaining it, the way we use our power. I may be new to this life, but I can recognize the difference between what I *must* do and what I *may* do. So don't do any numbers on me about predestination and compulsive behavior!" His voice was rising. With an effort, Garreth dragged it down again, to keep the whole town from hearing. "You abuse people because you hate them. You kill because you enjoy it. I understand why you do it, but that doesn't mean you have to, and it sure as hell doesn't justify it! You're a killer and you have to answer for it."

Her eyes flared. "You've decided that, have you? Tell me, how do you justify *that*? What gives *you* the right to judge *me*? That badge?"

The dread burst in him, like ice, like hunger cramps. He wanted to turn away and throw up. "No, not the badge." There was no responsibility, she said, because there was no one with greater power to punish her ... the same principle that punks like Wink lived by: *Get away with everything you can until you're caught.* And of course they never thought they would be caught. There was another principle, though, one that worked in human law and could apply equally to vampires. An awareness of it must have been working at him since the evening's first mention of the difficulty of taking her back to San Francisco. He drew a deep breath and said steadily, "I'm your peer."

She froze. "A jury of one?"

Acting to re-create order must be done with proper authority. He leaned back against the rail, fingers biting into it. "I'm all there is."

Lane stared at him. He avoided her gaze. After a moment, she gave up trying to trap his eyes and shrugged. "Very well. How does the jury find me? Guilty?"

He felt as though he were suffocating. "Yes."

"Then what sentence do you pass?"

The question stunned him. Something else he had not thought through. What *could* he do? Have her make some kind of anonymous cash gift to compensate the dead men's families? But that did nothing to restrain her from killing again. "I . . . have to think about it."

"Poor baby." She strolled back and reached out as though to stroke his cheek.

But before she touched him, her hands dropped to grab his upper arms. A knee drove hard up into his groin.

Pain exploded through Garreth. The world disappeared beyond a raging blue haze and he dropped to the floor, writhing and gasping in anguish.

Dimly, he felt her hands going through his jacket pockets and heard the jingle of keys. "Dumb mick," she hissed. "The world could have been yours. Now *I'm* imposing a sentence on *you*. Actually I'm doing you a favor by granting your wish. You will die, finally and irrevocably."

The heels of her boots rapped down the steps and away toward the bridge.

Garreth struggled to stand, to pursue her, but could not even make it to his knees, only continue to huddle groaning and cursing. Through the pain paralyzing him came the distant snarl of the ZX's engine. With it rang a grim echo in his head. *Setting one's self to alter things according to one's own judgment can end in mistake and failure . . . mistake and failure . . . failure.*

3

A decade later he managed to drag himself up the railing of the bandstand, and a couple of years after that the pain finally subsided enough for Garreth to walk. Anger helped, even directed at himself. *Dumb mick, all right. The maiden is powerful. When the hell are you going to get that through your thick skull and quit underestimating her, man?*

Reaching the bridge, he paused to breathe deeply and push self-recrimination aside. Flagellation did not solve the problem at hand, which was what to do now. With any other fugitive he could call for backup and count on help from every other officer in the area. Not this one. It would only needlessly endanger their lives. He really was the only one to deal with her.

But maybe he could let them help find her.

He broke into a run, angling through the park so he came out on Seventh Street, and raced down it toward City Hall. The wind had swung around to the north, he noticed, and it felt damp. A sign of snow coming?

A patrol car rolling up the street toward him braked to a stop. Maggie rolled down her window. "Garreth, I passed some girl driving your car a couple of minutes ago. When I realized it *was* your car, I swung around the block to catch her again, but by that time she was gone."

"That was La—Mada Bieber, Anna Bieber's

daughter." He scrambled into the passenger side. "Will you call Sue and have her ask Nat to be on the lookout for the car and woman? I need to talk to her."

Maggie eyed him skeptically. "She looked a whole lot younger than Mada Bieber."

"The night is kind to aging faces." He gave her a quick smile.

Maggie frowned. "How does she happen to have your car?"

Garreth grimaced. He would probably have to give some kind of explanation sooner or later. "She snatched the keys while we were sitting on the steps of the bandstand."

The curious stare became a suspicious frown. "What were you doing on Pioneer Island with a woman old enough to be your grandmother?"

He groaned inwardly. The last thing he needed to deal with now was jealousy. "Finding out she *is* my grandmother . . . and not very happy about the past crashing in on her." He reached for the microphone. "206 Baumen. Ask 303 to watch for a red 1983 Datsun ZX, local—"

"Baumen 206," Sue Pfeifer interrupted. "Be advised that vehicle is 10–19."

He blinked at the radio. The car was at the *station*?

Before he could ask about it, though, Sue went on, "206, will you please check the high school? 10–96 reported around the gymnasium."

Maggie grimaced. "Even on Thanksgiving someone has to be out making trouble."

They both checked all around the high school, but neither saw any sign of the reported prowler. All the doors and windows were secure. After ten minutes, Maggie called off the search and they drove on to the station, where Sue handed over Garreth's keys.

"This woman stuck her head in through the door and tossed the keys at me. She said to tell you she's sorry for stranding you and that she'll see you later."

Cold slid down Garreth's spine. He heard Lane's voice beneath Sue's cheerful tone and the words rang with threat.

Maggie said, "Sounds like she's cooling down."

He smiled grimly. "Yes." Cooling to subfreezing. The lady of ice and steel was out there planning how to kill him. He tried to imagine possible methods. Throw garlic at him and break his neck while he struggled to breathe? Wait and attack while he slept?

No matter. She was not going to have the chance. Lane had victimized him for the last time. He intended to find her first, and while he hunted, would think of some way to deal with her.

Blood smells from the two women swirled around him. His stomach cramped, reminding him sharply that he had still not eaten today. That had better be taken care of before he started the hunt.

Calling good nights over his shoulder, he headed for the door and his car.

His watch read midnight as he turned in the drive. Leaving the car running, he went to peer in through the windows on his side before opening the garage door. It was empty. The tool drawers caught his eye. Might there be something in them that would make an effective weapon? His gun was no good unless the bullets had suddenly transmuted to wood.

Wood. His gaze slid to the stack of firewood against the back of the house, and to the smaller pieces left from the tree trimming during the summer and saved for kindling. Garreth's gut

twisted. No! He turned away. Not that. It *would*
be setting himself up as judge. It would also be
murder. There had to be another answer, even if
it meant becoming her companion, after all, in
order to be her keeper.

He bent down for the garage door handle.

A flat thrum and hiss sounded from the direction of the shrubbery separating Helen's property
from that next door. Garreth reacted with all his
cop's training and instincts . . . spinning and
dropping. Not quite fast enough, however. Pain
exploded in his right shoulder. He fell backward
against the garage door.

With shock, he saw the feathered shaft of an
arrow pinning his uniform jacket to his shoulder.
But even then his training carried through. He
rolled for the cover of the car.

There he pressed against the front fender and
wheel and pulled at the arrow, gritting his teeth
against the pain as the shaft grated on the
underside of his collarbone. At the same time he
listened, straining for any sounds that would give
him Lane's position. The assailant must be Lane.
But the rumble of the car's engine drowned out
all other sound.

The arrow came free in a spurt of blood . . .
and fear. The arrow confirmed his assailant's
identity. Among those plaques on the Bieber
dining room wall were several for excellence in
archery. The arrow also told him how vulnerable
he was to her. Its metal point had been broken off
and the shaft sharpened in hurried, rough knife
cuts. An arrow, Garreth realized with sudden
chill, throwing it aside, was essentially a wooden
stake.

He pressed the jacket against his shoulder,
using the thick pile lining to soak up the blood,

and scooted toward the car door. The car would protect him. He could also use it to escape.

Then a sharp hiss sounded above the engine, and the rear of the car sank. Garreth swore. She had put an arrow in a rear tire. No matter; he could still drive; tires were replaceable. He reached for the door handle.

Heels rapped on the concrete of the driveway, approaching the car. Garreth froze. The moment the door opened, she would know what he intended to do. Could he open it and throw himself in faster than she could circle the car? He licked his lips. He would have to try.

He reached for the door handle again

"Don't move, lover," came a whisper. "Stay very still."

To his horror, her voice dragged at him like daylight. He wanted to obey. Grimly, he fought the power of it, fought to reach for the door handle.

The heels tapped closer, circling the rear end of the car. "You're weak. You hurt, poor baby. You want to curl up and wait for the pain to go away."

No. Move, you stupid flatfoot. Move! But his body, shocky from pain, blood loss, and hunger, would not listen to his mind. With all his will pushing his hand toward the door handle, the hand still fell back.

Lane appeared around the car. She held the bow with another arrow cocked, the bowstring half drawn.

Could two play the power game? Panting in gasps of pain and with the steam of his breath fogging his vision, he stared hard at her. "You don't want to shoot me." He crouched, presenting as small a target as possible, protecting his chest.

He poured his will at her. "Put down the bow and arrow. Lay it down."

She continued drawing back the bowstring. "Good try, but it won't work, lover. I've had more practice. Now, sit up," she crooned. "Give me a good target so it'll be over quick."

No. No! his mind screamed. His body slowly, inexorably straightened.

She smiled. "That's a good boy."

Desperately he fought to look away, fought to think of his pain, to become angry, but nothing worked. She held him, pinned him with her eyes like a butterfly specimen.

A second-floor window opened. "Is that you, Garreth?" Helen's voice called.

Lane's gaze shifted fractionally.

Free! He flung himself sideways.

The bowstring thrummed again, but this time *she* was late. The arrow clattered across the paving where he had been.

"Garreth?" Helen leaned out.

Like a shadow, Lane leaped for the shrubbery.

"Garreth, what's going on!"

He scrambled to his feet. "Stay inside where you're safe."

Lane was headed east. Garreth blocked out the pain in his shoulder and raced after the fading sound of her footsteps. Vampires healed fast, he reminded himself. The bleeding had stopped; the pain should disappear soon, too, then. In any case, he had no time to bother with it. He must catch Lane.

He saw only glimpses of her between trees, shrubbery, and buildings. His vampire hearing let him follow the sound of her flight, though. Minutes later he saw Maggie, too, headed west on Oak with light bar flashing. Helen must have called in about him.

Between the medical center and the hospital lay only open lawn. There he saw Lane clearly, but could not gain on her. Still well ahead of him, she raced past the doctors' offices and across the street into a yard. On the other hand, he was staying with her.

Three blocks later, approaching downtown, he remained just over half a block behind. Then she dodged north behind the Prairie State Bank. When he reached the alley entrance, she had vanished.

Obviously she had passed through the rear door into one of the buildings along the alley. The question was, which one?

The Prairie State Bank had no alley door, but the library on the back side of the block did. Might she have gone in there? He could imagine her lying in wait among the stacks.

He touched the door—*wrench*—and stood on a landing, between short flights of stairs leading down into a basement and up behind the circulation desk on the main floor. Garreth grimaced. The passage had renewed the lessening pain in his shoulder. With an effort, he ignored it and sniffed the air. It smelled of dust and paper and the musky odors of humanity which had been sinking into the walls and tables since Carnegie money put up the building. Traces of glues carried up from the basement. There was no fresh blood scent, though. Then it occurred to him that he had noticed no blood scent all the time he was with Lane. It would make sense that vampires could not scent blood in each other; they were not potential food sources. But he smelled no trace of her spicy-musky perfume, either.

He held his breath and listened. There were only the creaks and sighs of an aging building, and for a few minutes the roar of the furnace ... no footsteps, no hiss of breathing. No Lane.

Wrench. Pain sliced through his shoulder again. Garreth grimaced as he peered up and down the alley. This constant aggravation of his wound was going to make the search a really fun one.

Would she have gone into one of the stores? The main sections were all lighted and their interiors visible from the street, but back rooms and office space would not be. J. C. Penney lay closest.

Wrench.

But this time triumph helped him forget the pain. She was here . . . somewhere! The scent of her perfume hung fresh among the stale, fading odors of daytime occupancy. The entire main floor stretched before him with no sign of her, but he could not see it all. Clothing racks sat close enough together to use for cover.

He dropped to a crouch behind one so he could not be seen, either, and listened for any sound which should not be here. Nothing. Only the normal building creaks. The household-goods section lay downstairs. Could she have gone there, or up to the offices on the second floor? His hand itched for a gun, though he knew it would be useless. Old habits die hard. He had always had one on every previous building search like this.

Running crouched for the stairs up to the offices, he wondered why she had come in here. It was not as though she were a simple fugitive who only wanted to hide so she could escape.

The scent of her perfume in the stairway faded halfway up. Garreth continued the climb just to satisfy himself that she had not come on up, and it appeared not. He smelled no trace of her in the upper hallway.

Downstairs, plastic hangers rattled.

Garreth raced down the steps on tiptoes, cat-silent. Just in time to see a figure carrying a bundle under one arm vanish at the rear door.

Lane had changed clothes, to running shoes and a dark blue man's work coverall. Her hair was all pushed up under a dark stocking cap. The bundle must be her own clothes, then, wrapped up in her jacket.

He ran for the door, too, then hesitated. Outside, metal rang softly, like the lid of a trash dumpster being stealthily lowered . . . or someone crawling across the top. Garreth had a sudden mental image of Lane crouching atop the dumpster in wait for him.

He quickly considered his options. Opening the door would set off alarms. Try going through low and rolling? Not having tried it before, he could not be sure that was even possible.

He turned away and moved from rack to rack for the front door. Better to go around and head her off.

A glance out the window from the cover of the last rack showed him the street was clear.

Wrench!

He leaned back against the door clutching his shoulder and breathing through clenched teeth. That had been the worst one yet. It took most of a minute for the pain to subside to just a fierce throb.

"What's this—drinking on the job?" a voice sneered. "An outrage."

Garreth looked up to see a familiar blue van coasting to a stop opposite him and the Dreiling boy leaning across to the passenger window. He made himself stand up and let go of his shoulder. "A little late for you to be out, isn't it, Scott?"

"Oh, I'm on my way home right now, Officer. Gee, I hope the chief doesn't see you patrolling without your hat on, and without your gun, too. I didn't know cops ever took their guns off."

Snickering, the boy pulled back into the driver's seat and gunned the van away. Garreth glared after him. *Laugh on, punk; one of these days I'm going to have your head.*

Something brushed his face. He looked up . . . snow, not the feathery flakes of Monday but small and hard, rattling against the paving and store windows like icy grains of sand. He raced through the rain of it around the end of the block for the alley.

Each step of the way, he tried to put himself in Lane's place, to guess where she might go next, what her plan was. She had one. Her route, into Penney's first for a change of clothes, indicated that. But what it might be, he had no idea. Maybe just to keep him running until he wore down too much to resist. The way he felt, light-headed, nauseated, shaky, that would not be much longer.

Garreth reached the alley in time to see her at the rear door of the library. A moment later, she disappeared.

"Damn."

An ear against the door brought him the whisper of footsteps running up steps and away across wooden floors. At least she was not trying an ambush just inside. Steeling himself, he pressed against the door.

Wrench!

He made himself keep moving, but the effort brought a cold sweat, the first Garreth could remember since the alley in North Beach. His right arm felt heavy and numb. And ahead of him among the stacks, he heard the light dance of Lane's feet.

Her whisper carried clearly through the silence.

"This is a nice place to play hide-and-seek, don't you think, Inspector?"

He leaned against the end of a stack. "Let's talk."

"What's the matter? Haven't you found a weapon to use on me yet? Too bad, lover. You should have tried the hardware store. I think they have hammers and wooden stakes. Sport and Spinner up the street has bows and arrows. We could be armed equally . . . except those arrows have metal points, which can't hurt me, and I'm probably a better archer than you are."

He moved along the ends toward the sound of her voice. He stopped long enough to talk. "I had a chance to think while I was lying there in the bandstand and you're right, I can't beat you. So I want to join you."

"Would you join in the spirit of the hunt, though? I think not. You're too much like Irina . . . cautious, worried about human feelings and that they'll discover what you are."

While she talked, he moved again, following her voice. If he could get close enough, perhaps he could surprise her and grab her bow. But even as he formed the thought, he realized she was moving, too. By the end of her speech the sound of it came from somewhere above and behind him.

On top of the stacks? Garreth flattened against the books and peered up, hoping to catch some sight of her. "I thought you cared at least about your mother and wouldn't foul her nest."

"Don't worry, lover; I won't." Her voice was moving, coming closer. "Do I look like Mada Bieber to you?"

Not in her true face and new clothes. He backed away, around another stack. "Then you're not worried about the questions that'll come up if

I die?" A weapon. He needed something to defend himself with. "People know we were together and that we had a disagreement which ended with you taking off with my car."

A book. At least it might deflect her aim. He chose a moderate-sized one from the nearest shelf.

Her laughter floated around him. "No one will ever connect Mada Bieber with your death." Suddenly she was there, arching above him as she stepped from the top of one stack to another. She knelt, nocking an arrow. "I promise they won't."

He threw the book and dived sideways. She pulled back to dodge the book and he scrambled up around the cover of another stack.

Lane laughed. "Run, rabbit, run. Catch me if you can."

She vaulted off the stacks, but instead of coming after him, sprinted for the rear door. Cursing wearily, Garreth followed.

This time the pain of passage nearly knocked him to his knees. Only stubborn determination and anger kept him on his feet. Did she want to kill him or not? She could have managed it in there if she had really tried, but she seemed to be just playing with him. To torment him first?

Too late he happened to think that she might try to ambush him, but she did not. She was running across the street toward the alley in the next block south. He staggered after her.

Engines roared on Kansas Avenue. Across the intersection raced a blue van and a red pickup jacked high on its axles. Another engine rumbled to the other side of Garreth. Headlights flashed across him. Above the glare of the lights, he caught a glimpse of a light bar.

He dived across the street for the alley.

The patrol car braked and swerved after him, fishtailing on the snow crystals. "Mikaelian," Ed Duncan called. "Are you all right?"

Garreth swore and kept moving. "I'm fine. You go after the Dreiling kid."

The car pulled up alongside him and halted. Duncan jumped out. "Maggie said someone took a shot at you with a bow and arrow and you were on a foot chase after—"

"I said I'm all right! Get out of here; I'll handle it!" Garreth shouted.

"Maggie said one of the arrows had blood on it."

"*Damn it! Will you get the hell out of here!*" He shoved Duncan toward the patrol car.

"Imperialist pigs!"

The hoarse scream startled both of them. They spun in the direction of the sound.

Lane leaped squarely into the headlights of the car, an arrow nocked, bowstring drawn. "Death to all bourgeois yankee dog pigs!"

Duncan clawed for his gun. The bowstring sang. With a scream, Duncan went down, hip impaled by the arrow.

Lane streaked away up the alley. Garreth hesitated, torn between her and the wounded officer, then started for Duncan's car.

"No, you go after him," Duncan gasped. "I'll call in. Take my gun."

Garreth left the gun. After *him*. Yes, with her height and those clothes Lane did look male. The voice had been hoarse enough for a man, too. Suddenly he understood her confidence that she would escape suspicion, and why she had been playing with him. She had been waiting for another officer, someone to be a victim and a witness to the fact that a crazy foreigner was shooting police officers in Baumen.

Anger boiled up in him. Chance brought Duncan, but it could just as easily have been Maggie.

The icy chill of fear followed. With her witness ready, playtime was over. They had arrived at the finale and she lay in wait for him somewhere. Not in the Lutheran and Methodist churches on the back side of the block, nor did he think she would choose lighted stores or the Driscoll Hotel.

His eyes fell on the rear exit of the Driscoll Theater. There. Certainty rang like a bell in him. But of course the door was locked. He would have to go through it.

Garreth gritted his teeth.

Wrench!

A vestibule stretched between the door and curtained archway into the theater proper. Garreth huddled on the floor of it waiting for the pain to ease. Triumph and anger threaded through the anguish, though. Lane was here; he smelled her perfume.

While he fought down pain, he thought, mind racing. Just chasing Lane with no weapon, no way to catch her, was suicidal. Worse, the whole Baumen Police Department and sheriff's deputies from who knew how many surrounding counties would be descending on the area any time. She had a plan. He better come up with one, too. He must think of a way to fight her, and must settle the matter quickly, before anyone else could become involved or endangered.

Only one weapon occurred to him. Could he reach it? Maybe . . . if he could make it through two more doors.

Grimacing, he stood and moved cautiously out into the theater. The spicy-musky odor died among the others lingering there, popcorn and butter and candy mixing with the scents of sweat and human blood. The creaks and moans of the old

building hid any footsteps or breathing, but ...
she was here. He felt it in every nerve and bone
as he moved up one of the two aisles. She waited
with a final arrow ready for him. *Welcome to the
William Tell Sitting Duck Shooting Gallery.*

A bowstring thrummed. From above him.
Balcony!

Garreth flung himself up the aisle under the
balcony. The arrow sliced along the carpeting
behind him.

"That's the trouble with a bow, Lane," he
called. "There's no silencer on it. Now, you catch
me if you can."

He ran for the lobby and the front door, heart
thundering in terror. He was, he freely admitted,
scared shitless. Lane had all the advantages: a
weapon, experience, no injuries, and no conscience.

Wrench!

He staggered forward, fighting to stay on his
feet. *Don't fall, damn you; don't fall!* What did he
have in this contest? *Just my pure heart.*

He sprinted for the tracks and the far side of
the street.

The bowstring sang its deadly song behind him.
Fire burned across his left ribs.

Garreth stumbled. He struggled half a dozen
steps on feet and both hands but managed to
avoid a complete fall, then he was up again,
running as hard as he could.

The snow fell harder, sheeting the street like
graphite. Garreth slipped twice, once scraping his
palms as he came skidding down on them. The
nerves over his ribs and in his shoulder spasmed.
He gasped in anguish ... kept moving, not
daring to slow down, not daring to look back.

Weaver's Office Supplies loomed before him.
He hit the door—*wrench*—and landed heavily on
the floor inside. His head spun and he felt sweat

running down his face and underarms. On hands and knees, he crawled around the back of the cash register counter.

Inside the display case lay a row of open boxes, each holding a crucifix and rosary. Garreth tried the case. It was unlocked. He slid the glass open and reached in. His hand hesitated over a rosary, though, as he might over a bare wire suspected of carrying electric current.

Come on, man, pick it up. Church and holy water didn't hurt you, remember. The avoidance is only psychological.

Quickly, he scooped out the rosary, then crawled on through the store, past the steps leading up to the mezzaninelike second floor with its stock of office furniture, past the bookcases and shelves of stationery and envelopes. He flattened against the wall just beyond the door of the stockroom in the rear.

Only then did he take the time to examine the wound in his side. The arrow still stuck in his jacket but not in him. He pulled it loose from the fabric. The shirt, however, clung to his ribs, wet with his blood. Two holes and so much blood. The shirt would be ruined.

He laughed wryly at himself. *Worry about a new shirt when you're sure you'll need one.*

Footsteps whispered across the floor.

Garreth's heart lurched. He peered around the door. Lane stood just inside the front door, an arrow ready in her bow, her head tilted, listening. Garreth forced himself to breathe slowly and softly.

"Hello, Inspector," Lane said. "I smell you, and I see blood on the floor. Are you badly hurt?"

He needed to get close to her . . . behind her. *Come to me, blood mother.* He groaned softly.

Lane's head turned, hunting the source of the sound.

Garreth allowed himself a whimpering gasp.

Lane moved forward, silently now . . . past the stairs and bookcases, past the stationery shelves.

Garreth tossed the arrow into the far corner of the stockroom and gathered the rosary in both hands. Breathing as little as possible, ears straining for sounds of Lane's approach, he waited.

The clatter of the arrow brought her through the door swiftly, bow ready to fire. She spun toward the corner where the arrow had landed.

Garreth tossed the loop of beads over her head and drew it snug.

Lane reached for her neck, snarling. Then her hand touched the crucifix in the middle of the rosary. She screamed, shrieking the high, tearing sound of someone in mortal agony. Garreth needed all his control to keep the rosary tight.

"Garreth, let loose!" Lane cried. "I can't stand the pain!" She clawed at his hands. "I'll do whatever you want . . . anything . . . just take this thing off me. Please. *Please.*" She began sobbing.

Weakness and dizziness swept through him. He bit his lip. Was this capture too late? Had he become too weakened to stay on his feet?

He thought of Duncan bleeding in the alley, Duncan, who might have been Maggie. Grimly he said, "We're going to walk out of here and back to my place."

"Yes. Whatever you want, if you'll just take this thing off! Inspector, it's burning me! It's a hundred times worse than the barrier around dwellings. Help me. Take it off!"

He thought of Harry, of Mossman's and Adair's families, of his own shattered life. He thought of *I Ching*. *The maiden is powerful.* He kept the rosary tight.

"Garreth, *please!*" Lane screamed.

He adjusted his hold to give him a free hand for picking up the bow and arrows. "We'll go this way." He hoped. His knees felt weak.

Wrench!

Only his grip on the rosary kept him on his feet. The street spun around him. He shivered, suddenly feeling cold, a sensation he noted with dismay. Could he hang on long enough to reach his place?

Lane started screaming. "Help! Someone help me!"

Garreth jerked the rosary. "Stop that!"

She subsided, but he knew from the hiss of her breath that she remained in pain. Her hatred beat at him.

He angled for Maple Street. Police activity would be centering initially at the north end of the block near Oak. If they hurried past the south end, then stuck to alleys and backyards, they should reach his place without being seen. And then?

There was only one answer. But the deaths had to look like an accident, and it had to destroy their bodies completely. A car crash with the car burning should work best. It would solve everything. Lane would be punished and he would pay for her blood with his. He could stop fighting blood hunger; Grandma Doyle would be relieved; Brian could be adopted in clear conscience.

They crossed the tracks. Lane whimpered. He fought to keep his balance on the slick paving. His only regret was that he would not live to see this country under a good layer of snow. Running in it might have been fun.

Lane still reached for his hands, but each time her nails touched his skin, Garreth jerked the rosary and she subsided with a sharp gasp of anguish. He gritted his teeth, fighting dizziness and weakness.

Up the street, motors roared. Garreth looked around to see the Dreiling boy's van gunning up the street again, just in front of the red pickup. Garreth sucked in a breath of relief. He did not have to take her all the way home.

Before he could debate the rightness of the action or change his mind, he dropped the bow and arrows and caught Lane's chin with his freed hand. A quick jerk snapped her head around backward on her neck with a *crack* like a gunshot. Too fast for her to know what happened, he hoped. At the same time, he lifted the sagging body and leaped directly into the path of the van.

It had no chance to stop. The Dreiling boy tried. Brakes screamed. His tires found no traction on the icy paving, though, and the van spun end for end. Garreth kept moving, pushing himself and the slack Lane into its path. The gamble was that the van would hit something before it stopped, but the gamble paid off. In front of the hotel, the van answered his wish. The hurtling metal wrapped itself sideways around a solid old light pole, with Lane and Garreth directly between the two.

Wrench.

Garreth rolled on the sidewalk, shoulder and side burning with pain. "No!" he howled. He was not supposed to pass through the pole! He was supposed to die in the crash and fire *with* Lane.

But in spite of himself he felt . . . relief. Did he not really want to die, then? He had been relatively content here the past couple of months, he suddenly realized.

He realized something else, too . . . there was no fire, only the smell of spilling gas.

Lurching to his feet, Garreth scrambled for the

driver's seat. He ripped open the door and reached for the dazed boy. "Come on. It's going to blow!"

One hand searched the boy's pockets as he dragged him out. Good. There were the cigarettes and lighter Garreth expected to find. Flicking the lighter, he tossed it under the van and hauled the boy backward.

Flames engulfed the van.

The driver of the pickup ran up with a fire extinguisher. Garreth reached for it. "I'll do this. You take Scott into the hotel and go for the police officers who are in the alley."

He contrived to fall as he aimed for the van. The extinguisher "came apart" in his hands, spreading its contents all over the paving but not the flames. After that, he and the people who materialized out of the hotel could only stand back and watch the van and Lane burn.

Lane! Desolation swept Garreth, bringing another startling realization about himself. In spite of his outrage at her lack of respect for law and life, in spite of burning hatred for what she had done to Harry and him, her death hurt. Pain closed his throat, grief . . . grief for the child whose torment had driven her to seek the power of the vampire life and use it to vent her hatred on humanity, for the waste of intellect, for the voice that would never sing again. He wondered, too, if there might not also be regret for what might have been . . . companionship, the grand tour with so many wonders to delight the child still in her.

God, he hurt, and was so tired.

Garreth sat down against the wall of the hotel and leaned his head on up-drawn knees.

4

"What do you mean, you're calling the supervisor to find a room for me?" Garreth frowned at the emergency room doctor. "I'm not staying." Hunger cramps racked him.

The doctor scowled back. "You most certainly are. You may call those flesh wounds, but you've bled heavily. It's given you the most bizarre blood picture I've ever seen. You need to have a unit of blood and several days observation."

Knots raced through Garreth's gut. "Make the blood 'to go.' I'm signing myself out."

"I'm ordering you to stay." Danzig appeared in the doorway, regarding Garreth narrow-eyed. "Or would you assault another orderly and go over the wall again?"

Garreth set his jaw. "I hate hospitals."

Danzig and the doctor exchanged glances. The chief sighed. "Skip that for a moment, then. Just tell me what you know about Mada Bieber."

Garreth froze. "What does she have to do with this?"

"Nothing as far as I know, but Anna Bieber has been calling the station frantically. It seems she hasn't seen Mada since the two of you drove off together around eight-thirty."

Garreth closed his eyes. The one loose end. Everyone believed that the person who died in the van accident was a stranger, the man who shot Ed and him. How did he explain Mada

Bieber's disappearance? Then again, it occurred to him, why should he try? She had run away once before in her life.

He opened his eyes again. "Sue Pfeifer saw her last, turning in the keys to my car at the station."

Danzig frowned. "What?"

Garreth sighed. "It's a long story, the short of which is, in talking we discovered that she might well be my grandmother, after all. That upset her. I don't know why. Am I such a terrible person to have as a grandson? Anyway, she took off with my car. I was going to go looking for her. I thought maybe she'd decided to walk around thinking. This archer business made me forget all about her, though." He frowned in concern. "I hope that psycho didn't have friends who took her hostage or something."

"Hostage!" Danzig's eyes widened. "Oh, Lord."

Garreth caught the chief's gaze. God, how he longed for bed, and for the blood in his refrigerator. The smell of blood here was driving him crazy with hunger. "Please get my jacket; I'm going home. Helen can look after me, or Maggie can after she's off duty."

Danzig's face lost expression for a moment. "If you're going to be that stubborn about it, all right."

"Chief!" the doctor exploded.

Danzig shrugged. "You can't hold a man against his will if he's able to walk out under his own power."

Please let me be able to stand and walk.

"But when you're home"—Danzig turned on Garreth with a severe scowl—"you get into bed and stay there. I'll call Helen and have her make sure you do."

Garreth dropped his eyes. "Yes, sir," he said meekly.

5

Where do they end, the roads that lead a man through hell?

Maybe with the realization that the only hell is what people make for themselves, Garreth thinks, lying with his arms around Maggie three nights later, breathing in the sweetness of her blood smell and the musky scent of their lovemaking. Maybe it ends with retribution. He has penalties to pay for killing Lane and the manner in which he has used the Dreiling boy to destroy her; that is only just. As much as he dislikes the boy, he felt sorry for him at the hearing today, no longer looking arrogant but white-faced, frightened at the consequences of his recklessness, clinging to his parents' hands. Garreth commits himself to making friends with the boy. It might even help straighten him out. He commits himself, too, to giving Anna Bieber friendship and support, to becoming a great-grandson. He regrets that the cemetery plot containing Lane's ashes cannot be marked with her name, but he will tend the grave. That should keep him reminded of responsibility and accountability.

Maggie stirs in his arms. "Why don't we move more to my side of the bed. Your side is so lumpy, like you have rocks in the mattress."

"Nothing would be wrong with that," he answers, though he carefully shifts to her side, off his pallet. "Earth is healthy. It sets up positive

317

vibrations with the human body." Grinning, he adds: "My veins carry the blood of an ancient lineage who always keep close contact with the earth and, barring accident or murder, live very long lives."

She sighs. "You're crazy, Garreth."

"Ah, yes, but it's part o' me charm, Maggie darlin'."

She giggles and snuggles against his still-bandaged shoulder.

He smiles down at her. Maggie is not Marti—how can there ever be another Marti?—but she fills some of his needs, as he does some of hers. If he cannot share his soul with her, perhaps that will save him future pain when he has to give her up. His differences cannot be laughed away forever.

A gulf stretches between him and normal humans, but perhaps it is not as wide as Lane tried to make him think, and a few slender bridges can span it if he makes the effort to maintain them.

"What did you talk about with your ex-wife today?" Maggie murmurs.

"Brian." Dennis will adopt his son. Not that Garreth intends to give up all strings on him, though; he wants to keep track of his descendants. "Go to sleep. I want to run."

"You can't lay off until your shoulder and side finish healing?" She shakes her head and pulls the blankets over her head. "I always knew runners have a cog missing. Happy anoxia."

The bandages are nothing but props any longer, of course, hiding the fact that only slight scars remain of his wounds. But he does not tell her that. Sliding out of bed, he dresses in a warm-up suit.

The night outside is clear, the stars and sliver of moon bright as crystal in the icy sky. Garreth draws the air deep into his lungs and blows it out in an incandescent cloud of steam. He runs easily, taking quiet pleasure in his strength and endurance and in the vision that turns darkness to twilight. Briefly, he still wishes he could share this with a companion, then shrugs. Nothing is perfect and the solitude has a loveliness he is coming to enjoy.

The frozen ground streams beneath his feet. When something moves in his peripheral vision, he smiles. Three coyotes are falling in behind him, tongues lolling in predatory laughter.

He glances back. "Hi, gang."

Facing forward again, he lengthens his stride. Far ahead, a herd of cattle lies dozing. With his shadow escort pacing him, he aims for them.

Nothing is perfect, but this is not bad. It is enough.